RECKONING

A DERRICK ANDERSON ADVENTURE

MATTHEW GUNNOE

TWISTED SKIES
PUBLISHING

Reckoning: A Derrick Anderson Adventure
Copyright ©2024 Twisted Skies Publishing

Icon has been designed using images from Flaticon.com
Cover has been designed using images from Canva.com

Trade Paperback ISBN: 979-8-9903356-3-9

Published by Twisted Skies Publishing
Wichita, KS 67220

https://www.twistedskiespublishing.com

DEDICATION

To Kenny:
I'm honored to have a brother like you to look up to.
Dicky, Dicky!

To Steve and Becky:
Thank you for being there when I needed someone
most.

To Amanda:
For being my cheerleader!

CHAPTER 1

The gentle rocking of the boat on the calm Gulf waters was soothing, the rhythmic sound of the light waves lapping against the hull creating a tranquil melody. Derrick sat back in the captain's chair, feet propped up as he held a fishing rod lazily in one hand. He had just dropped a line in the water, more for the relaxation than any serious intent to catch something today. The sun was high, but not unbearable, casting a warm glow over everything. It was one of those perfect days, the kind that lingered in your memory like a photograph.

Lydia was stretched out on the deck, her skin gleaming as she soaked in the sun. Her eyes were closed, a peaceful smile on her face as the warmth of the day wrapped around her like a soft blanket. Today was her birthday, and Derrick had surprised her that morning with a pair of earrings that shimmered in the same shade as her eyes—a soft blue that reminded him of the ocean in the early dawn. She'd been delighted, hugging him tightly before gently putting them on, her laughter ringing out as she admired herself in the boat's small mirror.

Madeline was fast asleep in the forward berth, curled up with her little green stuffed turtle. The gentle hum of the ocean had lulled her to sleep not long after they set off, her tiny hands clutching the toy as if it were a lifeline. Every now and then, Derrick would glance through the cabin door to check on her, smiling at the sight of his little girl dreaming peacefully.

Everything was perfect.

But then, the phone rang.

Derrick frowned, glancing at the screen. The number was one he hadn't seen in years. The Chief. He hesitated, thumb hovering over the "Decline" button.

A few minutes later, the phone rang again with the same ID. Derrick sighed as he swiped to answer, reluctantly putting the phone to his ear. "Chief."

"Derrick," the Chief said, his voice as familiar as it was unwelcome. "Sorry to bother you. I know it's been a while."

"You could say that," Derrick replied, trying to keep his tone neutral. "What's up?"

There was a pause on the other end, which immediately made Derrick's instincts flare. The Chief was never one to dance around the issue, and the fact that he wasn't getting straight to the point meant this was going to be something Derrick didn't want to hear.

"We've got a situation," the Chief finally said.

Derrick closed his eyes for a second, already feeling the weight of the conversation settling on his shoulders. "What kind of situation?"

"It's an officer... one of ours. He's gone missing," the Chief said, his voice careful.

Derrick's brow furrowed. "Sir, it's been years. How could I possibly be of any help?"

"It's Tae."

Derrick froze, his grip tightening on the phone. "What?"

"You guys are still friends, right?"

"Usually," Derrick replied, trying to lighten some of the tension.

The Chief hesitated again, and Derrick could almost hear the man gathering his thoughts, trying to figure out how to deliver the news. Tae and his site chief had a... disagreement. Well, 'disagreement' might not be accurate. They had a fight. The next morning, Tae vanished... and to make matters worse, he took a hard drive full of classified intel with him."

Derrick sat up straighter in his chair, gripping the phone tightly. "You think Tae went rogue?"

"We don't know," the Chief admitted. "But it looks bad. We've labeled him an enemy of the state, and the military has been deployed to hunt him down... at all costs. I'd much rather see him face trial than whatever they have planned.

Derrick's mind was racing, trying to piece together the information. Tae was a friend. A close friend. There was no way he'd betray them like that. "Why don't you just track his phone?" Derrick asked, hoping there was some simple explanation.

"We tried," the Chief said. "We found it in his room. Broken in half."

Derrick clenched his jaw. Tae wasn't careless. If he broke his phone, it was intentional. "What do you need me for?" Derrick asked, already knowing the answer but hoping there was some other option.

You and Tae were close. Any idea where he could be?"

He thought back to Tae's visit a few weeks ago. They'd spent the day catching up, laughing, and sharing old stories. Before Tae left, he handed Derrick a small note, something cryptic as always. Derrick hadn't thought much of it at the time, figuring it was just another one of Tae's puzzles. But now... "There was this note he left..."

"Derrick, this conversation never happened. Would you be willing to help us find him before the military does? I've got everything arranged. You'd be a contractor with your own funding for travel. I'll work on expediting any visas you'd need, but no one can know of this operation... oh... and stay out of the embassies. I know it's a lot to ask, but you really are Tae's only hope."

Derrick sighed. "You're not leaving me much of a choice, are you?"

"Expect a package tomorrow morning... and Derrick... thanks."

Standing at the back of the boat, Derrick's gaze was locked on the vast, endless stretch of water around him. The gentle lapping of the waves against the hull seemed distant, drowned out by the storm brewing in his mind. He clenched his jaw, his thoughts racing. "What did you get yourself into, buddy?" he muttered under his breath, barely audible above the sound of the sea. His shoulders tensed as the weight of Tae's predicament settled deeper.

Noticing his concerned look and the way he gripped the railing, Lydia quietly joined him at the stern. Her presence, as always, brought a calming energy, though Derrick didn't turn to face her. "What's going on, honey?" she asked softly, her hand resting on the small of his back in a comforting gesture.

"Tae's in trouble," Derrick finally said, his voice quiet, as though speaking the words would make the situation even more real. He then explained everything—the fight, the missing hard drive, Tae's sudden disappearance. When he finished, he sighed, guilt weighing down his words. "I'm sorry... I couldn't refuse."

Lydia listened intently, her expression serious but understanding. "You shouldn't have," she replied gently. "Tae's our friend. He needs us. When do we leave?"

Derrick blinked, turning to face her, surprised. "We?"

She smiled softly. "Yes, we. I'm not letting you do this alone. Besides, it adds to our cover if it's a husband and wife traveling. Momma and Daddy will gladly look after Madeline for a while. They've been begging for some time with her already."

Derrick's tension eased slightly as he processed her words. With Lydia by his side, maybe they had a better chance at finding Tae—and getting through whatever lay ahead.

***

Later that afternoon, while Lydia was out birthday shopping with her mom, Derrick had the house to himself. It was the perfect opportunity to take his mind off Tae for a bit and execute his plan: bake her a cake from scratch—or, well, mostly from scratch. He wasn't much of a baker, but how hard could it be to follow the instructions on a box of cake mix?

Pulling out the necessary ingredients, Derrick felt confident. He preheated the oven and added everything to the stand mixer as instructed. As it blended into a smooth, pink batter, he couldn't help but feel pleased with himself. "This isn't too hard," he thought, smiling. Pouring the batter into the cake pan, he slid it into the oven and placed it on the middle rack.

Feeling triumphant, Derrick decided to relax on the couch while it baked. He scrolled absentmindedly through old text messages from Tae, laughing at some of the riddles and jokes his friend had sent over the years. But just as he was reminiscing, the unmistakable smell of something burning wafted from the kitchen.

Heart pounding, Derrick leaped off the couch and ran to the oven. He yanked the door open to find a charred, blackened mess in place of the perfect pink cake he'd envisioned. His stomach sank as he realized the obvious: he had forgotten to set the timer.

"Knew that was going too well," he muttered under his breath. Tossing the ruined cake into the trash, Derrick pulled out another box of strawberry cake mix, determined to get it right this time.

In his haste, however, he cranked the mixer up to high, causing flour, sugar, and pink batter to explode from the bowl like a sugary volcano. "You've got to be kidding me!" he shouted in frustration. Grabbing a towel, he frantically started wiping up the mess, knocking over the bottle of vegetable oil in the process. The slick liquid cascaded down the cabinet, pooling on the floor. Distracted, Derrick didn't notice.

After what felt like ages cleaning up the counter, Derrick removed the mixing bowl to transfer the batter. But as his bare foot hit the oil-soaked floor, he slid across the kitchen like a hockey puck, crashing into the cabinets with a heavy thud. The bowl he had been holding spun out of his hand, flipping through the air before splattering batter across the room.

A large blob dropped from the ceiling and landed squarely on Derrick's face. "I hate baking," he groaned, wiping his eyes with the now sticky towel.

With batter dripping down his forehead, he threw the towel into the ever-growing pile of chaos in the corner of the kitchen.

Out of breath and with his patience dwindling, Derrick realized he had only one box of cake mix left. He couldn't afford any more mistakes. Carefully, he mixed the batter by hand, refusing to risk another "explosion" with the mixer. Pouring it into a fresh pan, he triple-checked the timer this time and pulled a chair from the dining room to sit in front of the stove like a hawk, watching it bake.

Finally, the timer went off, and Derrick cautiously pulled the cake from the oven. To his relief, it was the perfect shade of pink, just as it should be. He placed it gently on the cooling rack and let out a long, relieved breath.

But as fate would have it, disaster struck once more. Turning to put the empty pan in the sink, Derrick's foot found the oil puddle again. He slipped, crashing into the cabinets. The cake pan flew from his hands and landed directly on top of his perfectly baked cake, caving in the center.

"No, no, no!" Derrick scrambled to lift the pan, but the damage was done. A gaping hole now marred the middle of what had been his last chance at a flawless cake. He stared in disbelief, then turned away in disgust, only to slip once more on the oil, this time landing hard on his backside.

Sitting on the floor, Derrick noticed his toes throbbing from where they'd collided with the cabinet earlier, the skin already turning a deep shade of purple. But the pain in his foot was nothing compared to the disappointment swelling in his chest. The kitchen was a war zone—batter dripping from the ceiling, the floor slick with oil, broken eggshells scattered around him. And the cake... well, it was a disaster.

Then, as he sat there in the middle of the chaos, an idea struck him. He wasn't out of options just yet.

With no more cake mix left, Derrick grabbed the cans of strawberry icing from the counter. If he couldn't fix the cake, he could at least make it look presentable. Carefully, he filled the hole in the middle with icing, smoothing it out until it was barely noticeable. He used all three cans, layering it thick to cover up the imperfections. As a final touch, he cut up fresh strawberries and arranged them on top, spelling out "Lydia" in neat letters.

Stepping back to admire his work, Derrick sighed in relief. The cake wasn't perfect, but it was good enough—and, more importantly, Lydia would never know the difference.

"Well," he muttered, wiping the sweat from his brow. "At least it's done."

Derrick limped up the front steps of the Evans' house, carefully balancing the cake box in his hands. His toes still throbbed from earlier, but the sight of Lydia's beaming smile as he entered made the pain worth it. He set the cake down on the table, a wave of relief washing over him.

Lydia's eyes lit up as she took in the sight. "You made this?! It's so beautiful!" she exclaimed.

Derrick, blushing from both the praise and the memory of the kitchen catastrophe, shrugged. "Sorry, it's a bit lopsided."

But Lydia wasn't bothered by the imperfection. She pulled him into a tight hug, her arms squeezing him as if to say thank you a hundred times over. "I think it's perfect!" she said, her voice full of genuine warmth.

Jeb, watching with amusement, grabbed a knife and sliced into the cake. As he lifted a piece, the icing-filled hole was immediately visible. "Well, that's interesting," he said with a chuckle. "I bet there's a story behind that."

Derrick looked away, trying to suppress a grin. "There might be…" he muttered.

Later, after the party, Mary walked back with Lydia and Derrick, carrying a drowsy Madeline in her arms. As they opened the door to the house, Mary gasped, taking in the disaster that was once a functioning kitchen. "Derrick! What happened?!"

Lydia laughed, shaking her head with a knowing smile. "Actually, this is pretty clean for him cooking," she teased, playfully nudging Derrick, who could only respond with a sheepish grin.

***

The next morning, Derrick was jolted awake by the sound of the doorbell echoing through the house. He rubbed the sleep from his eyes, groggily pulling himself out of bed. Lydia was already downstairs, sipping her morning coffee in the dining room, the aroma drifting faintly through the air.

When Derrick opened the door, he found a man in a FedEx uniform standing there, a small package in hand. The driver handed him the parcel, his expression unreadable.

"Package for Mr. Anderson," the man said, his voice formal but detached.

"Do I need to sign for it?" Derrick asked, already feeling uneasy.

"No records," the driver replied before turning away and walking briskly down the path.

Derrick frowned. Something didn't feel right. "Where's your truck?" he called after him, but the driver had already disappeared, vanishing faster than he should've been able to.

He stood there for a moment, the early morning sun casting long shadows across the driveway. Something gnawed at the back of his mind, but he shrugged it off for now, closing the door behind him.

Back in the dining room, Derrick set the package on the table where Lydia sat, her coffee mug in hand. "What is it?" she asked curiously, her gaze shifting between him and the unmarked box.

"Let's find out," Derrick muttered, tearing open the packaging. Inside was a sleek Swiss bank debit card and several documents with bold red stamps reading "TOP SECRET."

Derrick's brow furrowed as he pulled the contents from the box. "This doesn't seem entirely legal," he said, a note of worry creeping into his voice.

Lydia leaned forward, taking a closer look at the documents. "The Chief did say this was off the books," she reminded him, tapping her fingers on the table. "But how do we even know where to start looking?"

Derrick leaned back in his chair, the weight of the situation pressing down on him. "I've been trying to figure that out ever since the Chief called. Tae's last known location was Somalia, but we can't start there without drawing unwanted attention."

Lydia watched as Derrick's gaze drifted toward his office. He suddenly stood up, snapping his fingers. "Wait... that note he gave me... could it actually be a clue?"

He retrieved the cryptic note Tae had handed him weeks ago, unfolding the small, worn piece of paper. Clearing his throat, Derrick read aloud:

"Visit this globe in a circle,

but don't take your spinning compass.
Bring Lydia as she knows
how to talk to their 'formal' residents."

Derrick raised an eyebrow. "Why wouldn't I bring my compass? He knows I love my compass!" He looked baffled, clutching the note like it might give him more answers if he stared hard enough.

Lydia smiled, seeing how Tae's riddle had already thrown Derrick off track. "Focus, honey! It's got to mean something. Why would the compass be spinning? Don't they always point north?"

"They do..." Derrick muttered, the wheels in his head starting to turn as he paced the room. "But they spin at the poles!"

Lydia leaned forward, intrigued. "But what's the 'globe in a sphere'? And why is the word 'formal' in quotes? Why would I know how to talk to them?"

Derrick paused, mid-thought, before his eyes lit up with realization. "The North Pole has no real marker since it's covered in water half the year, but the South Pole..."

His voice trailed off as he grabbed his phone, frantically typing a search. After a few seconds, he turned the screen around to show Lydia. "Look—there's a sphere on a pole surrounded by a ring of flags at the South Pole. It's literally a globe in a circle!"

Lydia squinted at the image on his phone, excitement bubbling inside her. "Okay, but what about the residents? No one actually lives at the South Pole."

"Penguins!" Derrick exclaimed. "They live there, and you worked with them for years. That must be what Tae meant by 'formal' residents."

Lydia's eyes widened, sparkling with excitement. "You mean I can see them in their natural habitat?" she asked, practically bouncing in her seat. The idea of going to Antarctica, of seeing the penguins she'd once studied, thrilled her.

Derrick chuckled, nodding. "Looks like Tae planned this out better than I thought."

Lydia grinned, already mentally packing her things. "Let's go find Tae!"

***

The gravel crunched softly underfoot as Derrick and Lydia walked side by side, Madeline nestled securely in Derrick's arms, her tiny hands gripping his jacket. The street was quiet, the sun filtering through the trees and casting dappled shadows across the path. Lydia took a deep breath, admiring the calmness of the afternoon. "It's such a beautiful day, isn't it?" she remarked, her eyes drifting to Madeline, who seemed content with her face buried against her father.

Derrick, though, wasn't as relaxed. His brow was furrowed, his thoughts clearly elsewhere. Lydia noticed the tension on his face and gently nudged him with her elbow. "It'll be fine, Derrick. My parents love spending time with her. She's in good hands with them. Trust me."

Derrick sighed, his gaze distant. "It's not that I'm worried about them watching her. I know she's safe with them. I'm just... still concerned about Tae. This whole thing doesn't feel right. Something's off. It's not like him to just vanish."

Lydia stepped in front of him, forcing him to stop walking. She reached out and placed a reassuring hand on his chest. "And that's why we're going to find him," she said, her eyes steady with determination. Derrick took a deep breath, grounding himself in her confidence.

When they reached her parents' porch, Derrick broke the lingering tension by asking, "Did your mom say what she was making?" His face brightened when Lydia smiled and replied, "Roast chicken."

Jeb met them at the door as Lydia opened it, his face lighting up when he saw Madeline. The little girl squirmed excitedly in Derrick's arms, her tiny voice bursting with joy. "PAPA! PAPA!"

Jeb wasted no time whisking Madeline away to the living room, immediately making silly faces at her. The sound of her giggles filled the house, and Derrick chuckled softly, exchanging a glance with Lydia. "Never would've guessed that when I first met him," Derrick said with a smirk.

Lydia smiled warmly. "I kept telling you he was a big softie."

Dinner was a feast. Derrick leaned back in his chair, completely stuffed after polishing off more than his fair share of Mary's famous roasted chicken. It was one of his all-time favorite meals, and tonight had been no exception.

"There's more in the kitchen if you're still hungry," Mary teased, eyeing Derrick's empty plate.

He groaned, holding his stomach. "You trying to make me explode?"

Mary laughed as she and Lydia began clearing the table. When Derrick offered to help, Mary waved him off with a playful grin. "No, thank you! I've seen the mess you can make!"

While the dishes clattered softly in the kitchen, Lydia leaned closer to her mom. "Could you join us in the living room for a moment? We need to talk to you and Dad."

Mary's brow furrowed slightly with curiosity, but she nodded. "Of course, dear. Is something wrong?"

In the living room, Jeb sat on the couch with Madeline on his lap, but he quickly noticed the serious expressions on Derrick and Lydia's faces. "What's going on?" he asked, sensing the tension in the air.

Lydia sat down next to Derrick, taking his hand for support. "Mom, Dad, we need to ask a big favor," she began carefully.

Derrick cleared his throat, his voice serious. "Tae's gone missing," he explained. "The Chief called us to help find him. He thinks Tae is in grave danger."

Her parents exchanged worried glances, the gravity of the situation sinking in. "What do you need us to do?" Jeb asked, his voice steady but concerned.

Derrick hesitated, struggling to find the right words. Lydia, sensing his unease, gently squeezed his hand and spoke for him. "We need to leave as soon as possible, but we can't take Madeline with us. We were hoping she could stay with you while we're gone."

Jeb's face broke into a wide smile, clearly thrilled at the idea of having more time with his granddaughter. Mary chuckled, seeing the excitement in her husband's eyes. "I think that's a yes, honey," she said, her voice warm with reassurance. "Take all the time you need. Just make sure you come back safe... Both of you."

As the first light of dawn began to break over the horizon, Derrick and Lydia stood outside her parents' house, the early morning air cool against their skin. Mary held Madeline, who waved cheerfully at her parents. "Bye-bye," she cooed in her small voice, unaware of the gravity of the journey they were about to embark on.

Lydia knelt and kissed her daughter on the forehead. "Be good for Grandma and Grandpa, Sweetie. We'll be back soon, okay?"

Madeline giggled and snuggled closer to Mary. Derrick stepped forward and hugged Jeb, who clapped him firmly on the back. "Stay safe, son," Jeb said in his deep voice. "Bring Tae home."

Derrick met his gaze. "We will," he promised.

As they drove toward the airport, the reality of what they were about to do settled in the air between them. The car was quiet, save for the low hum of the engine. Lydia finally broke the silence. "How do we know Tae's even leading us on a real hunt?" she asked, the uncertainty clear in her tone.

Derrick gripped the steering wheel tighter. "We don't," he admitted, glancing at her. "We don't even know if he's still alive. This clue... it's all we have."

Lydia nodded, the unspoken fears lingering between them as they pulled into the private terminal at the airport. The Gulfstream G700 sat waiting on the tarmac, sleek and ready for the long journey that lay ahead.

Stepping out of the car, Derrick couldn't help but feel a sense of awe as they approached the plane. This was no ordinary trip. They were heading into the unknown, to the frozen expanse of Antarctica—one of the most remote places on Earth—and the fate of their best friend hung in the balance.

Inside the jet, the cabin was luxurious, with plush seating and all the amenities they would need for the long flight south. Derrick and Lydia settled into their seats, strapping themselves in as the pilot and co-pilot went through the final pre-flight checks. The engines roared to life, filling the cabin with a steady rumble.

Lydia reached over and took Derrick's hand, her fingers trembling somewhat. She squeezed it tightly, her voice barely above a whisper. "We're really doing this, aren't we?"

Derrick looked into her eyes, seeing the uncertainty, the fear—and the hope. A single tear threatened to escape from the corner of her eye. He gave her hand a reassuring squeeze. "We are," he said softly.

The Gulfstream began to taxi down the runway, gathering speed. The familiar landscape of home blurred, then disappeared beneath the clouds as they soared higher into the sky. What awaited them at the South Pole was a mystery, but they were ready to face it—together.

CHAPTER 2

After a quick refueling stop in Santiago, Chile, Derrick and Lydia were ready to get back into the air. The plane's engines roared as Captain Reynolds closed the door and asked with a grin, "Alright! Who's ready for Antarctica?"

Rain poured down in sheets as the Gulfstream G700 taxied to the runway, the wet tarmac gleaming under the airport lights. Derrick watched from the window as the city of Santiago slowly disappeared into a thick cloud bank beneath them. Climbing higher, they eventually broke through the clouds, revealing the stunning Andes Mountains, their snow-capped peaks towering above the clouds.

"That must be Cerro el Plomo," Derrick said, pointing to one particularly majestic peak. Lydia nodded, admiring the beauty of the mountains from their vantage point.

As the hours passed, the vibrant green of the Andes gave way to the deep blue of the ocean below. Soon enough, the water was replaced by endless white icy plains as they neared the Antarctic continent. Lydia stared out the window, her eyes wide with fascination, hoping to catch a glimpse of a penguin colony in the distance. Derrick, on the other hand, reclined in his chair, his head tipped back as he tried to catch a quick nap.

"Derrick! How can you sleep at a time like this? It's so beautiful!" Lydia exclaimed, her voice filled with awe.

Groggily, Derrick opened one eye, squinting at the bright, snow-covered expanse outside the window. "It's nothing but white... forever," he muttered.

Lydia gasped, nudging him playfully. "How dare you! It's breathtaking. There are more people in Bloomfield than those who've had the privilege to see this!"

Derrick chuckled at her enthusiasm, but her words stayed with him. She was right—this was an experience most people could only dream of.

Lydia practically bounced in her seat when the pilot announced that they were approaching the Amundsen-Scott South Pole Station. Derrick sat up to get a better view, and there it was: a high-tech, elevated facility standing in stark contrast to the vast whiteness around it. The station, a marvel of engineering, looked like a futuristic outpost in the middle of nowhere.

As the plane touched down, the roughness of the ice runway immediately became apparent. The engines' reverse thrusters roared longer than usual, fighting to slow the plane on the slick surface. Finally, they came to a stop, and the pilots carefully taxied the aircraft toward the station.

Derrick opened the door, and an icy blast of air instantly hit him. The minus forty-degree temperature was like a punch to the lungs, stealing his breath. He winced, regretting not putting on more layers before stepping out.

"Come on, move it, slowpoke!" Lydia urged, practically dragging him along. "I want to see the penguins!"

At the base of the stairs, a man dressed in a full-length parka greeted them. "Mr. and Mrs. Anderson, welcome to the South Pole! I'm Station Chief Dobson. We don't usually get Spooks down here, especially not twice in as many weeks."

Derrick's ears perked up. "Twice?" he asked, exchanging a glance with Lydia.

"Yeah, another guy came through last week. Short fellow, strange smile," Dobson explained.

Derrick's heart quickened. "That must have been Tae."

"Yup, that's him. Name fits his personality," Dobson confirmed with a chuckle. "Come on inside—it's freezing out here!"

Inside the station, they were led to their rooms. Dobson pointed to two adjacent doors. "Here we are, berthing pods 244 and 246. Apologies for the single rooms; it's all we've got."

Derrick stared, a little confused. "Wait, did you say… birthing pods?"

Dobson laughed. "Berthing, with an 'e.' It's a Navy term for a bunk. Here, let me show you."

He opened the door to reveal a tiny room with a single bed, a dresser, and a small desk. It was no luxury suite, but it would do.

Lydia peeked inside and immediately asked, "Where's the bathroom?"

"Down the hall," Dobson replied. "Men's on the left, women's on the right. Shared showers and stalls."

Derrick muttered under his breath, "Now would be a good time to get constipated."

Over the next hour, Chief Dobson led them on a tour of the facility. The hallways, painted in bright colors, reminded Derrick of his old high school, except these walls were covered in memorabilia from past expeditions to the pole.

As they passed the communications room, Lydia's eyes lit up. "Ooooh… so many radios," she said, her voice filled with admiration.

Dobson noticed her excitement and explained, "Those are our primary forms of communication, especially during emergencies. Internet's unreliable here due to environmental conditions."

Derrick, who had been listening quietly, suddenly perked up. "I can fix that for you," he offered with a grin.

Lydia whipped around and firmly said to Dobson, "NO! No, he won't!" She shot Derrick a glare, making Dobson chuckle.

The tour ended in the conference room, where a group of scientists had gathered to greet their new visitors. Dobson gestured for Derrick and Lydia to join them at the table.

"So, you two will be with us for a few days, right?" Dobson asked. "Anything you'd like to do while you're here?"

Lydia, without missing a beat, replied, "I'd love to check out the radio room, if that's okay."

Dobson smiled. "Thought you might say that. Maria, our radio expert, will show you around."

Derrick, getting to the heart of their mission, added, "Our main reason for coming is to find Tae. He left us a clue to come here, and we think he may have left something behind for us to follow."

Dobson nodded. "I remember something about that from the cable that was sent. He left an envelope for you. We can grab it after this."

Before leaving, Derrick asked one last thing. "And... is there any chance we could see the penguins while we're here? I know it would mean a lot to Lydia."

Dobson grinned. "We've got a colony of Emperors not far from here. We'll head out tomorrow morning."

Lydia's face lit up with joy, a wide smile spreading all the way across.

As the group prepared to head in different directions, Lydia turned to Dobson with a serious look. "One more thing, Chief. While I'm gone, do *not* let Derrick go anywhere unsupervised. Full surveillance. I mean it."

Derrick looked offended. "What? I wouldn't do anything stupid! I just wanted to check out the electrical room, see how this place runs."

Lydia's eyes widened. "*Especially* not the electrical room!"

Dobson laughed heartily as Lydia gave Derrick one last stern look before heading off with Maria.

Dobson led Derrick through the narrow hallways back to his office, where he retrieved a small, white envelope from the wall safe. The atmosphere in the room felt tense as he handed the envelope to Derrick with a cautious expression. "Tae gave me this and told me to only give it to you," Dobson said, his voice low. "I have no idea what it is or why he brought it here, but he seemed very skittish about it. If it wasn't for the fact that he and Lucas worked together many years ago, I probably would have reported it."

Derrick began to open the envelope, curiosity gnawing at him, but Dobson quickly held up a hand to stop him. "Don't open it here. I don't want any part of it. The less I know, the better."

Understanding the gravity of the situation, Derrick nodded and tucked the envelope into his pants pocket. "How about I get you a tour of the power plant now?" Dobson offered with a smile, clearly wanting to change the subject.

The two made their way to the facility's power plant, where they met Lucas, the station's electrical engineer. Lucas greeted them warmly and agreed to show Derrick it's inner workings. They entered an underground tunnel leading to the plant, the air thick with the sound of howling wind outside.

"Wow, those winds are getting pretty wicked," Derrick remarked as they walked. "Is that normal here?"

Lucas nodded. "We usually get some wind, but this storm looks stronger than normal. Last winter, we had winds over 100mph. Sounded like the entire plant was going to tear apart, but she held fast."

Handing Derrick a pair of ear protection with built-in microphones, Lucas explained, "We run CAT diesel engines that power our generators. It gets *really* loud in there. These headsets will help us talk."

As they stepped into the plant, Derrick was immediately overwhelmed by the sight of the massive engines. "I feel like an ant at a picnic," he said through the comms, looking up at the towering machinery.

Lucas laughed. "We've got triple redundancy here—one engine running, one on standby, and the third offline for maintenance. We even have a fourth engine inside the station that powers the heaters and lights in an emergency."

The sound of the building creaking from the wind outside grew louder as Lucas explained the engine system's integration with the generators. But their conversation was interrupted by a loud *snap* coming from the massive breaker panel on the wall. The storm had caused the primary generator breaker to trip.

Lucas grinned as the second engine roared to life, taking over without a hitch. "That happens occasionally during storms. The electricity in the air sometimes causes a breaker to trip. No worries—we'll just flip it back on, and that engine will become the standby node."

As Lucas walked toward the panel, Derrick eyed the towering breaker switches with caution. "You sure you shouldn't put on some protective gear? That thing's big enough I'd want to be flipping it from Peru."

Lucas waved him off with a chuckle. "These aren't like your typical breakers. We flip them all the time."

But as Lucas reached for the two-foot breaker and pulled it down, there was a deafening *boom*. The breaker exploded, launching Lucas across the room and spraying white-hot sparks into his face. Derrick's instincts kicked in. He grabbed a Nomex jacket hanging on the wall, slid under the shower of sparks, and threw the coat over Lucas's face. Dragging him away from the spray, Derrick felt the heat searing the jacket's fabric, but he didn't stop until they were safely out of the immediate danger.

The entire station went dark. Red strobe lights flashed, and the klaxon alarms blared throughout the facility. Lydia, sitting with Maria, jumped at the sudden noise. "What was that?!"

Maria looked just as confused. "I don't know. I've never seen that happen before."

Lydia's heart sank as a voice came over the PA system.

> *"ALERT! ALERT!*
> *Fire detected in power plant.*
> *Emergency personnel status 1, electrical precautions!*
> *Personnel, muster stations!"*

"Where's Derrick?" she whispered, her voice thick with fear.

Back in the plant, Derrick removed the jacket from Lucas and felt his stomach drop. The skin on his face was blackened, melting from the bone. He was barely breathing, each ragged breath a struggle. Derrick knew there was little he could do, even if he had a full medical kit. This was beyond saving.

"Lucas, I'm here. Just focus on breathing," Derrick urged, though he knew it was a losing battle. Grabbing the radio from Lucas's belt, Derrick called for help. "Mayday, Mayday, Mayday! Anyone there?"

Lydia and Maria rushed down the hallway toward the muster station when two firefighters ran past them. Lydia froze as she heard Derrick's voice crackling over one of their radios. "Maria! That's Derrick calling for help!"

Derrick checked Lucas's pulse and felt his heart sink further. Nothing. Lucas was gone. Derrick's breath came in sharp gasps as he looked around at the wall now engulfed in flames. He wasn't far from joining him if he didn't stop the electrical fire.

His eyes darted around the room, landing on a rescue hook hanging on the wall. He grabbed the hook, his mind racing. The fire was intensifying, the heat unbearable. "I've only got seconds," he muttered, his voice barely audible over the crackling of the fire. Grabbing another Nomex jacket, he approached the electrical panel with the hook, positioning it at the breaker.

With a grunt, Derrick yanked the breaker down, just as the pole began to bend under the pressure. The spray of electricity stopped abruptly. He stumbled back, his heart racing. But now the fire was growing, and he had to act fast.

Derrick spotted several CO_2 canisters stacked near the damaged engine. An idea formed in his mind. He could choke the fire, but it would also choke him— removing all the oxygen from the room. It was a desperate move, but he was out of options.

Securing the canisters with ratchet straps, he aimed them at the flames. "Not the best plan," he muttered, coughing violently from the smoke filling his lungs. His hands shook as he reached for the handles. Whispering, "I love you, Lydia," he pulled the handles open, releasing the gas.

The firefighters finally managed to raise the door with hydraulic spreaders. Black smoke billowed out as they rushed inside.

Lydia, sitting on the floor at the muster station with a borrowed radio, listened in agony as the firefighters reported back.

"Entry made. One signal-7. One unconscious, not breathing. Transporting to medical."

Lydia's heart pounded. "Where's medical?" she demanded, her voice shaking.

A bright light pierced through Derrick's eyelids, intensifying the headache that throbbed behind his temples. The muffled sounds of distant voices echoed in his ears as he struggled to make sense of his surroundings. "What's going on? Why is the ground moving, and what's on my face?!"

Slowly, he opened his eyes, his vision blurry at first but gradually sharpening. The medical team was hovering around him, a mask secured over his face, delivering precious oxygen.

"He's back!" a nurse exclaimed, removing the bag mask and replacing it with a non-rebreather. The world around him continued to spin as Derrick blinked, trying to ground himself in reality.

"What happened?" Derrick asked, his voice hoarse, as memories of the fire began to trickle back to him in fragments.

"You were oxygen-deprived from the fire, but you'll be fine," the doctor assured him. "Just lie back and relax."

But Derrick's mind was racing. Panic seized him as he sat up, the image of Lucas's lifeless body flashing before his eyes. "Lucas... what about Lucas?" he asked, his voice shaking with dread.

The doctor's face darkened, and he shook his head. "Sir, he's gone. Thanks to your efforts though, everyone else is safe. But Lucas didn't make it. Now, please, lie back down."

Before Derrick could react, Lydia and Maria appeared, rushing around the corner. The moment Lydia saw Derrick, she burst into tears, pushing past the medical team to throw herself onto his chest, clinging to him as if he might vanish if she let go.

The doctors decided to keep Derrick in the medical room overnight for observation. Despite their reassurances, the weight of Lucas's death pressed down on him like a lead blanket, replaying in his mind over and over. He couldn't shake the image of Lucas's face—blackened, burned, and beyond saving. The helplessness he felt in that moment gnawed at him.

Lydia refused to leave Derrick's side. She stretched out across two chairs beside his bed, her eyes red from crying, her hand resting on his as if her presence alone could anchor him. Eventually, the doctor administered a sedative to help Derrick sleep, and slowly, he drifted off, slipping into the dark, dream-filled depths of unconsciousness.

...Derrick screamed, watching in horror as Lucas's body was hurled against the wall by the blast of

fire and sparks. He rushed to his side, heart pounding in his chest as he pulled Lucas away from the flames.

Lucas's skin was blistered and charred, his breath coming in ragged gasps, each inhale an excruciating effort. Derrick's hands trembled as he tried to assess the damage, his voice shaking. "Stay with me, Lucas. Stay with me."

"It... hurts... Derrick," Lucas rasped, his voice a shadow of what it had been, his words barely audible. His breathing grew shallow, each breath a struggle.

Suddenly, Lucas convulsed violently, his body seizing in Derrick's arms. His eyes rolled back, and a guttural growl escaped his throat. Derrick stumbled backward, his heart racing in terror as Lucas's skin began to crack and peel away, revealing something dark and twisted beneath.

Horns sprouted from Lucas's forehead, and his eyes glowed an eerie, malevolent red. The creature hissed as it emerged from Lucas's body, its voice low and venomous. "You left me to die, Derrick, just like so many others before me. Now, you'll pay... but not with your life. That would be too easy. You'll pay with her soul... in HELL!"

Derrick's heart lurched as the demon lunged at Lydia, its claws raking the air, reaching for her. Derrick fought with everything he had, but the demon's grip was iron, pulling Lydia closer to its grotesque, twisted face.

"NO!!!!" Lydia screamed, struggling against the creature's hold as the fire blazed brighter, the heat intensifying. The room warped around them, the walls melting away as flames consumed everything.

"You cannot escape," the demon snarled, dragging her toward a fiery abyss that had opened on the floor. Derrick leaped after her, his skin blistering as he descended into the burning pit, but it was too late. Lydia's screams echoed in his ears as she was swallowed by the flames...

Derrick woke with a violent jolt, his body drenched in sweat. The alarms on his heart monitor were screaming as his chest heaved, his breathing erratic. Lydia stood in the corner of the room, her face pale with fear as the doctors rushed in. Derrick's eyes darted around wildly, trying to separate the remnants of the nightmare from reality.

Two doctors approached, their voices calm but firm. "It's okay, Derrick. You're safe. Just breathe," one of them said as a nurse read his vitals aloud. "Pulse: 165, Blood Pressure: 210/110, Respirations: 55!"

Derrick's body trembled uncontrollably. "What happened?! What's going on?!"

One of the doctors quickly drew a dose of Valium and injected it into Derrick's IV. The medication worked swiftly, and the panic that had gripped him began to subside, his breathing slowing as the sedative took effect.

"It was a nightmare, Derrick," Lydia whispered, her voice trembling as she walked to his side and took his hand. "You're safe. Nothing here will hurt you."

Derrick's eyes fluttered closed, fragments of the nightmare still haunting him. "Lydia... demon... fire..." he muttered, his voice barely audible as his body finally began to relax.

After Derrick had returned to sleep, one of the doctors pulled Lydia aside for a quiet conversation. "Does he get these night terrors often?"

Lydia sighed, glancing back at Derrick's sleeping form with a look of deep concern. "He used to... a lot, actually. He's struggled with them for years, but after we got married, they seemed to settle down. I don't know what's changed."

The doctor nodded, his expression thoughtful. "Nightmares like that... they can be triggered by stress or trauma. With everything that's happened today, it's not surprising."

Lydia bit her lip, watching Derrick's chest rise and fall as he slept. "I just wish I knew how to help him," she whispered.

***

The storm had calmed overnight, and by morning, the sky was a brilliant blue. Derrick sat in the cafeteria, having been released from medical just a couple of hours earlier. He stared out the large windows, lost in thought, Tae's new cryptic clue lying on the table in front of him.

"...This is KIOW. Twenty-four hours ago, hundreds of..." Derrick's mind drifted as Lydia returned with a tray of breakfast.

"Hey, sweetie. You okay? I got you some food," Lydia said gently, setting the tray down. She could see the weight of the previous night still hanging on him.

Derrick glanced up, his expression somber. "Why does it seem like someone ends up dying everywhere I go?" he muttered.

Lydia placed a hand on his shoulder. "Honey, you didn't do it. In fact, you're the reason the station didn't burn down last night. I'm so proud of you."

Looking down at the biscuits and gravy with a side of bacon, Derrick smiled faintly. "She knows exactly what I like," he thought. "Thanks, honey. Grab some for yourself. I'm fine, and we have a hot date soon with some very formal guests."

Lydia sat beside him, placing her hand on his knee. "Derrick, we don't have to go. You've been through a lot. It's okay."

"Honey, I wouldn't miss the look on your face for the world," Derrick said, his smile growing as he saw the excitement spark in her eyes.

Dobson led them to the ceremonial South Pole, located just outside the main building. "Tae said you had to take a picture with it to prove you were here. Such a weird little guy," he said with a chuckle.

After snapping a picture, they climbed into a snowcat. "The colony is a few miles north. Won't take long," Dobson said as he maneuvered the vehicle out of the station's lot.

Lydia, bouncing in her seat with excitement, asked, "I can't wait! Which way is north?"

Dobson glanced into the rearview mirror, trying to determine if she was joking. When Lydia turned to Derrick, he realized she wasn't. Turning around, he whispered, "Lydia... everything is north from here."

After a few seconds of processing, Lydia flushed. "I know... I was just joking... and... oh, shut up and take me to the penguins!"

Dobson slowed the snowcat as they approached the top of a hill. Lydia had been eagerly peering out of every window for the past thirty minutes, trying to spot the colony. As they crested the summit, a vast black mass stretched out to their left, moving like a sea of life.

Lydia gasped, her eyes wide with delight. "DERRICK!!! THERE THEY ARE!" The joy on her face was even better than Derrick had imagined.

The snowcat coasted down the hill toward the colony. Once they arrived, Dobson advised them to be quiet when getting out, so as not to scare the penguins. Lydia carefully opened her door, sliding down the side of the vehicle. A few penguins cautiously approached her, nuzzling her arms with their beaks. Lydia knelt down, tears welling in her eyes as a baby penguin waddled up to her and let out a soft peep. She picked it up, cradling it in her hands as tears spilled over. "Madeline would love you," she whispered, overcome with emotion.

Meanwhile, on the other side of the snowcat, Derrick was having a very different experience. A large adult penguin waddled toward him, braying loudly. "Hello, Mr. Penguin. How are you today?" Derrick said with a laugh, but his amusement faded as the five-foot-tall bird continued its advance.

The penguin trumpeted again, this time more aggressively, and started pecking at Derrick's abdomen with surprising force. "Hey, what the—?!" Derrick exclaimed, trying to bat it away. His swats only irritated the bird further, and it began pecking harder. When it started to hurt, Derrick shoved the penguin away, knocking it over. "Stay down, jerk! What did I ever do to you?!"

The penguin struggled back to its feet, staring Derrick down. "Don't do it," Derrick warned, but the penguin charged, braying loudly before pecking him in a very sensitive area. Derrick doubled over in pain, gasping. "That's it, you freak! You're going to regret picking a fight with me!"

With adrenaline surging, Derrick landed a punch on the penguin's beak and then tackled it to the ground. The two rolled in the snow, the penguin flailing its wings as Derrick tried to wrestle it into submission.

Hearing the commotion, Lydia and Dobson rushed around the vehicle to find Derrick on the ground, grappling with the penguin. Derrick had the bird in a chokehold, yelling, "Just wait till I find an orca! He's going to have a nice meal tonight!"

"Derrick! Stop!" Lydia screamed, startling him. He released the penguin, which scampered away, braying in protest.

"What the crap, Derrick?!" Lydia exclaimed, her hands on her hips, staring at him in disbelief.

Derrick stood up, his parka ripped and blood seeping through his shirt. He gestured at the retreating penguin. "He started it!"

***

Derrick was hunched over the sink, carefully cleaning his wounds when Lydia quietly slipped into the bathroom. He looked up at her through the mirror, raising an eyebrow. "You know, this is the men's room, right?"

Lydia tiptoed closer, a playful smile tugging at her lips. "I know. I just wanted to check on you. I'm sorry for yelling at you earlier. I just couldn't believe you would hurt an innocent penguin."

"Innocent?" Derrick scoffed. "You mean that murder bird?"

Lydia picked up a cotton ball and poured peroxide on it, sighing as she dabbed it on a wound on his arm. The sharp sting made Derrick wince. "You sure do live a hard life, you know that?" she murmured.

"I don't want to imagine how much harder it would be without you," Derrick replied, turning to face her. He leaned in and kissed her, the tenderness of the moment melting away the tension from earlier.

Later, Derrick opened the door to his berthing pod and stared at the tiny room, his mood sinking. The space felt smaller than ever, and his claustrophobia gnawed at him. Lydia, sensing his unease, stepped across the hallway from her own room. "It's only one night," she said, trying to sound upbeat. "We head out tomorrow. I love you, honey."

He smiled softly and returned the sentiment before closing the door behind him.

He removed his shoes and crawled into the cramped bed. The mattress was comfortable enough, but the room seemed to close in on him. He tossed and turned for hours, his thoughts swirling until exhaustion finally took over, pulling him into a fitful sleep.

...Derrick woke to the sound of smoke detectors blaring. The glow of orange flames illuminated the room. Panicked, he flung open the door, only to be met with a wall of fire that threw him back to the floor. The heat was unbearable, and the air was thick with smoke. From the other side of the house, he could hear Lydia and Madeline screaming. Their cries pierced through the crackling flames, urging him forward.

He crawled through the intense heat, his skin blistering as the hair on his arms burned away. He had to save them. The floor beneath him began to sag with each movement, the wood glowing orange as the flames ate away at the foundation. "I have to keep going," he told himself over and over. But just as he neared the living room, the floor gave out beneath him, and he plummeted into the fiery abyss, flames surrounding him as he fell...

Derrick jolted awake, screaming, his chest heaving as he gasped for air. The room was pitch black, adding to his disorientation. He scrambled out of bed, only to trip over the chair and crash to the floor. The impact sent a jolt of pain through his body, but before he could even try to stand, the door burst open.

Lydia rushed in, her eyes wide with concern. She saw Derrick lying on the floor, his feet tangled in the chair, and her expression softened with pity.

Still breathless and rattled from the nightmare, Derrick looked up at her. "Can I please sleep on *your* floor?" he asked, his voice shaky.

***

The next morning, Derrick stood on the observation deck, watching as the plane touched down on the ice once more. He sighed with relief, the sight of the aircraft a welcome reprieve from the chaos of the past few days. "I've never been so glad to see an airplane in all my life," he thought.

Chief Dobson escorted them to the plane's stairs outside the main entrance. After shaking Derrick's hand, Dobson thanked him again for his efforts in saving the station. Then, turning to Lydia, he smiled. "You know, we're always looking for people to run our radios down here. Think about it. If you're interested, give me a call," he said, handing her his business card.

Lydia tucked the card into her pocket, smiling politely as she boarded the plane.

Captain Reynolds greeted them as they settled into their seats. "Where are we going next?" he asked, his tone light.

Derrick pulled out the clue Tae had left behind and read it aloud:

"In the heart of the desert
where sands do flow,
To a village

where ancient traditions still glow.
Seek the place where the sun
kisses the dunes,
And stars sing their secrets
under the moon.
Travel to a land
where history is grand,
Where Bedouins roam
in a vast, golden land.
To Timimoun you must go,
where the Sahara's breath is deep,
There you'll find wisdom
in the chief's keep.
He holds the key to your quest,
In his tent, you'll find answers
that are best.
Speak greetings from
'The Great White Man,'
In this desert oasis,
you'll find your stand."

Derrick looked at the captain and said, "Timimoun… Algeria."

CHAPTER 3

Derrick peered out the small plane window at the vast desert stretching endlessly below. As they descended toward Timimoun, the plane dropped lower and lower, close enough to the ground that a dust cloud began trailing behind them. "There's actually a runway here, right?" he thought nervously, just before a strip of asphalt appeared beneath the plane, and the tires made contact with the ground.

As they disembarked, a man in a golf cart greeted them with a wide smile. "*Marahabal asmi Lotfi. Marhaba pekem fe Timmimo*n!" he exclaimed. Lydia's eyes widened, and she looked at Derrick, whose grin grew wider as he responded, "Tahiati. Hill ant ma Herzl?"

Lotfi let out a hearty laugh. "Nice! You speak Arabic... well, sort of. Hop on, I'll take you to de counter."

Climbing into the cart, Lydia shot Derrick a skeptical glance. He met her gaze with an innocent look. "What?" he shrugged. "I couldn't sleep one night, so... Duolingo."

Lotfi led them to a small counter under a bright yellow sign that read "*Herts*."

Confused, Derrick blinked at the sign. "I thought this was *Hertz*?"

Lotfi beamed proudly. "Oh no, we are a much smaller company dan dat car place."

"Dat car place?!?" Derrick asked, even more perplexed.

"Oh yes!" Lotfi nodded. "We here at Herts rent camels, not cars. Dat's why our motto is, 'We get you der, but it Herts.'"

Lydia groaned, pinching the bridge of her nose as a headache began to form. "Did he just say camels?"

Derrick, sensing the storm brewing, offered, "Why don't you go find some coffee for us, and I'll straighten this out."

Lydia sat on the hard wooden seats of the smallest airport terminal she'd ever seen, sipping on a lukewarm cup of coffee. When Derrick approached, his expression said everything she needed to know.

"We're taking camels, aren't we?" she asked, already resigned to the idea.

Derrick sighed. "Yeah. But hey, imagine the stories we'll be able to tell!"

Not long after, Lotfi appeared, leading two camels. Grinning, he handed Derrick and Lydia the reins, clearly amused by the situation.

Lydia eyed her camel and then Lotfi. "So... how do we make these guys move?"

Lotfi chuckled. "You'll pick it up quickly. To get on, just say 'Suk.'"

Lydia tried it out, and the camel obediently knelt down. "Okay, that's not so bad," she said, cautiously mounting the creature.

"And to get it to stand up?" Derrick asked, still looking at his camel with suspicion.

"Qum," Lotfi replied, stifling a laugh as Derrick awkwardly tested it out. The camel rose gracefully, leaving Derrick clinging on with wide eyes.

"And how do we make it go?" Derrick asked, trying to sound confident.

"Yalla," Lotfi answered with a wink. "And for stopping... well, you'll figure dat out."

Lydia, warming up to her camel, gently petted its head. "You aren't so scary after all, are you, cutie?" she cooed, and the camel responded by nuzzling her face and letting out a soft grunt.

"I tink he like you," Lotfi said, clearly enjoying the scene.

Derrick, inspired by Lydia's success, reached out to pet his camel. The animal let out a deep, guttural sound that Derrick mistook for a grunt.

Lotfi's eyes widened. "Uh... dat no good."

Before Derrick could react, the camel spat directly at him. "Ugh! Uncool, dude!" he exclaimed, wiping the spit from his face as Lydia tried, and failed, to stifle her laughter.

The sun beat down on them mercilessly as they made their slow journey eastward across the Sahara, the village mentioned in Tae's clue still hours away. The camels plodded steadily through the sand, their long shadows stretching across the dunes.

After a while, Derrick started humming absentmindedly.

Lydia, adjusting her headscarf to block more of the sun, shot him a look. "That was a horse, not a camel," she said dryly, recognizing the tune.

Derrick shrugged. "Yeah, but he doesn't have a name either, so it's the same difference."

Lydia rolled her eyes, but a small smile tugged at her lips. Despite the heat, the camels, and the strangeness of their current situation, there was no one else she'd rather be on this adventure with.

The sun was beginning to dip toward the horizon, casting shadows across the desert when the village emerged in the distance, like an oasis mirage. The small, tented structures blended seamlessly with the golden dunes, appearing almost like they were born from the sand itself.

As Derrick and Lydia approached, a group of children sprinted from the village, their laughter and excited voices filling the air. They surrounded Lydia's camel, their hands waving in the air as they repeatedly cried out, "Mallak! Mallak minn al-samaa!"

Lydia glanced at Derrick, a puzzled look on her face. "What are they saying?"

Derrick grinned, the amusement clear in his eyes. "They're calling you an angel from Heaven."

A blush crept up Lydia's cheeks, and she smiled warmly at the children. "How do you say, 'Thank you very much'?"

"Shukran Gsilla," Derrick replied, puffing up with pride.

One of the children broke away from the group, running up to Derrick and yelling gleefully, "Wajh qird! Wajh qird!"

Derrick's expression quickly soured. Lydia, hearing the unfamiliar words, smiled and asked, "What did they name you?"

"Oh, uh..." Derrick hesitated, eyes darting. "It was something like 'Knight on his steed.'"

Lydia giggled, turning her attention back to the children, who were now waving happily at her. Derrick, meanwhile, glared at the child who had shouted at him. "Stupid little twerp," he muttered under his breath.

As they rode into the village, the chief stepped out of his tent to greet them. Derrick, trying to maintain some dignity, pulled out Tae's clue and recited, "Salam! Nahin masafron arasalham al-rajel al-abeedh al-azim!"

The chief chuckled, a deep, hearty sound. "You mean Tae?" The children who had followed them laughed too, clearly amused.

Derrick, confused, looked around. "Does everyone speak English here?!"

The chief smiled. "It's more common than you would expect."

Derrick and Lydia commanded the camels to lower themselves to the ground, dismounting with practiced ease. The chief walked up to Derrick, stepping unusually close. Derrick's confusion grew as the chief leaned in, their noses nearly touching. After a brief pause, the chief wiggled his nose back and forth, brushing it against Derrick's in what seemed like a strange, but intentional, gesture.

Derrick stood frozen, his eyes wide, unsure of what just happened. The child who had called him a "monkey face" earlier sidled up to him and whispered, "That mean he like you."

Still bewildered, Derrick followed Lydia and the chief into the large tent at the center of the village. The chief motioned for them to sit on a couple of floor cushions. "Please, have a seat," he said warmly, pouring two cups of tea and handing them over.

"So, you're looking for the wisdom of the Great Tae?" the chief asked, a twinkle of amusement in his eyes.

Derrick raised an eyebrow. "That's a first," he thought. Out loud, he said, "Yeah, we've been following clues he left behind. We think he's in danger and need to find him before it's too late."

The chief nodded slowly, taking in Derrick's words with a thoughtful expression. "Ah, from the Sunaj? He mentioned this threat."

"Sunaj?" Derrick repeated, his brow furrowing in confusion.

The chief nodded again. "Yes. Tae seemed very troubled when he was here... like a gazelle being hunted by a dabu."

Derrick's heart began to race. "Did he say anything about why he was so scared?"

The chief sipped his tea and shook his head. "We didn't talk much, but he left this for you." He reached into his robe and pulled out a sealed envelope, handing it to Derrick.

Derrick took the envelope, turning it over in his hands, the weight of it feeling heavier than it should. "Did he say anything else?"

The chief leaned back. "Najla spent more time with him. She might know more. I'll have someone take you to her after we finish our tea."

One of the chief's handmaidens led Derrick and Lydia through the village to a modest tent. She stopped at the entrance and explained with a polite smile, "Men are not allowed in the tents of unmarried women." With that, she disappeared inside to fetch Najla.

Moments later, a young woman with bright eyes and a welcoming smile emerged. "Marhaba! I hear you are friends of Tae. I miss that goofy little guy. How is he doing?" Najla asked warmly.

Derrick and Lydia exchanged a quick glance before Lydia replied, "Well, unfortunately, we think he might be in some danger, and we're trying to find him. Do you remember anything from his visit that might help us?"

Najla's smile faltered as concern clouded her face. "Oh no! Tae in danger? Yes, please help him. I'll tell you anything I can. Let's sit by the fire and have some tea while we talk."

The three of them moved toward the central fire pit of the village. The flames crackled warmly, casting flickering shadows across the sand as they settled onto the soft cushions. Najla handed them cups of tea, and as they sipped, she began recalling Tae's visit.

"We sat just outside the camp one night and watched the stars," she began, her voice soft and nostalgic. "We saw what he called the *'devil's stars.'* He told stories about how they were metal monsters flying high in the sky." Najla's eyes twinkled with amusement. "His imagination was powerful. Almost as much as his kiss."

Derrick, in mid-sip, nearly choked on his tea, spitting it out onto the ground. "Excuse me?" he sputtered, caught completely off guard.

Najla looked concerned. "Oh no, is the tea not good? Let me get you some more!" She reached for the teapot.

"No, no, it's fine," Derrick assured her, wiping his mouth, though the color had drained from his face. "You just, uh, surprised me. Please, continue."

Najla smiled gently. "The next morning, Tae said it was time to return to the real world... again with his imagination. He kissed me, and then we left his tent. I watched him ride off west on his camel."

Derrick blinked, struggling to regain his composure. "Wait... you two left *his* tent?"

Najla's grin turned mischievous. "He had gentle hands," she added with a wink.

Derrick's face turned a pale shade of green, and he quickly stood, muttering an excuse about needing fresh air. Lydia bit her lip to suppress a laugh as Derrick hurried off, clearly rattled by Najla's revelations.

Once he was out of earshot, Lydia turned to Najla with a friendly smile. "I love how you style your hair. Can you show me how you do it?"

Najla beamed, grateful for the change in topic. "Of course! I'd be happy to show you. Come, I have some beads and oils inside my tent. You'll love them."

Derrick lay in the tent, staring up at the woven fabric ceiling, still reeling from the earlier revelation about Tae and Najla. His stomach had finally settled, but his mind was stuck on the word the chief had mentioned. "Sunaj... Sunaj... What language is that? Is it a name? A place?" He turned the word over in his mind, trying to puzzle out its meaning.

As he pondered, Lydia stepped through the curtain into the tent. She was dressed in a flowing, ankle-length Bedouin dress, her face partially veiled with jewels woven into her intricately braided hair. Only her sparkling eyes were visible beneath the fabric.

"Um! Occupied!" Derrick blurted, not immediately recognizing her. But as she moved closer and the light from the oil lamp caught her eyes, his breath hitched. "Oh... wow..." was all he could manage.

Lydia, noticing his awe, playfully swayed her hips as if preparing to perform a belly dance. "Najla hooked me up. What do you think?"

Derrick's response was limited to staring at her with his mouth agape, speechless.

Lydia sat down beside him, her expression shifting to something more teasing. "You know, that Tae guy has excellent taste in women."

Derrick's excitement instantly faded, his mood crashing back to reality.

Later that evening, with the desert night cooling around them, Derrick and Lydia indulged in a Bedouin tradition—stargazing. They lay together on a blanket, mesmerized by the sky above. The moon had yet to rise, and the Milky Way spilled across the sky in a dazzling array of stars.

"This view sure beats Bloomfield," Lydia murmured, awe evident in her voice.

He pulled her closer, but Lydia wrinkled her nose almost immediately. "What's that smell? Is that your breath?!"

Derrick hung his head, embarrassed. "I forgot my deodorant on the plane."

"Derrick! You'll have to use mine then."

He cringed at the suggestion. "I'm not using yours. I'll be fine till we get back."

Lydia's expression was firm. "Uh. I don't think so. I'm not riding back to Timimoun with three animals that stink."

***

The next morning, Lydia woke early, quietly sifting through her bag until she found her deodorant. After using it herself, she tiptoed over to Derrick, who was still asleep. Giggling to herself, she gently applied the deodorant to his underarms while he snoozed.

Later, as Derrick dressed and pulled on a clean shirt, he caught a floral scent. "Man, Lydia sure does smell good today," he thought, until he noticed that the scent followed him. "Why do I smell like lilacs?!" he asked aloud, realization dawning as he spotted Lydia grinning mischievously.

"Lydia! Why?" he groaned.

"Because you smelled like a sweaty monkey!" she teased, stifling a laugh.

Derrick shot her an exasperated glare. "Chief told me what the kids called you," Lydia added, giggling.

As they prepared to leave the village, the chief came out to see them off. Derrick approached him and extended his hand. "Salam, my friend."

The chief took Derrick's hand, catching the floral scent. With a knowing smile, he replied, "Al-salam ya ragel al-zahra."

Derrick's face flushed bright red.

As they rode away on their camels, Lydia couldn't resist asking, "See, no one noticed. By the way, what did the chief say when you left?"

Derrick stared straight ahead, his voice flat. "He called me 'Flower Man.'"

Lydia burst out laughing so hard she almost toppled off her camel.

Once back on the plane, Derrick opened the envelope, revealing a note with the riddle and a key. He read the clue to Lydia.

"To a land down under where kangaroos leap, Across oceans wide and waters deep.

*A city's harbor sparkles with light,
where sails of white are a glorious sight.*

*In this iconic structure by the sea,
Culture and arts blend harmoniously.*

*Seek out a place where music and
drama thrive, where performances
bring the stage alive.*

*Find your way to a locker that's more
than it seems, A number that holds the
next clue in your dreams.*

*Four one three is the code none too
bleak, within its hold, the answers you
seek."*

Derrick jotted down a few keywords in his notepad, already analyzing the clue. "'Down under,' kangaroos... Must be Australia. City harbor sparkles, iconic structure, culture, and arts... the Opera House?"

Folding the note back up, Derrick looked at Lydia. "Looks like we're off to Sydney."

CHAPTER 4

As the G700 began its fifteen-hour journey to Sydney, Derrick and Lydia settled into the cozy luxury of their private cabin. After finishing up in the lavatory, Derrick stepped out, feeling refreshed. He found Lydia sitting on the couch, scrolling through her phone and giggling.

"What's so funny, honey?" Derrick asked, sitting beside her, curious about what had her so amused.

"I just talked to Izzy. She's going to pick us up from the airport and show us around!" Lydia grinned, clearly excited.

Derrick's eyes widened in shock. "Honey! We weren't supposed to tell anyone what we were doing!"

Lydia rolled her eyes at his overreaction. "Come on, Derrick. It's Izzy. She's letting us stay at her place for a couple of nights, and she's taking us to a wildlife refuge. How could I not tell her?"

Derrick chuckled nervously. "That sounds... fun," he said, though visions of chaotic wildlife encounters flashed through his mind.

Lydia grinned mischievously. "I promise, no penguins this time... or camels."

The hours of the flight passed quickly, and soon their plane was descending over the shimmering city of

Sydney. From their window, the sunlit Opera House came into view, its iconic white sails gleaming like a beacon. Derrick pointed toward it.

"You know… the clue is just right there," Derrick said. "We could be in and out of the Opera House before anything gets a chance to kill us."

Lydia playfully smacked his arm. "Where's your sense of adventure?! We've never been to Australia before, and we haven't seen Izzy in years!"

Derrick relented with a grin as they headed to the terminal, passed through customs, and made their way to the arrivals exit. Outside, Izzy was waving a sign excitedly, her chestnut brown hair blowing in the breeze.

"Welcome to Australia!" she exclaimed, throwing her arms around Lydia in a tight hug. Then she turned to Derrick, her eyes twinkling with mischief. "I'm going to hug you now."

Derrick winced, his nose scrunching up. "I wish you wouldn't," he replied, half-joking, knowing full well what was coming. Despite his protests, Izzy enveloped him in a hug anyway, laughing at his discomfort.

Once the bags were loaded into Izzy's SUV, they set off toward her apartment, laughter filling the car. Lydia and Izzy quickly fell into fast-paced, animated conversations, sharing stories, inside jokes, and catching up. Derrick, however, was more focused on Izzy's reckless driving, gripping his seat as they narrowly avoided collision after collision.

When they finally arrived at Izzy's apartment, Derrick stumbled out of the vehicle, breathing a sigh of relief, thankful to have survived the ride. Lydia, meanwhile, was awestruck by the breathtaking view of Sydney's skyline from the floor-to-ceiling windows in the living room.

"That view is *gorgeous!*" Lydia exclaimed, gazing out in admiration.

Derrick set down their bags near the closet, intending to join the girls, but before he could even say a word, Lydia and Izzy darted off for a tour of the apartment. Feeling like a third wheel, Derrick sat down on the couch and sniffed his armpit.

"I remembered deodorant this time, didn't I?" he muttered to himself.

But his peace didn't last long. Lydia and Izzy scurried back out of the bedroom, both looking excited. "Get up, Derrick! Izzy is taking us out for some Sydney rock oysters!" Lydia exclaimed.

Derrick's head dropped with a sigh. "Ugh. I barely survived the last ride with her," he mumbled under his breath, bracing himself for another round of heart-stopping traffic encounters.

Glass windows surrounded their table, offering a stunning view of the Sydney Opera House and Harbor Bridge. The golden lights reflected off the water's surface, creating a picturesque setting. Derrick, however, seemed unimpressed by the beauty around him as he studied the menu in front of him, growing increasingly horrified by each dish.

"Smoked eel... bone marrow pasta... pig jowl," Derrick muttered under his breath. "Is there *anything* edible on this menu?"

Izzy, catching sight of his discomfort, snatched the menu from his hands with a grin. "Don't bother. You have to order the rock oysters. It's practically a law here."

Having read through the less appetizing options, Derrick decided to take her advice. "Okay, sure. I've never had oysters before. What do they taste like?" he asked, lifting his wine glass for a sip.

Lydia laughed, her eyes gleaming mischievously. "Oh, they're like a fishy, slimy... snot ball."

Derrick's eyes widened in horror. He sputtered, nearly choking on his drink, and quickly downed the rest of the wine to recover.

To his surprise, Derrick found the oysters far more enjoyable than Lydia had described. By the time he had polished off three plates, he was feeling rather satisfied.

After paying the bill, they headed back to Izzy's apartment. On the drive, Derrick couldn't stop squirming in his seat, causing the car to shake slightly.

"Would you quit fidgeting?" Lydia snapped, growing annoyed. "What are you doing back there?"

"My back itches," Derrick replied, rubbing against the seat. "Must be that new laundry detergent."

As they stepped out of the elevator into the brightly lit hallway of Izzy's building, Lydia stopped in her tracks. She noticed something odd about Derrick's arm and grabbed it to take a closer look. Red blotches had begun to spread across his skin.

"Derrick, are you allergic to oysters?" she asked, her voice tinged with concern.

"I don't know. I've never had them before," he replied, scratching his shoulder vigorously.

Lydia lifted his shirt to inspect further, gasping at the sight of angry red welts covering his back. "Derrick! You've broken out in hives! Are you feeling okay?"

Derrick paused, looking puzzled. "Well, that would explain the itching," he said nonchalantly, still rubbing his back against the wall as they entered the apartment.

A few hours and six Benadryls later, Derrick sat slumped by the window, staring vacantly into the distance. His eyes were glazed over, and he had the dazed look of someone deep in a medication-fueled haze.

"Um... am I the only one seeing this?" Derrick mumbled, his voice slurring slightly. "There's a Hatman up on the parking garage, and he's playing baseball with a kangaroo. How does he even hold that bat with those tiny arms?"

Lydia exchanged a worried glance with Izzy before gently suggesting, "Why don't you lie down for a bit?"

Derrick nodded sluggishly, struggling to his feet. He swayed unsteadily and muttered, "I feel like... I'm leaking."

"EWWW!" Izzy exclaimed, laughing as she rolled her eyes.

Lydia guided Derrick into the bedroom and helped him into his pajamas. But before she could fully pull his shorts on, Derrick collapsed onto the mattress with a heavy thud, already snoring.

Smiling fondly, Lydia shook her head. "What am I going to do with you?"

From the living room, Izzy called out, "You could exchange him for a newer model! One that doesn't leak!"

Lydia returned to the couch after tucking Derrick in. It had been a while since they'd had a chance to catch up, and both were eager to share the latest developments in their lives.

Sipping her tea, Izzy glanced over at Lydia. "So, did you ever make it out to Elmo? Is that really a place?"

Lydia smiled with fondness in her eyes as she thought about the trip. "Yes, actually. I managed to convince Derrick to stop there on our way to Bloomfield last year."

Izzy's eyebrows shot up. "Really? How did that go?"

Leaning back, Lydia started reminiscing...

...The bustling streets of DC were nothing compared to the intricate web of highways that crisscrossed Dallas, as Lydia soon discovered. Navigating the labyrinth of highway intersections left her awestruck and a little anxious as they climbed the exit onto US-80.

"Are they serious here?!? These highway intersections are MASSIVE!" she exclaimed, eyes wide in disbelief.

Derrick chuckled, maneuvering through the heavy traffic. "You're not in Kansas anymore, little missy," he quipped in his best John Wayne voice.

As they left behind the metroplex's urban sprawl, Lydia marveled at how quickly the landscape shifted to rural surroundings. The highway felt like it went on forever as they made the sixty-mile trek from the airport to Elmo.

Off in the distance, two gas stations appeared beside the road. They were a welcome sight to Lydia, who was trying not to show her desperateness.

"Derrick, can we stop there? I'm going to need to pee, and I think Madeline needs a break," she said, shifting in her seat.

Derrick grinned as they passed the city limit sign. "Sure, we can stop. Earl's store always has great tacos!"

"We're here?!?" Lydia gasped, sitting up in excitement. "You weren't kidding when you said this was a small town!"

Derrick parked the car in front of the store, and Lydia wasted no time jumping out and darting towards the building.

As he unbuckled Madeline from her car seat, she pointed to the store excitedly and exclaimed, "Mama!" Derrick laughed. "Yeah, Mama should have gone at the airport, huh?"

Entering the store, Derrick was greeted by a familiar voice calling his name. "Derrick Anderson! Well, I never!"

Behind the counter stood a rugged, elderly man sporting a large, white cowboy hat. "Hey, Earl. How ya been?" Derrick replied, walking up to hug him.

"Who's this little one?" Earl asked, playfully tickling Madeline's stomach.

Hearing the commotion, Myrtle, Earl's wife, emerged from the back room and gasped. "Thelma owes me $20!" she exclaimed, wiping her hands on the towel around her waist. "We made a bet on whether you would ever set foot back in town again!"

Breathing a sigh of relief, Lydia walked out of the bathroom and saw Derrick talking with the elderly couple. Joining them, she put her arm around him and greeted them with a warm smile. Derrick introduced them, saying, "Myrtle, Earl, this is my wife, Lydia, and our daughter, Madeline."

Earl's eyes widened. "Dang, son!" he exclaimed, extending his hand. Myrtle playfully smacked Earl with her towel. "Smooth as always, dear." Turning to Lydia, she added, "You'll have to forgive him. He's an uncultured animal." Lydia laughed and thanked Earl for the compliment.

"Gimmie, gimmie!" Myrtle said, reaching out to play with Madeline. As they chatted, Earl asked, "What brought y'all back here? Come to visit your parents?"

Derrick's shoulders slumped slightly. "We wanted to introduce Madeline to them." Glancing over at her, Earl smiled. "They would have been so proud."

Derrick navigated the worn road, his tires bumping over potholes as Lydia peered out at the small, weathered single-story homes. Memories of her own upbringing flooded back, and she couldn't help feeling a twinge of guilt for the privileges she'd been blessed with. *Sensing her thoughts, Derrick spoke softly, "We didn't have much, but Dad made sure we never went without. They scrimped and saved every penny to send me to MIT. He was so proud that he could put his son through college. I never told them it didn't cover even a quarter of the costs."*

On the right, a black wrought-iron fence marked the entrance to the cemetery. Derrick turned onto the gravel path leading through the grounds, eventually parking on the east side. He turned off the engine and took a deep breath.

Exiting the car, he unbuckled Madeline while Lydia retrieved a bouquet of flowers from the back seat. Together, they walked to a granite headstone bearing the name "Anderson."

Lydia handed the flowers to Derrick, who knelt by the grave and gently cleared away a few weeds. "Hi, Mom. Hey, Dad," he began, his voice filled with a mix of sadness and gratitude. "I'm sorry it's been so long. I wanted to let you know — I made it. I graduated. Thank you for always believing in me! Oh! I found someone... and she actually married me! Mom, Dad, this is Lydia. Guess what else? You have a granddaughter. You'd adore her, Dad. She has your eyes."

Lydia didn't expect it to hit her as hard as it did. Tears welled in her eyes. She knelt beside Derrick, her hand finding his as he shared stories of the adventures he'd experienced since their passing.

After leaving the cemetery, they drove through town, passing a small house. "That's where I grew up," he said, pointing to the modest home with the sprawling yard. "The window on the right was my bedroom, though I was hardly ever in there. I was always outside, tinkering with things."

Lydia smiled, imagining a young Derrick taking apart machines and causing trouble. "I love this town," she said softly, resting her hand on his leg. "It made you who you are today. I love it for that."

Later, while Lydia changed Madeline in the airport restroom, Derrick sat at Gate A12 at DFW, checking the weather for Bloomfield. "Hmm… looks like we might get some storms while we're there," he muttered. "Maybe I should add the damage waiver for the rental…"

***

The next morning, Derrick woke to a beautiful Australian sunrise, rising out of the Pacific Ocean in the distance. Lydia was already on the balcony, drinking a cup of coffee like usual. She smiled as he joined her. "Hi, honey. You feeling better?"

Still amazed by the colors saturating the sky, Derrick replied, "Wow… so… beautiful."

***

The drive-thru wildlife refuge was a few hours outside of Sydney. As they pulled in, Lydia's eyes lit up at the sight of a couple of quokkas lounging by a tree. "Oh... my... stars!!! They are so blasted cute!" she squealed, captivated by their perpetually smiling faces.

The landscape unfolded before them into a breathtaking expanse of wilderness. As they ventured deeper, they passed mobs of kangaroos lazily grazing and packs of dingoes slinking through the underbrush. But just as they were beginning to enjoy the tranquility, the vehicle sputtered and lurched to a halt.

Derrick felt his stomach drop. "What now?" he muttered, trying to keep his cool. He opened the door and called to Izzy, "Pop the hood, will ya?"

Izzy shook her head, scanning the surrounding bush with unease. "It's not safe out there, Derrick! Everything here wants to kill you."

Derrick forced a laugh, trying to hide his growing apprehension. "How's that different from anywhere else?" But as he stepped out into the wild, he became acutely aware of how vulnerable he was.

Lifting the bonnet, Derrick's hands shook slightly as he inspected the engine. Relief washed over him when he saw that the serpentine belt had merely popped off and was still intact. "Just a minute, ladies," he said, trying to sound more confident than he felt.

As he fumbled with the belt, his mind raced with thoughts of everything that wanted to eat him hiding in the bush. He hadn't heard anything approach, so when a small shadow suddenly appeared at his side, he jumped out of his skin. A kangaroo stood there with its head cocked curiously.

His heart pounded in his chest as he let out a surprised scream. This sent the animal into a defensive frenzy. It reared back, its forearms flailing in a bizarre boxing stance before launching a powerful kick.

Derrick barely dodged the attack as his adrenaline surged. "Stupid little rat!" he snapped. "You picked the wrong person to mess with!"

From the window, Lydia's voice cut through his panic. "Derrick! Don't you dare punch that cute little kangaroo! What is wrong with you?!"

Distracted, Derrick looked back at her, "He started it!" But the kangaroo took advantage of his lapse in focus and delivered a swift kick to his abdomen that sent him sprawling backward onto the ground.

Derrick gasped for air having the wind knocked out of him. As he regained his bearings, a rustling to his right caught his attention. Turning his head, his blood ran cold—he was face to face with a taipan, one of the most venomous snakes in the world.

His eyes were wider than saucers as he slowly slid away until he was out of the snake's striking range. Standing on shaky legs, he took a moment to steady himself.

But before he could fully recover, another noise came from the weeds beside the road. "Oh, what now?!" he groaned. A small, brown lizard emerged from the grass with its beady eyes locked onto him.

Derrick let out a nervous laugh. "Oh, it's just a stupid lizard. Thank goodness."

The lizard then flared out its neck in a menacing display and charged at him.

"Holy crap! It's a Dilophosaurus!" Derrick yelled, his mind flashing back to Jurassic Park as he instinctively covered his eyes.

In full-blown panic mode, he bolted back to the SUV with the frilled lizard hot on his heels. Scrambling up onto the front tire, he hauled himself onto the roof. "This place is a blooming nightmare!"

Inside the car, Lydia struggled to contain her laughter, tears streaming down her face as she watched Derrick slide back down off the roof.

As he was finishing up on the engine, Lydia suddenly screamed, seeing a large spider crawling up Derrick's arm. Without hesitation, he swatted it away onto the ground.

Izzy's face went pale. "Derrick, do you know what kind of spider that was?"

Wiping his hand on his pants, he said, "No idea. Just another creepy-crawly, right?"

"It's a huntsman spider," Izzy said, her voice tinged with worry. "And I think it just bit you."

Derrick glanced down at his arm, unamused, as it began to feel like it was on fire. "Oh, great. This is when you tell me it's deadly."

Izzy chuckled a little. "No, they're usually not, but you aren't going to enjoy the next few hours."

Back at the apartment, Derrick sat staring out the window with an ice pack on his arm. Izzy was putting the finishing touches on dinner when Lydia sat down next to him. "Rough day, huh?" she said sympathetically.

Derrick continued to glare out the window. "I hate this country."

Grinning, Lydia laid her head on his shoulder. "Just one more night."

Derrick struggled to sleep that night as he kept having off-the-wall dreams caused by the spider venom. Jerking awake from one of the dreams, he yelled out, "Sulfuric acid goes on top of the cheese!"

Lydia smacked him with a pillow and rolled over. Before he could explain, she stopped him. "Derrick, there isn't a planet in the known universe where that statement would ever make sense. Go back to sleep!"

Derrick was very tired the next morning. Even coffee struggled to keep him awake for any amount of time. After loading up into Izzy's car, she drove them to the Opera House, where they found a bank of lockers. "What was the number again," Lydia asked.

Pulling the clue and key from his pocket, Derrick read it and said, "Locker 413." Unlocking it, he found a small safe.

Izzy suddenly became very interested in what was in it after he removed it. "You going to open it?" she asked.

"I will when we get back to the plane. I don't want anyone to overhear what's on it. You never know who you can trust right now," he said, tucking it under his arm.

As they got back into the SUV, Izzy tried again to get him to look at it. "How do you know where you are going to go next if you don't start figuring out the clue now? Why don't you look at it? Three heads are better than one."

Hearing commotion coming from the back seat, Lydia turned around to see Derrick holding the box and contorting his arms. "You okay, honey?"

Frustrated, Derrick growled," Stupid Tae! He made it have a lock where you needed five fingers to open!" Placing his four fingers on the corresponding pads, he struggled to orient his right-hand pinky to fit.

Lydia laughed. "Need a hand?"

Derrick shot her a glare as the lock disengaged. "No... I needed a pinky." After opening the box, he removed the clue and read it to himself.

> *"Float down the roads*
> *in your long, stick driven boat.*

Stay in the Gritti Palace and
Marco Polo will find you."

He paused for a moment before looking at Lydia. "Venice," he said confidently.

"That's it? No other clues?" Izzy asked, her curiosity still evident.

Lydia shot a quick glance at Izzy, something about her sudden interest making her uneasy. Derrick, however, didn't notice and continued explaining. "He mentioned stick-driven boats and Marco Polo. The Venice airport is named after Marco Polo, and its roads are canals. It's pretty clear."

After dropping them off at the airport, Izzy watched as Derrick and Lydia headed into the terminal. As soon as they were out of sight, she pulled out her phone and made a call. "They're on their way to Venice," she said quietly. After a pause, she added, "No, I don't think they suspect anything yet."

CHAPTER 5

The Grand Canal shimmered under the fading light of the setting sun, reflecting the old-world charm of Venice. Gondolas glided smoothly across the surface, their gentle swaying matching the rhythm of the city. Derrick and Lydia sat in one of these gondolas. Lydia's head rested on Derrick's shoulder as they approached their hotel. She closed her eyes listening to the sound of the lapping water and distant chatter from nearby cafes.

As their gondola docked, Derrick helped Lydia onto the private pier. The hotel's sharply dressed doorman greeted them with a warm smile, his polished shoes clicking on the wooden planks. "Welcome to the Gritti Palace!" he said, his voice smooth and welcoming.

Stepping inside the hotel, they were immediately enveloped in the serene, luxurious atmosphere. The bustling waterways of Venice seemed a world away as they entered the lobby, which was a masterpiece of Venetian splendor. Crystal chandeliers hung from the high ceilings, casting a soft, golden light over the polished marble floors. Rich tapestries adorned the walls, depicting scenes of Venice in its golden age, while antique furniture and plush fabrics added a sense of timeless elegance.

Derrick and Lydia were greeted by the concierge, who led them to the reception desk. As they checked in, Lydia couldn't help but marvel at the attention to detail. The air was faintly perfumed with the scent of fresh flowers, and a soft classical melody played in the background, adding to the ambiance.

The concierge escorted them through the grand corridors to their suite. When the door opened, the room exceeded their highest expectations. Velvet armchairs and a king-sized bed draped in luxurious linens beckoned Derrick, while Lydia was immediately drawn to the large windows that offered a breathtaking view of the Grand Canal below.

"Wow!" Lydia exclaimed, her voice filled with awe. "This is incredible!"

Derrick placed their bag on the floor and collapsed onto the bed, pulling the comforter over himself. The soft fabric enveloped him, and he felt sleep beginning to pull him under.

As Lydia explored the intricacies of the marble bathroom, Derrick was on the verge of drifting off when a knock at the door jolted him awake. "Go away," he mumbled, still half-asleep. But the knocking continued and was more insistent this time.

Groaning, Derrick dragged himself out of bed and opened the door. A man stood there, looking slightly out of place in the luxurious surroundings. His clothes were ordinary, and he had an air of nervousness about him.

"Marco?" Derrick asked cautiously.

The man nodded slightly and handed him a small envelope. "Be careful. Your presence has been noted," he said quietly before quickly disappearing down the hallway.

Lydia stepped out of the bathroom just as Derrick shut the door. "Who was that?" she asked, noticing the puzzled look on his face.

Derrick stared at the envelope in his hand as his mind raced. "It was Marco," he replied, distracted. Tearing into the envelope, he read the note inside.

> "I quit! O' S-hoot.
> Just ride down this snake
> through the jungle.
> Captain Bongo will lead the way.
> -------------------------
> 38-57-6 77-8-48."

Lydia frowned, confused. "Why do his clues never make any sense?"

Derrick rubbed his forehead, feeling a headache coming on. "His favorite class was cryptography. This is just him having fun."

***

Later that evening, Derrick and Lydia found themselves seated at Osteria alle Testiere, a small, intimate restaurant Lydia had spotted in an advertisement at their hotel. The warm candlelit ambiance was exactly what Lydia had hoped for, creating the perfect setting for a romantic evening. Derrick, on the other hand, looked less impressed as he scanned the menu with a growing sense of dread.

"Why do fancy restaurants always have the grossest-sounding foods?" Derrick grumbled, flipping through the list of dishes with a frown.

Lydia couldn't help but laugh. "Do you want me to ask if they have chicken nuggets for you?" she teased, rolling her eyes.

Derrick shot her a scorching glare but didn't respond. His attention was split between the menu and two men seated across the room. They were wearing Hawaiian shirts, an odd choice for a romantic, upscale restaurant in Venice. Something about them didn't sit right. They were out of place.

Lydia continued listing the things she wanted to do before they left Venice, but Derrick's focus remained on the two men. His instincts told him something was off.

Sensing his distraction, Lydia sighed. "And we can rent a couple of horses and ride naked on the beach."

Derrick nodded absentmindedly. "Sounds good."

Lydia smacked his arm playfully. "Derrick Anderson! Have you even heard a word I've said?"

Turning his gaze back to her, Derrick's expression grew serious. "We're being followed."

Lydia's heart skipped a beat. "Where?" she asked, trying to sound calm though a chill ran down her spine.

"The two guys in the corner," Derrick explained quietly, barely moving his lips. "They've been watching us since we sat down."

Lydia discreetly pulled out her compact mirror and pretended to touch up her makeup, using it to glance over at the men. "How do you know they're not just two guys having dinner?" she whispered, trying to rationalize.

Derrick shook his head, his voice low and steady. "In a place like this? And look at their boots—U.S. military issue."

Lydia exhaled sharply, her frustration barely contained. "Derrick, you're just being paranoid. Nobody knows we're here. How could they be following us?"

Derrick's expression remained grim. "When Marco dropped off that clue, he said our presence had been noted. Someone knows we're here. It could be a leak... or worse."

As they walked back to the hotel, Derrick held Lydia's hand tightly, his eyes scanning every shadow as they strolled along the canal. Venice was quieter now, the evening settling into a peaceful lull. The sound of water lapping against the gondolas was almost calming, but Derrick couldn't shake the feeling of being watched.

As they passed a man sitting on a bench, reading a newspaper, Derrick noticed him glance up at them more than once. His suspicion deepened.

"Hey," Derrick said, tugging Lydia's hand gently, "why don't we check out that alley? I heard there are some great ice cream shops hidden away from the main drag."

Lydia hesitated, casting him a skeptical glance. Derrick wasn't usually the type to suggest venturing into narrow alleys, but the thought of gelato was too tempting. She followed him, trusting his instincts.

Sure enough, tucked away in a quiet corner, they found a small, charming gelato shop. As Lydia ordered, Derrick kept his eyes on the alley, watching for any sign of their mysterious pursuers.

Lydia handed him a cone and narrowed her eyes playfully. "This is an SDR, isn't it?"

Derrick chuckled, taking a bite of his gelato. "A little *surveillance detection route* never hurt anyone," he said, licking the dessert with a smirk.

Later that night, back in the safety of their suite at the Gritti Palace, Derrick finally felt a small sense of relief. They had made it back without incident, and now, maybe, he could relax—if only for a moment. Lydia immediately grabbed a notepad and began planning their sightseeing for the next day, while Derrick moved toward their suitcase, ready to pack for their departure.

He paused, noticing something off. "Didn't I leave this open when we left?" he muttered, suspicion creeping back into his voice.

***

A few hours earlier, the door to their hotel room had quietly clicked open. A man and woman dressed in tactical gear slipped inside.

"You check the suitcase. I'll handle the bathroom," the man instructed, his voice a low whisper. They meticulously searched every corner of the room, rifling through personal belongings, looking for something specific.

"Found anything?" the woman asked as she opened the drawers.

"Nothing," the man replied, frustration seeping into his voice. "It's not here. They must have it on them."

The woman smirked as she opened the cabinet doors, revealing a small hotel safe. Entering the override code, she opened the safe, but it was empty.

"Nothing," she confirmed, her tone flat.

Stepping out into the hallway, the man dialed a number on his phone. "Sir, we didn't find it. I think he's carrying it," he reported, his voice hushed. After a brief pause, a curt voice responded. "Understood," the man said before hanging up.

***

The next morning, as Derrick packed their suitcase, his mind was still on edge. The events of the previous night lingered, and he couldn't shake the feeling of being watched. Slipping the envelope from Marco into his shorts pocket, he made sure it was secure.

"Figured out the numbers yet?" Lydia asked as she tied her hair back, her excitement bubbling as usual.

Derrick sighed. "No, but I think I've cracked the first part of the riddle. The 'snake through the jungle' is the Amazon, and the first letters spell out Iquitos, a river town in Peru."

"Peru?!" Lydia's eyes sparkled with excitement. "Too bad Mike never got his clearance to go there. We could have had dinner!"

Derrick smiled weakly, his thoughts still clouded by the realization that they were in more danger than he initially suspected. After checking out of the hotel and leaving their luggage at the front desk for safekeeping, Derrick and Lydia set out to explore Venice, trying to make the most of the time they had left. The hotel agreed to hold their bag until they returned... for a *nominal* fee.

By mid-afternoon, Derrick was running on fumes. They had spent hours touring St. Mark's Square, admiring the grandeur of St. Mark's Basilica, Doge's Palace, and the vibrant colors of Venice's skyline. Lydia was having the time of her life, soaking in every moment, while Derrick's mind kept wandering back to the night before.

Lydia browsed a nearby boutique, chatting with the shop owner while Derrick sat on a bench just outside. He tried to relax, but something was gnawing at him. His instincts were screaming, and as he glanced up, his blood ran cold. One of the men from the restaurant was casually watching the store. His heart began to race as he quickly texted Lydia.

"I need to take a walk. Meet me at the store's entrance."

Blending into the crowd, Derrick followed the man, keeping his distance but never losing sight of him. The man walked with an air of confidence, as if he knew he was being tailed but didn't care. As Derrick trailed behind, he noticed something even more unsettling— the other man was actually shadowing him now.

Derrick quickly made his way back to the store, finding Lydia at the register as she finished her purchase. He slipped his arm around her, pulling her close and whispering in her ear. "We need to leave. The two guys from last night are here. Act normal."

Lydia's heart skipped a beat, but she didn't show it. She smiled at the cashier, thanked her, and calmly walked with Derrick out of the store. As they stepped into the bustling square, Derrick's gaze locked onto a third man speaking with the others. His heart stopped.

It was Obadiah.

Lydia gasped when she saw him, her eyes widening in shock. "What's he doing here?!"

"Run!" Derrick shouted, grabbing her hand as they sprinted through the crowded square, weaving between tourists and dodging groups of people.

Derrick and Lydia sprinted through the bustling streets, weaving through the crowd as they made their way toward the hotel.

Lydia dashed inside to grab their bag while Derrick stayed outside, scanning the narrow street for any sign of the operatives. His heart pounded as he spotted Obadiah rounding the corner in pursuit.

Having just gotten the bag, Lydia turned to see Derrick shoving an antique cabinet in front of the entrance. The heavy piece scraped across the floor, with its delicate china rattling ominously. "Derrick, don't—" Her words were cut short by the sharp sound of porcelain shattering against the marble floor as the cabinet tipped over, blocking the door.

"Back door!" Derrick shouted, grabbing her hand once more. They bolted toward the canal pier, their footsteps echoing off the wooden planks as they skidded to a stop at the water's edge.

Lydia looked around, panic creeping into her voice. "Now what?"

"Boat!" Derrick replied without hesitation, spotting a wooden motorboat tied up nearby. They leaped into it, and as Lydia clambered with their suitcase, Derrick fired up the engine. The smell of gasoline mixed with the briny air as the boat rumbled to life. Without a second to spare, Derrick slammed the throttle in reverse, lurching the boat backward as they shot out into the canal.

For a moment, Derrick felt a surge of triumph—until he glanced back and saw another boat closing in fast. The narrow canal walls blurred past in a dizzying mix of stone bridges and dark water. Lydia's knuckles turned white as their pursuers matched every twist and turn.

Noticing a small compartment near the steering wheel, Derrick yanked it open to reveal a flare gun and three flares nestled inside.

"That'll work!" he exclaimed, snatching the gun and loading it with the first flare.

Still clutching the edge of the boat, Lydia noticed him and yelled in a panic, "Derrick! What are you doing?!"

"Buying us some time," he replied, aiming the barrel over his shoulder. The boat rocked beneath them as he fired the first flare. Lydia ducked as the bright red streak of light arched through the evening sky before landing just short of the oncoming boat.

The flare exploded in a burst of light and smoke, momentarily blinding their pursuers, but Derrick knew it wasn't enough. Without hesitating, he loaded another flare and fired... this time aiming directly at the boat's windshield.

The flare hit its mark, shattering the glass in a fiery burst. The pursuing boat veered sharply and the driver struggled to maintain control as the smoke filled the cabin. But they didn't stop.

Derrick gritted his teeth as he loaded the last flare.

"Make this one count," Lydia whispered, her voice barely audible over the engine's roar.

With a deep breath, Derrick aimed carefully, timing the shot with the boat's erratic movements. He squeezed the trigger, and the flare shot out with a loud pop, streaking toward the pursuing boat.

The flare blew through the windshield, past the driver's head, and slammed into the boat's engine. It ignited in a flash of flames and smoke. The boat jerked violently to the side, losing speed as the engine sputtered and died.

Lydia cheered as the flaming wreck drifted aimlessly while the pursuers scrambled to extinguish the fire.

Derrick let out a sigh of relief. "That should keep them busy for a while."

Rewarding him with a kiss on the cheek, Lydia knew they still weren't out of danger. "Let's not stick around to find out," she urged.

Derrick eased off the throttle, letting the boat's speed gradually decrease. His adrenaline began to ebb as he scanned the canal ahead for a safe place to dock.

"There," he whispered, spotting a small, secluded dock tucked between two old buildings. He carefully steered the boat toward it and gently coasted into the wooden planks. Jumping out, the boat rocked slightly as he quickly tied the mooring line to a post. Then, he turned back to Lydia, who was still clutching the suitcase.

"My Dear," Derrick said softly, reaching out to help her out of the boat. Lydia smiled as she grasped his hand, admiring his calmness after such an adventure. It didn't take long for her to realize his anxiousness, feeling his fingers trembling.

They hurried along the narrow walkway leading away from the dock to a dimly lit street. Derrick spotted a taxi idling near the curb, its driver leaning casually against the door.

Derrick wasted no time, flagging the cab down. The driver eyed the disheveled pair but said nothing as he opened the door for them.

"Airport," Derrick instructed as he helped Lydia into the backseat. He tossed the suitcase in beside her before climbing in himself. The cab driver nodded, pulling away from the curb.

As they sped through the streets of Venice, Derrick leaned back in his seat, finally allowing himself a moment to relax. He glanced over at Lydia, who was staring out the window. He reached over, giving her hand a reassuring squeeze.

"Derrick," she began softly. "Why was Obadiah there?"

"I don't know," Derrick sighed. "But I think I need to have a chat with the chief."

CHAPTER 6

Each time the plane touched down in a new place, it was like stepping into a different world. But this landing was something else entirely. Derrick couldn't tear his eyes away from the vast expanse of green that stretched endlessly beneath them. The dense rainforest seemed untouched by time, and a wide river meandered through it like a silver serpent glistening in the sunlight. The sheer beauty of the scene took his breath away.

"It's hard to believe places like this still exist," Derrick muttered, glancing over at Lydia, who was equally captivated by the view on the other side of the plane. "Everything back home feels so... artificial compared to this."

Lydia, alight with excitement, turned to him with a grin. "I can't wait to get down there—no internet, no distractions... just us and nature. It's going to be amazing!"

After landing and making their way to the terminal, they were greeted by a young woman holding a sign with their names on it. "Hola! Señor y Señorita Anderson! Mi nombre es Sofia."

Lydia grinned at Derrick and then addressed Sofia in fluent Spanish, surprising the guide with her ease. Switching to English, Sofia smiled and said, "I didn't expect you to speak Spanish so well. We just do that for the tourists. Come on, let's head to the boat!"

The moto-taxi ride through the bustling town was an adventure in itself. The streets were alive with color and noise, vendors calling out their wares, children laughing as they ran by, and the occasional honk from a passing vehicle. Sofia pointed out various landmarks, sharing snippets of their local history as they passed.

About halfway through town, a sudden, sharp snap from beneath them brought their journey to an abrupt halt. The vehicle sputtered and then stopped altogether. Sofia, her face showing a hint of panic, quickly got out and began inspecting the engine, though it was clear she wasn't sure what she was looking for.

Derrick, sensing her frustration, stepped out to offer help. "Mind if I take a look?" he asked, already crouching down to peer underneath the vehicle. The problem was immediately apparent—a broken chain dangled uselessly, dragging along the ground. "Well, there's your problem," Derrick muttered, half to himself.

Sofia tried calling for help but wasn't getting through to anyone. Derrick, noticing a metal paperclip on the front seat, asked, "Can I use this?" Without waiting for an answer, he grabbed the clip and crawled back under the vehicle.

After a few minutes of fiddling with the chain, he emerged, brushing the dirt off his hands. "Try it now," he suggested.

Sofia turned the key, and to her delight, the moto-taxi roared back to life. Overcome with gratitude, she gave Derrick a quick, tight hug. "Thank you so much, Señor! You are a miracle worker!"

The rest of the ride to the pier was smooth, though Derrick couldn't help but notice Lydia giving him a playful, sideways glance. "What? Do I have something on my face?" he finally asked, feeling her gaze on him.

Lydia's grin widened. "Oh, nothing. Just admiring my handy husband," she teased, her voice full of affection.

When they arrived at the pier, Derrick's confidence faltered slightly as he saw their boat. It was a quaint, two-story vessel that looked more charming than sturdy. On the sun deck railing, a small monkey waved at them with his tiny paw, adding to the boat's rustic charm.

Lydia's face lit up with delight. "He's so cute! What's his name?" she asked Sofia, already smitten with the little creature.

"That's Bongo," Sofia explained as she helped them aboard. "He's our boat's ambassador. Very friendly—he might even sneak into bed with you if he takes a liking to you!"

As the boat pulled away from the dock, the sounds of the town faded, replaced by the gentle lapping of the river against the hull and the distant calls of birds hidden within the dense foliage. The mist rising from the river gave everything an ethereal quality, making the world beyond the boat feel like a distant memory. Derrick and Lydia stood at the railing, watching Iquitos disappear into the distance, both lost in their thoughts.

Lydia was brought back to reality by a gentle tug on her leg. She looked down to find Bongo, the little monkey, saluting her with a cheeky grin. She squealed in delight and knelt down to hug him, her heart melting at his antics. Meanwhile, Derrick noticed Bongo glancing at him with what could only be described as a mischievous glare.

"Did you see that?" Derrick asked, his brow furrowing in confusion.

"See what?" Lydia replied, still focused on the adorable monkey.

"That thing just snarled at me," Derrick said, sounding perplexed and slightly offended.

Lydia giggled. "Oh, please, Derrick. Bongo doesn't know you yet. He'll warm up to you."

As if to prove her wrong, Bongo shot Derrick a playful smirk before sticking out his tongue and scampering off. Derrick sighed inwardly. "This is going to be a long trip."

The evening air on the upper deck was warm and inviting, the lanterns casting a soft glow over the dining area. Derrick pulled out Lydia's chair with an exaggerated flourish, causing her to burst into laughter. It was a moment of levity, a needed contrast to the intensity they had been navigating lately.

Sofia arrived at their table, balancing two glasses filled with a clear liquid. "This is Brazil's national drink, Caipirinha," she explained, placing the glasses before them. "And yes, we know we're in Peru, but we save the Pisco Sour for formal dinner tomorrow night."

Derrick took a sip, immediately surprised by the refreshing mix of sweetness and the sharp tang of lime. "This is good," he said, finishing his drink with unexpected speed and holding his glass out for more.

Lydia watched him, a smile tugging at her lips as Sofia leaned in to whisper, "Doesn't he know that has alcohol in it?"

Lydia chuckled softly, shaking her head. "He'll find out soon enough."

As the evening went on, Derrick's head began to spin slightly. The world around him felt pleasantly wobbly just as the chef arrived with the appetizers. "Tonight," he announced, "we have ceviche mixto, prepared with the freshest seafood."

Derrick, his judgment clouded by the Caipirinhas, eyed the dish. The tangy aroma of lime was irresistible, and he dug in without hesitation. The burst of flavors delighted him until Sofia casually mentioned the dish's key feature: "It's raw seafood, Señor, marinated in lime juice."

Derrick's fork froze mid-air, a look of disbelief crossing his face. "Raw?" he asked, his back starting to itch as the word clam drifted into the conversation.

Lydia sighed, immediately sensing where this was going. "I have the Benadryl in the room," she said, already preparing for the worst.

The main course arrived soon after: skewers of tender, grilled meat, with sides of roasted vegetables. Derrick, now cautious, hesitated. "What exactly is this?" he asked.

Sofia smiled warmly. "It's beef, Señor. Grilled to perfection."

Derrick took a bite and found it delicious. He devoured the skewers until Sofia revealed the truth with a proud grin: "It's beef heart, a delicacy."

Derrick's face fell, his hand automatically reaching for the Caipirinha. Lydia, noticing his discomfort, leaned in. "You know that has alcohol in it, right?"

Without missing a beat, Derrick downed the rest of his drink. "That's what I'm counting on."

Later that night, back in their room, Derrick found sleep elusive. The combination of raw seafood, unfamiliar meats, and more alcohol than he realized had left his stomach in knots. He tossed and turned, seeking a cooler spot in the bed when he felt something soft and hairy beside him.

Smiling sleepily, Derrick leaned in, assuming it was Lydia. But just as his lips brushed against fur—something Lydia definitely didn't have—his eyes flew open. He found himself face-to-face with Bongo, the mischievous monkey grinning at him.

Derrick's scream echoed through the small room, startling both Lydia and Bongo into a chorus of surprised shrieks. Lydia shot up in bed, rubbing her eyes groggily. "What's going on?"

"Why is there a monkey in our bed?!" Derrick demanded, scrambling out from under the covers.

Lydia, now fully awake, blinked at Bongo, who was nestled comfortably between the pillows. "Bongo must have been scared and wanted company," she said, scooping the tiny creature into her arms like a child.

"Scared? This is his home!" Derrick argued, exasperated.

Lydia rolled her eyes, hugging the monkey close. "If this cute little guy wants to sleep in our bed, that's where he'll sleep."

Derrick sighed in defeat, grabbing a pillow from the bed. "Fine," he muttered, trudging toward the bathroom. "I'll go sleep in the tub. I've already spent most of the night in that room anyway."

As Derrick closed the door behind him, he heard Lydia giggling. Bongo let out a contented sigh, and Derrick, slumped against the bathroom door.

"This trip is going to be the end of me," he thought.

***

Derrick groaned as he shifted in the cramped bathtub, every muscle in his body protesting. His head throbbed in sync with the gentle rocking of the boat, and the dim light filtering in through the small bathroom window felt like a cruel spotlight shining directly on his misery. He had spent the entire night curled up in the tub, trying to keep his nausea at bay, but it was relentless.

A soft nudge on his shoulder woke him. Lydia's concerned voice filtered through the haze of his discomfort. "Honey, you feeling any better? It's breakfast time if you're hungry."

Derrick winced as he unfolded himself from his fetal position, stumbling out of the bathroom. The mere thought of food made his stomach churn, but he knew he needed to attempt to face the day. As he squinted at the dim light in the room, Lydia innocently reached for the curtains.

"No! Don't!" Derrick croaked, but it was too late. The sunlight streamed in, flooding the room with unforgiving brightness. Derrick winced, clutching his head. "Curse you, sun! Curse you!" he growled, the throbbing in his skull intensifying.

On the top deck, Lydia breathed in the fresh jungle air, listening to the call of macaws overhead. The peacefulness of the Amazon was overwhelming, the dense greenery surrounding them like a natural fortress, untouched by the modern world. The moment felt magical, like they were the only people in existence, floating down the endless river.

Suddenly, Bongo screeched from somewhere behind her, disrupting her peace. Lydia turned just in time to see the mischievous monkey dart past her, Derrick's underwear flapping on his head like a tiny victory flag.

Derrick appeared moments later, out of breath and furious, charging after Bongo. "Get back here, you stupid mangy primate!" he yelled, his frustration evident.

Lydia barely suppressed a laugh as she called after him, "Derrick... why does Bongo have your underwear on his head?"

"He stole them, put them on his head, and then ran off laughing," Derrick huffed, panting as he tried to catch his breath.

Bongo paused just long enough to rip the underwear off his head, fling them over the side of the boat, and mock Derrick with a taunting shake of his tiny rear end.

Derrick's eyes widened in disbelief. "You jerk! Those were my last clean pair!" he shouted, resuming his pursuit.

Sofia arrived just as Bongo made his escape. "What's going on?" she asked, bringing Lydia a drink.

Lydia chuckled, shaking her head. "Just two monkeys playing tag."

By dinnertime, Derrick was still recovering from his culinary misadventures the night before. When Sofia brought out a tray of Pisco Sours, Derrick's stomach churned at the mere sight of the drinks.

"I think I'll pass on that tonight," he said, pushing the glass away.

Sofia looked surprised. "But, Señor, you enjoyed the other so much last night. You'll love this one."

Derrick grimaced at the memory. "Can I just have some water, please?"

The chef soon arrived with the first course, proudly announcing, "Inchicapi soup! A traditional Peruvian dish made with hen."

Derrick eyed the bowl suspiciously. "What part of the hen, exactly?"

The chef laughed but didn't answer, leaving Derrick to poke at the soup cautiously.

Upon finishing the inchicapi, the chef returned with the entrees. "And for our main course, my specialty, tacacho with cecina… and for you, Mr. Anderson, that is fried plantain balls with smoked pork."

Derrick managed a grateful smile, relieved to hear something more familiar.

After the meal, Lydia was swept up in the romantic atmosphere. Sofia and the chef played soft traditional Peruvian music, and Lydia pulled Derrick onto the makeshift dance floor. As they swayed to the melody, Derrick found himself lost in her eyes, the stresses of the day slipping away. "You look so beautiful tonight," he whispered, causing Lydia to blush.

From the corner of his eye, Derrick noticed Bongo watching them from a distance, his little face twisted into what seemed like jealousy. Derrick chuckled at the absurdity of it all. Even the monkey wanted Lydia's attention.

Later, when they returned to their room, Derrick was startled to find Bongo curled up in their bed, snuggled under the blankets.

"Oh, no. I don't think so, you hairy monstrosity!" Derrick growled, grabbing a shoe and chasing the monkey off the bed. Bongo screeched indignantly before leaping onto the windowsill, returning Derrick's glare with a mischievous screech of his own before darting out of sight.

Lydia poked her head out of the bathroom, her eyes sparkling with amusement. "You okay out there?"

"Just dealing with a pest," Derrick muttered.

That night, Derrick was jolted awake by something smacking him in the face. Disoriented, he opened his eyes to find Bongo standing triumphantly on his chest, holding Derrick's own shoe in his tiny paws. Before Derrick could react, Bongo crawled over to Lydia and gently tapped her shoulder with the shoe, then dropped it beside her with a playful look.

Derrick lunged for the shoe, but Bongo darted toward the window, his cheeky grin never faltering. Just as Derrick was about to throw the shoe at him, Lydia stirred, groggily opening her eyes. "Did you just hit me with your shoe?" she mumbled.

"It wasn't me! It was that hairy beast!" Derrick pointed at Bongo, who now perched innocently on the windowsill.

Lydia, still half-asleep, shook her head. "Why would you blame him? He's just a sweet little monkey."

Fed up, Derrick hurled the shoe at Bongo, but the monkey ducked, and the shoe sailed straight out the window and into the river. Bongo immediately ran into Lydia's arms, clinging to her like a scared child.

"Serves you right, Derrick," Lydia teased while stroking Bongo's fur. The monkey, sensing his victory, stuck out his tongue at Derrick before snuggling into Lydia's embrace. Derrick sighed in defeat.

***

The next morning, as the boat pulled into port, Derrick and Lydia were enjoying the last few moments of their river journey. The thick mist hovering over the water was slowly burning off, revealing the vibrant greens of the rainforest and the bustling activity of the nearby port town. They were chatting with Sofia when the captain approached, a wide grin plastered across his face.

"I hope you enjoyed your trip! We sure enjoyed having you on board, especially Bongo here," he said, gesturing to the little monkey who stood proudly beside him. "I think he even has a little something for you."

Bongo held out an envelope, his mischievous grin intact. Derrick hesitated for a moment before taking it, laughing at the sight of the troublemaker now acting like a model citizen. "I forgive you, you little hairy monster," he said, smiling as he opened the envelope.

Inside was the next clue from Tae:

> *"To an island city where gardens bloom,*
> *A bustling port with a vibrant loom.*
> *Where cultures mix and flavors delight,*
> *Under the equator's warm, bright light.*
> *Seek a place where apples might be.*
> *Not in an orchard, but where you dine*
> *with glee.*

In a global chain known far and wide,
A waitress awaits with secrets to
confide.
Mei Ling Tan to be your guide."

At the airport, while waiting to be transported to their plane, Lydia excused herself to use the restroom. Derrick wandered over to a vendor selling hats and spotted a fedora that caught his eye. Feeling a wave of playfulness, he tried it on, tilting it at just the right angle and grinning at his reflection.

When Lydia returned, she took one look at him and rolled her eyes dramatically. "Are you kidding me? You're really going for the Indiana Jones look now?"

Derrick flashed her a wide grin, pulling the brim lower over his eyes. "What do you think? I'm ready for the next adventure."

"Dork," she muttered under her breath, but she couldn't hide the small smile tugging at the corners of her mouth.

As they boarded the plane, Derrick leaned back in his seat, still wearing the fedora, and began humming "The Raiders March." Lydia sighed, pretending to be exasperated. "Seriously?"

He didn't move, but his grin grew wider. "I thought it was fitting with the new hat and all the traveling. Don't you think?"

Lydia shook her head, playfully swatting him on the arm. "You only wish you were as cool as him."

Derrick gasped.

Before bed, Lydia called her parents to check in on Madeline. The screen flickered to life, revealing her dad grinning widely. But it wasn't just his usual smile that caught Lydia off guard—his face was smeared with bright, garish makeup. Lydia's eyes almost popped out of her head.

Derrick was lounging beside her and casually sipping his cola when he noticed her reaction. He leaned over to see what had startled her. The moment his eyes landed on the screen, he nearly choked on his drink. The sight of Jeb with lipstick, eyeshadow, and a poorly drawn mustache, combined with him cheerfully declaring in a high-pitched voice, "I'm pretty," was too much.

Derrick's laughter turned into a coughing fit, and he sprayed cola all over Lydia's lap. "Ewwwww, Derrick! Gross!" she yelped, jumping up to avoid the sticky mess.

Laying the phone down, Lydia went to get some towels to wipe off with. Derrick slowly leaned his head over to take another look. "Uh... Having fun, sir... er... madam?"

Jeb's expression remained unruffled. "Nice hat," he remarked dryly.

102 | P a g e

Returning, Lydia pushed Derrick aside, handing him a towel. "Here, you human fountain. Clean that up!" she ordered, picking the phone back up.

Madeline joined Jeb on the screen as she snuggled up against him. "Mommy! Papa pwetty!" she giggled, pointing at Jeb's colorful face.

Lydia's heart melted at the sight of her daughter. She fought back tears while managing a smile. "He sure is, sweetheart. Are you having fun with Grandma and Grandpa?"

Madeline's eyes sparkled as she nodded vigorously. "We get nuggies and ize queem," she announced with a joy only a child could have.

Jeb gasped in mock outrage, playfully shaking his head. "You traitor! That was supposed to be our secret!" he exclaimed, wrapping Madeline in a warm hug as she giggled uncontrollably.

The conversation continued for another half hour, filled with stories of Madeline's adventures and antics. Eventually, Mary appeared in the background, signaling it was time for Madeline to get ready for bed.

Madeline kissed the phone and said, "Wuv you, Mommy! Miss you!" Then she headed off to bed.

Lydia watched as her little girl turned around and waved one last time before Mary gently led her away and disappeared from the screen.

"She's been asking about you both," Jeb said, his voice softening. "She misses you, but she's having a great time. We've been keeping her busy with all sorts of activities."

Lydia smiled, though the ache in her chest was undeniable. "I miss her so much. We'll be home soon."

Jeb nodded. "I know, sweetheart. She's a tough cookie... just like her mother."

As the call ended, the cabin went silent. Lydia took a deep breath, trying to shake off the wave of emotions that had hit her.

"She's in good hands," Derrick said softly, squeezing her hand. "We'll be back home with her soon."

Lydia's eyes lingered on the blank phone screen for a moment longer before turning to Derrick. "I know. It's just hard being so far away."

Derrick pulled her in for a hug, which caused her to finally release the tears she had been holding in.

CHAPTER 7

Somewhere over the vast expanse of the Pacific Ocean, Derrick's phone buzzed, breaking the quiet drone of the aircraft. He glanced at the screen— *Chief* showed on the screen. With a quick swipe, he answered. "Hey, Chief. What's up?"

"I just wanted to check in and see how things are going. Sounds like you're on a plane. Heading somewhere?"

The Chief's tone was casual, but something felt off. "Yeah, we're on our way to the next location, but there's something I've been meaning to talk to you about. When we were in Venice, we were followed... chased. It was Obadiah. Any idea why he'd be there?"

There was a brief pause on the other end... the kind that makes you think twice. "Unfortunately, I do," the Chief finally responded. "Obadiah is the leader of the Nightfall Clandestine Group. They've been tasked with finding Tae. This means the situation just became a lot more dangerous. Derrick, you need to find him—Tae might have been onto something crucial, but we won't know unless you bring him back... alive."

Derrick's grip tightened around the phone as he glanced at Lydia, who was quietly listening beside him. "Understood."

"Where's your next stop? I need to know in case something goes wrong."

Derrick hesitated, unsure of how much to divulge. After a moment, he gave in. "Singapore, sir."

"Got it. And Derrick... keep your head on a swivel."

***

Derrick awoke to the soft light of dawn filtering through the plane's windows. He turned to see Lydia snuggled up beside him, her peaceful expression bringing him a brief moment of calm.

The usual hum of the aircraft's engines was absent, so he went to the front, where the pilot met him.

"Good morning, sir! We landed about an hour ago, but we let you sleep since it was still early."

Derrick nodded in appreciation.

The sun was just beginning to rise, painting the tarmac with shades of blue, red, and orange. He gently woke Lydia, who stretched and yawned as she took in their new surroundings. She had a busy day planned— shopping at the Raffles City Mall before following the clue to their much-anticipated lunch at Applebee's.

The MRT ride to City Hall Station was a blur of soft chatter and the rhythmic clatter of the train on the tracks. As they stepped off the train, the bustling energy of Singapore encircled them. The city was alive with the sounds of commerce, the scent of street food mingling with the crisp, clean air of the shopping district.

Lydia's eyes sparkled with excitement as they entered the Raffles City Mall. "I saw a store called Génue online," she said, her voice brimming with anticipation. "There's this dress I've been dying to get ever since."

Derrick chuckled, squeezing her hand. "Lead the way, my love."

Navigating through the mall's stylish corridors, they finally found Génue. Lydia flitted between racks, trying on different colors and styles, her enthusiasm infectious. Derrick watched her, a soft smile playing on his lips as she twirled in a flowy pink dress that made her glow. He couldn't deny it—she looked stunning. After she was done, they made their way to Applebee's, shopping bags in tow.

The restaurant was buzzing with activity as they requested Mei Ling Tan, as the clue had instructed. A middle-aged woman with a warm smile, Mei Ling led them to a cozy booth near the back, away from the noise.

"We're here for the clue our friend, Tae, left. Do you happen to have it?" Derrick asked.

Mei Ling's smile widened as she nodded. "Ah yes, I remember him well. He sure did love his Applebee's. But he told me not to give it to you until after you've had a meal."

As they waited for their food, Lydia reminisced about when they were preparing the nursery. "Remember when we were painting Madeline's room?" she asked, a mischievous glint in her eye.

Derrick chuckled, the memory clear in his mind. "How could I forget?"

...*Lydia was finishing taping the edges of the nursery walls when Derrick returned from Home Depot, balancing two cans of paint and a large box in his arms. He fumbled through the doorway, the box almost slipping from his grasp.*

Lydia peeked out, raising her eyebrows. "Honey... you were just supposed to get paint," she said, giggling.

Derrick's face was full of excitement. "I know, but check this out! This sprayer is going to make the job so much easier!"

Despite her skepticism, Lydia watched as Derrick set up the sprayer. To her surprise—and relief—it worked like a charm. He moved around the room with childlike glee, spraying the walls with the perfect shade of pink.

"It works! It works!" he shouted in triumph. But just as he was about to finish the last wall, there was a loud pop, and the paint sputtered to a stop. Confused, Derrick inspected the spray gun, his excitement turning to concern as he traced the hose back to the pump.

"Oh, there's the problem," he said, turning to Lydia with a sheepish grin. But his smile faded as he saw her standing there, covered in pink paint from head to toe. "Oh, honey! I'm so sorry! Don't be mad... I'll get you cleaned up!"

Lydia's eyes narrowed, a slow, almost menacing smile spreading across her face as she wiped paint from her eyes. "Oh, I'm not mad..." she said, her tone far too sweet to be genuine.

Derrick's heart skipped a beat as he realized she was out for revenge. He tried to make a run for it, but Lydia was faster. She tackled him to the ground, smearing the wet paint from her clothes all over him, both of them laughing until they were breathless...

Derrick gazed at Lydia, his heart swelling with love. "We've had some pretty amazing times, haven't we?"

Lydia nodded, her eyes sparkling. "You've made my life more exciting than I ever imagined."

Just then, the waitress returned with their meals. As she placed Derrick's plate down, she subtly tucked a small piece of paper beneath it. Derrick discreetly retrieved it, unfolding it out of sight.

The words on the paper were cryptic but clear:

"In a place where history climbs,
Beware the vandals in time.
Seek within where shadows loom,

Find what you seek in Khufu's tomb."

Derrick leaned in close, whispering to Lydia, "Cairo."

Lydia's eyes widened in surprise. "How did you figure that out so fast?"

He pointed to the name Khufu. "That's the pharaoh buried in the Great Pyramid."

Lydia noticed some additional writing on the paper Derrick was holding. "What's that on the back?" she asked. "What is 'Operation Midnight Halo'?"

Derrick's face immediately soured at the phrase. Lydia could see the unease in his eyes, but before he could explain, Mei Ling returned to top off Derrick's already full glass of water, her expression suddenly serious. "We have visitors," she warned quietly.

Derrick's gaze flicked to the entrance. "Nightfall is here," he gasped. "Two at the front door."

Lydia scanned the other side of the room. "Two more by the side entrance. They don't seem to have spotted us yet."

Seeing a passing waiter who was laden with a tray of dishes, he grabbed the clue and instructed, "Grab your bag and meet me in the kitchen." He rose from the booth, slipping into the crowd, using the waiter's tray as cover. Moving hastily, he reached the kitchen door with Lydia close behind.

"How did you do that without knocking that tray out of his hands?" Lydia whispered, a hint of jesting in her voice.

Acting as if they belonged, they slipped through the bustling kitchen, dodging chefs and servers as they made their way to the back door. Derrick cautiously pushed it open, peering outside. The coast was clear.

They hurried across the parking lot toward the main road as Derrick scanned for their next move. That's when he saw it—a helicopter parked near the entrance.

A mischievous gleam sparked in his eyes. Lydia noticed and sighed. "Derrick, that's a horrible idea."

"You don't even know what I'm thinking," he protested.

"Doesn't matter. Any idea that makes you smile like that is bound to end badly."

Crouching behind a car, Derrick laid out his plan. "I'm going to sneak up there, take out the pilot, and then we'll fly that thing back to the airport. Nightfall won't be able to follow us."

Lydia's skepticism was evident. "Are you sure you can fly that?"

Derrick flashed a confident smile. "Of course! A helicopter is a helicopter! Just wait here until I get it started, then hop on."

With that, Derrick began his approach, darting from car to car until he was just a few yards from the aircraft. He took a deep breath, preparing to rush the cockpit. But as he rounded the final vehicle, he found himself face to face with the pilot, who was standing casually by the helicopter, clearly expecting him.

"Oh, hey there. Nice helicopter. Mind if I take a look?" Derrick asked, trying to sound nonchalant.

The pilot didn't buy it. "Nice try, Anderson. How about you come along quietly?"

"Uh, Anderson? Who's that? I'm Johnny Smith... you know, like the apple guy," Derrick stammered, trying to play it cool.

The pilot's patience wore thin. "So, we do this the hard way, then," he said, pulling a pistol from his holster. But before he could raise it, there was a loud clang, and the pilot's eyes rolled back as he crumpled to the ground. Behind him stood Lydia, holding a metal pipe and shaking her head.

"Smooth there, Johnny. Now get in and start this thing before anyone else shows up," Lydia ordered, dragging the unconscious pilot behind a nearby car.

Derrick jumped into the cockpit, his hands moving swiftly over the switches. "Flip, flip, little turn... add the fuel, then watch it burn!" he sang to himself as the ignitors clicked.

"Stop messing around and get us out of here!" Lydia hissed. "They could come out any second."

Derrick shot her a mock glare. "It's not that simple. If I rush it, we'll hot start and fry the engine."

He continued with the startup sequence and the jet engines roaring to life. "Throttle detent... blades turning... oil pressure rising," he called out, half to himself.

Just as Derrick pulled the helicopter into a hover, several Nightfall operatives burst through the front door, drawn by the sound of the rotors.

"Time to go!" he shouted, yanking the collective and sending the aircraft into a rapid ascent.

The sudden motion threw Lydia to the floor. "Hey! A little warning next time?" she snapped, just as a barrage of bullets clanged against the helicopter's floor.

"They're shooting at us!" Lydia exclaimed, her voice tinged with panic.

"Relax! This thing has armor against small arms fire. We're fine," Derrick reassured her, weaving the helicopter between the mall and the towering steeple of St. Andrew's Cathedral.

But even as he spoke, the engine began to sputter, having taken several rounds. The master alarm blared as the helicopter started shuddering violently.

Lydia's eyes narrowed. "You were saying?"

Derrick's optimism wavered as the fire warning light flashed, and the engine flamed out. "I've got this. Nothing to worry about!" he declared, though his confidence sounded increasingly forced.

With only forty feet of altitude, Derrick barely had time to react. Entering an autorotation, he aimed for the only open space in sight... the soccer fields of a nearby country club.

"Hold on!" Derrick yelled as the helicopter plummeted, crashing onto the field with a bone-jarring thud.

Derrick instinctively began the emergency shutdown procedure, but Lydia wasn't waiting around. She grabbed his arm, yanking him from the cockpit. "Leave it! We need to go—now!"

They were sprinting across the field as the helicopter exploded into flames behind them. Derrick dove to the ground in a dramatic roll, instinctively taking cover from the blast. Still on her feet, Lydia glanced back at him with a mix of amusement and disbelief.

"New to this whole spy thing, huh?" she quipped.

As they made it to the MRT station a few blocks away, they stopped to catch their breath. The relief was short-lived when Lydia pointed out a group of four men in tactical gear running past. "I told you they'd be here soon," she said, a hint of smugness in her voice.

Derrick's blood ran cold as he spotted a fifth figure trailing behind the group. It was Obadiah.

"How is he here again?" Derrick muttered, his voice laced with frustration and dread.

Obadiah's gaze suddenly locked onto Derrick's, his eyes narrowing in recognition. After a tense moment, he turned and continued toward the helicopter with the rest of the team.

"And now he knows..."

CHAPTER 8

The sky outside the plane was pitch black when Derrick's phone rang, jolting him awake. He fumbled to answer, expecting the usual calm tone of the chief on the other end. But the voice that greeted him was anything but calm.

"Derrick, what were you thinking!? I just got word about the crash in Singapore. Do you have any idea what kind of mess you've caused? You stole a U.S. military helicopter and crashed it on foreign soil! What was it even doing there in the first place?!"

Derrick's frustration simmered to a boil as he tried to process how the chief knew so many details about something that had just happened. "Sir, what makes you think I had anything to do with that? Oh... and *'why was the helicopter there?'*, you tell me. Obadiah and his team brought it. They shot us down while we were trying to escape."

A heavy silence filled the line before the chief spoke again, his voice more subdued. "I'm sorry, Derrick. I didn't mean to be accusatory. I don't know how they keep finding out where you're going. Are you sure you haven't told anyone else?"

Derrick's irritation flared. "No one else... except you."

As the plane touched down at Cairo International Airport, the sky outside was still dark. The engines whined down as the aircraft taxied to a stop. The flight had been long, and Derrick was eager to stretch his legs. When the door finally opened, a blast of hot, dry air rushed into the cabin, wrapping around him like a blanket. It was a stark contrast to the cool, climate-controlled environment of the plane. Derrick stepped out onto the tarmac, feeling the heat instantly searing his skin, even in the pre-dawn darkness. The warmth of the air was mixed with the faint scent of desert sand and exhaust fumes from the airport.

Lydia's eyes sparkled as the hotel shuttle pulled up to the Marriott Mena House. Nestled in an oasis of lush gardens, it was a paradise amid the desert landscape. But it was the view that truly took her breath away—the majestic pyramids of Giza stood just beyond the hotel grounds. The early morning light cast a long shadow across the desert floor. "It's like a dream," she whispered to Derrick, who smiled, admiring the view with her.

Their luxurious suite offered an unobstructed view of the pyramids, which seemed close enough to touch. The cool breeze from the air conditioning inside the room was a welcome relief from the heat outside, but Lydia found herself drawn to the balcony repeatedly, enchanted by the view.

After a restful night, they awoke the next morning excited about the day's adventure. Having secured permits from the local government, they would be exploring the inner chambers of the Great Pyramid.

The sun was just rising as they made their way onto the Giza Plateau. It cast an eerie red hue over the sands, leaving Derrick somewhat unsettled. "Isn't there a curse on this place or something?" he said, his nerves showing in his voice.

Lydia chuckled at his superstitions. "You're such a weenie, Derrick."

Their guide, a local man named Hassan, met them at the entrance to the Great Pyramid of Khufu. He was a small, wiry man with quick eyes. Greeting them with a smile, he said with pride in his voice, "Hello, friends. Welcome to the Great Pyramid! I will take you inside to the inner chamber where few get to go."

After clearing security, they followed Hassan through the pyramid's narrow, dimly lit passages. The air inside was cool and musty, a stark contrast to the heat outside. The sound of their footsteps echoed off the stone walls as they descended deeper into the ancient structure. Derrick's unease continued, but he pushed it aside.

Finally, they reached the inner chamber. It was a small, claustrophobic space with walls covered in ancient hieroglyphs. The air was thick with dust, and the dim light barely illuminated the room. A large, imposing sarcophagus dominated the center of the room.

Hassan stood by the door watching them with suspicion as they moved about.

"Here we are," Derrick whispered, his voice barely more than a breath in the stillness. "It has to be here somewhere."

Their initial search of the chamber offered little in the way of clues.

Lydia, drawn more to the history around her, examined the hieroglyphics with fascination. Her gasp broke the silence as she spotted something. "Derrick! Look at this! Someone scratched *'Lincoln Bedroom'* into the wall here. How could anyone deface something so precious?!"

Derrick moved closer, squinting at the vandalism. That's when he saw it—a tiny smiley face and the name *"Tae"* etched just below the phrase. "Honey, you're not going to like this," he said, bracing himself for her reaction.

But before he could explain, the ground began to tremble violently. Dust and debris started raining down from the ceiling. Panic flashed across Hassan's face. "Earthquake!" he shouted, and without another word, turned and bolted back through the entryway they had come from, leaving Derrick and Lydia behind in the rapidly destabilizing chamber.

Derrick grabbed Lydia, pulling her close to shield her from the falling debris. The walls seemed to close in around them as the sound of stone grinding against stone filled the air. A loud crash echoed through the chamber as the sarcophagus toppled over, spilling its ancient contents.

"I've got you," Derrick said into Lydia's ear, reassuring her.

As the shaking finally stopped, Derrick quickly checked Lydia for injuries. "You okay, honey?" he asked, trying to keep his voice calm.

Her trembling hand pointed toward the entrance as her voice shakily replied, "We're trapped."

Derrick's mind raced as he took in their situation. The entrance was blocked by heavy stones that had shifted during the quake. Lydia pushed against one with all her strength when she called out, "Can you give me a hand here, Derrick?"

Scanning the chamber for anything he could use for leverage, Derrick's eyes landed on the dismembered mummy lying on the floor. Without thinking, he reached down and grabbed the detached arms with a grin. "Hey! Lucky us. I just happened to find an extra pair of hands lying around."

Lydia turned, her eyes wide in horror. "Derrick! That's a desecration! Put those down!"

His grin faded as he quickly dropped the arms. "Sorry, I didn't realize you had 'mummy' issues."

Despite herself, Lydia couldn't help but smile, even in the face of their predicament. "Focus, Derrick. We need a real plan."

Derrick continued searching the chamber until he spotted a long, sturdy staff lying on the ground. It was adorned with intricate hieroglyphs, clearly a valuable artifact, but at that moment, its worth as a tool outweighed its historical significance. He grabbed it and hurried to Lydia's side.

"This should do the trick," he said, wedging the staff between two stones to create leverage.

Lydia gasped again when she saw the staff. "Oh, Derrick! You can't use that! It's a treasure!"

Derrick shot her a look. "Would you rather Khufu himself lend us a hand? Just get ready to push."

Reluctantly, Lydia got into position, and together they heaved with all their might. Slowly, the stone began to shift, revealing a small gap. "It's working!" Lydia exclaimed.

With one final push, the rock dislodged and rolled to the other side of the chamber. When it did, the staff snapped in two. Lydia's stomach turned, seeing the broken artifact, until Derrick grabbed her and said, "Honey, we need to go."

They squeezed through the gap, emerging back into the pyramid's passageways. Derrick retraced their steps from memory and finally reached the entrance. Their bodies were aching, and minds frazzled... but they were free.

Outside, they blended in with the crowd of emergency workers and snuck off to a secluded spot nearby.

Derrick collapsed onto the ground as Lydia knelt beside him, pressing a quick kiss to his lips. "Next time, let's avoid places that can collapse on us... deal?" he joked, managing a smile on his tired face.

Lydia laughed as the tension finally broke. "Deal. Now, how about we get cleaned up and get some dinner?" I hear there's a Pizza Hut nearby with a great view of the pyramids. We can finish watching the sunset behind them from there."

Later, as they sat in the Pizza Hut enjoying their meal, the news on the nearby TV caught their attention. The footage showed the quake's aftermath, including the blocked pyramid entrance and damage to the inner chamber. Video onsite showed one of the police officers holding the broken staff Derrick had used. The anchor mentioned that authorities were searching for two Americans seen entering the pyramid just before the earthquake happened.

Lydia looked worried, but Derrick reassured her that no one could link them to the damage. That was until Hassan appeared on the screen, giving a description of the "*persons of interest.*"

"That little weasel!" Derrick muttered. "Maybe we should head back to the plane."

Lydia nodded in agreement as she scanned the room. A number of the customers were looking at them with suspicion.

They quickly paid for their meal and left the restaurant. They were able to make it back to the jet without being stopped. Rushing aboard, Derrick instructed the pilots to take off without delay. Captain Reynolds glanced at Lydia and asked, "Did he desecrate another tomb?"

Derrick innocently gasped. "Another?"

Laughing, Lydia shook her head. "Let's not stick around to find out what the authorities call this one."

CHAPTER 9

Derrick and Lydia stood in the bustling crowd outside the White House, the air buzzing with anticipation. It wasn't every day they found themselves in front of the nation's most iconic residence, and Derrick could feel the excitement mingling with the cool breeze that rustled the leaves of the nearby trees. He gently pulled Lydia closer, his arm draped around her shoulder, as they moved through the security checkpoint and entered the grand building.

Inside, the tour was already in full swing. The low hum of conversations filled the air as tourists marveled at the lavish decor and historical artifacts. Derrick, however, found it hard to focus on the beauty around him. His thoughts kept drifting back to the clue they needed to find, hidden somewhere in the Lincoln Bedroom—a room that wasn't part of the standard tour.

"Ready?" Derrick whispered to Lydia as they followed the group through the East Room, the rich tapestries and gleaming chandeliers barely registering in his mind.

"Let's do this," she replied, her voice steady but her eyes darting around, scanning for any potential escape routes.

As the tour guide led them into the Green Room, Derrick spotted a narrow hallway branching off to the right, away from the main tour path. It was now or never. He nudged Lydia gently, and without a word, they slipped away from the group. They moved silently as they disappeared down the corridor.

The White House was a labyrinth of hallways and rooms, each more ornate and filled with history than the last. Derrick and Lydia moved purposefully, their footsteps muffled by the thick, plush carpet underfoot. The distant murmur of the tour group faded behind them and was replaced by the quiet hum of the building's ventilation system. Turning a corner, they found themselves in an empty hall.

"Which way now?" Lydia whispered, her voice barely audible as she glanced around, her heart pounding in her chest.

"Up those stairs," Derrick replied, pointing to a narrow staircase tucked away at the end of the hall. "The Lincoln Bedroom should be on the second floor."

After climbing the stairs, they paused at the top to catch their breath. Just as they were about to continue, they heard voices coming from around the corner—footsteps growing louder.

Derrick and Lydia pressed themselves against the wall, hoping to stay hidden in the shadows. The voices were getting closer, and suddenly, they found themselves face-to-face with President Green... and his Secret Service detail.

"Freeze!" two of the agents shouted, drawing their weapons and moving toward them.

The other agents swarmed the President and ushered him away from the area.

Before Derrick and Lydia could react, the President raised his hand, his voice cutting through the tension. "Stop! Stop!... Derrick? Lydia? Is that you?"

...Derrick and Lydia had prepared their home to welcome Senator Green and his wife, Katherine. The guest room was meticulously arranged, with crisp white sheets adorning the bed and a vase of fresh flowers adding a touch of warmth to the nightstand. Hosting the Greens during the election campaign had felt like a privilege—over the years, they had become close friends, and Derrick and Lydia were more than happy to offer them a warm place to stay.

"Do you think they'll be comfortable?" Lydia asked, fussing over a pillow for what must have been the third time.

Derrick smiled, wrapping his arm around her shoulders. "They'll be more than comfortable. You've made this room look like it's straight out of a five-star hotel."

Lydia chuckled, leaning in to kiss his cheek. "Let's hope so. It's only for a few weeks, but I want them to feel at home."

The doorbell rang, signaling their guests' arrival. Derrick and Lydia exchanged a quick look of excitement before hurrying downstairs. When they opened the door, Senator Green and Katherine greeted them with warm smiles, their faces lighting up at the sight of their friends.

"Welcome!" Lydia said, hugging Katherine warmly while Derrick shook the senator's hand.

"Thank you both so much for having us," Senator Green said, sounding genuinely appreciative. "It's such a relief to have a place to stay during this crazy time."

"Our pleasure," Derrick replied. "Come in and make yourselves at home."

As the days passed, the house buzzed with the energy of the campaign. The dining room often doubled as a makeshift office, papers and laptops strewn across the table as the Greens worked tirelessly. But no matter how busy the days became, Derrick and Lydia always made sure the house felt like a sanctuary, a place where their friends could unwind at the end of a long day...

Back in the White House, the Secret Service agents hesitated, loosening their grip somewhat on Derrick and Lydia's arms.

"Mr. President, it's good to see you," Derrick said, relief evident in his voice as he recognized the familiar face of his friend.

"What are you doing here?" President Green asked, a smile spreading across his face as he took in the sight of Derrick and Lydia, clearly out of place but somehow fitting into the surreal situation.

"It's a long story," Derrick began, quickly explaining their search for the clue hidden in the Lincoln Bedroom, feeling slightly sheepish as he recounted their impromptu detour.

President Green listened intently, his expression one of both curiosity and concern. When Derrick finished, he turned to his detail, his decision made. "It's okay. Let them go. They're friends."

The agents released their hold and stepped back, their postures only slightly relaxing as the tension in the air dissipated.

"Follow me," the President said, gesturing for them to come along. "I'll take you to the Lincoln Bedroom."

They walked in silence, flanked by the President's detail as he led them through a series of corridors, each one grander than the last. Finally, they reached a large, wooden door that looked like it hadn't been touched in years.

"Here we are," President Green said, pushing the door open with a sense of ceremony.

Inside the Lincoln Bedroom, history seemed to come alive. The room was filled with heavy antique furniture, and each piece seemed to tell a story.

Intrigued, President Green joined in as they started searching the room—looking under the bed, behind paintings, and inside the intricately carved armoire.

Lydia focused on the ornate desk, carefully rifling through the drawers and examining every inch of the surface, her fingers brushing over the worn wood.

"You sure you're not too busy for all this?" Derrick asked the President, pausing his search to look over at his friend. "It seems like your schedule would be full all the time."

The President smiled, a hint of mischief in his eyes. "This job can be pretty dull sometimes—speeches, emails, phone calls. I wouldn't miss a treasure hunt for anything!"

About thirty minutes later, Lydia suddenly shouted, "There!" as she pulled out a small, worn envelope from behind a framed photo of Lincoln.

The President and Derrick hurried over. Their curiosity was piqued as Lydia carefully opened the envelope. Inside was a handwritten note, another clue for their journey.

> "From the base,
> you can see the top of the world.
> But it's not the view, it's the journey.
> Find Pedro and give him three carrots,"

Derrick read aloud, his brow furrowing in concentration.

"This one seems more confusing than the others," Lydia said, her voice tinged with resignation as she tried to make sense of the cryptic message.

"Top of the world... top of the world..." President Green repeated, his mind clearly working to connect the dots. "I heard that phrase recently in a documentary I was watching. What was it about?"

Suddenly, his face lit up with realization. "Everest! It was on Sir Edmund Hillary last week. 'From the base'... Base camp! Sounds like you are looking for Everest's base camp."

Derrick shook the President's hand, his excitement evident. "Thank you, sir! I wish you could join us on this journey. It sounds like we could use your brain!"

"If you need anything from me, don't hesitate to call," the President said, handing Derrick a card with a phone number. "This is my secretary's number. It's the only one these guys will let me give out," he added, nodding at the Secret Service officers beside him with a wry smile. Wishing them adieu, President Green left them with his trademarked phrase as he turned to head back to work. "Dicky Dicky, Derrick, and good luck."

They thanked the President again as he left the room before the Secret Service escorted them back downstairs. Rejoining the rest of the tour, Derrick smiled, knowing the group was blissfully unaware of the adventure that had just unfolded.

As they walked down the driveway of the Executive Mansion, Lydia held Derrick's hand, a sense of disbelief and excitement coursing through her. "Not many people can say they've been given a tour of the Lincoln Bedroom... by the President! Maybe we should have asked if we could catch a ride in his helicopter back to the airport," she joked, her eyes sparkling with the thrill of the day.

Derrick chuckled, pulling out the clue to examine it once more. "Now all we have to do is find Pedro when we get there. I wonder what the significance of the three carrots is?!?" he mused, his mind already turning toward the next part of their journey.

CHAPTER 10

As Derrick and Lydia stepped back onto the plane, the familiar hum of the engines greeted them. The cabin was quiet, and the seats were still cool from the air conditioning. Lydia pulled out her phone and quickly dialed home, eager to check on Madeline. After a few rings, Jeb answered, and the screen filled with the image of Madeline perched on his shoulders, her small hands gripping his ears as she waved enthusiastically at the camera.

"Hi, Maddie!" Lydia's face lit up with a smile as she waved back. "Have you been a good girl for Papa?"

Madeline grinned mischievously and pulled on Jeb's ears, stretching them out like a playful monkey. Jeb chuckled, looking up at her with an amused expression. "That's her new thing," he said, his voice full of affection. "We've been having a blast, honey. We were just watching some old war movies. Who knew she liked guns and explosions so much?"

Lydia's heart skipped a beat, her mind instantly flashing to Derrick's influence. "Daddy!" she exclaimed, concerned. Not so much for the violence but the idea of Madeline turning into a little Derrick.

Jeb burst into laughter. "I'm just kidding, honey. We've been watching those colorful horses she loves so much. She's been teaching me all their names. I take it you haven't found Tae yet?"

Lydia sighed, the weight of the search evident in her face. She was about to respond when Madeline's face appeared closer to the screen, her big eyes filled with longing. "Mommy home?" she asked, her voice small and tinged with sadness.

Lydia's heart clenched. She felt a wave of guilt and longing wash over her, and her voice cracked as she replied, "Almost, Maddie. Almost. You know I love you and wish I could be there right now, right?"

Madeline nodded solemnly, her little lips forming a pout. "Come home soon," she added softly, her words hitting Lydia like a punch to the gut.

Sensing that Lydia was on the verge of tears, Mary appeared on the screen, gently taking the phone from Jeb and moving to a quieter room. "She's doing fine, dear," Mary reassured, her voice calm and comforting. "She misses you but gets distracted easily by your dad... or ice cream."

Lydia managed a small chuckle through her tears, wiping at her eyes. "Thank you, Momma. We didn't expect it to take this long."

"Do you have any idea how much longer it will be?" Mary asked, her tone filled with concern.

"Honestly, no," Lydia admitted. "We're going as fast as we can, but the clues just keep coming."

"It's okay," Mary said gently. "It's important you find him. Just stay safe."

As the pilots went through their final checklists, Derrick and Lydia settled into their seats, bracing themselves for the long flight ahead. The hum of activity outside the plane grew quieter as the cabin door closed, sealing them in for the fourteen-hour journey to Kathmandu, followed by a short flight to Lukla, the gateway to Everest Base Camp.

The plane taxied smoothly down the runway, and soon they were airborne, the city lights of Washington, D.C., shrinking below them. Derrick glanced over at Lydia, who was staring out the window, her face illuminated by the last rays of the setting sun. Her eyes were distant, lost in thought.

"You miss her too, don't you?" Derrick asked softly, sensing the heaviness in her heart.

"Of course I do," Lydia replied, her voice wavering as tears welled up in her eyes. "I miss her little morning hugs... the way she wraps her arms around my neck and squeezes so tight." A tear slipped down her cheek, and she quickly brushed it away, but Derrick could see the deep ache in her eyes.

Derrick's own heart tugged at the sight of Lydia's pain. He thought about how much Madeline needed them, how much they both missed her. But he also knew that if they didn't find Tae, if they didn't finish this mission, he would be as good as dead. Nightfall wouldn't stop until they had him, and Derrick couldn't let that happen—not to Tae, not to the person who had always had his back.

He glanced at Lydia again, wondering if she was here to keep him out of trouble or because she cared just as much about finding Tae. Either way, having her by his side was a comfort he couldn't deny.

As the hours dragged on, Derrick tried to distract himself by binge-watching the first season of *Agent Inept*, a show about a bumbling spy who somehow managed to complete his missions despite his constant mistakes. Derrick found the perfect mix of absurdity and cleverness hilarious, but Lydia, who had dozed off with her head resting on his shoulder, couldn't believe the CIA would ever trust someone so incompetent with such important tasks.

By the time the last show ended and Lydia stirred awake, they were nearing their destination. The plane began its descent, and Derrick felt a familiar twist of nerves in his stomach as the busy Kathmandu airport came into view.

After clearing customs, Derrick and Lydia hurried to their gate for the final leg of their journey—a short but nerve-wracking flight to Lukla. The sight of the small, twenty-seater aircraft waiting on the tarmac made Derrick's heart skip a beat.

As they boarded the plane, Derrick couldn't help but notice the tiny details that set his anxiety on edge. "I've already counted three missing bolts just walking up the stairs," he whispered to Lydia, his voice tight with worry.

She patted his leg and gave him a reassuring kiss on the cheek. "I know, honey, but remember what happened when we asked our pilot about taking us in? He said something in a foreign language, which definitely wasn't 'Sure! No problem'."

The descent into Lukla was harrowing. The mountains rose like jagged teeth around them as the runway loomed closer, looking impossibly short. Derrick's knuckles turned white from gripping the armrests, and his breath came in shallow gasps.

"I can't watch," Derrick muttered, squeezing his eyes shut as the plane touched down with a jolt. The passengers erupted into relieved applause as the pilot slowed the aircraft and taxied towards the terminal.

Lydia squeezed his hand, her voice filled with relief. "We made it," she said softly, though Derrick could hear the undercurrent of tension in her tone.

Lukla was a bustling village filled with trekkers and climbers preparing for their journey to Everest Base Camp. The air was thin and crisp, filled with the sounds of chatter, the clinking of climbing gear, and the occasional roar of a distant avalanche. Derrick and Lydia gathered their gear and headed to the Sherpa meeting point, scanning the crowd for Pedro.

"He should be here somewhere," Derrick said, his eyes darting around as he clutched the three carrots in his hand like they were the key to everything.

They wandered through the crowd, Derrick calling out, "Pedro? Pedro?" with increasing desperation. He approached several people, offering them a carrot and asking if they were Pedro, only to be met with confused looks.

A donkey nudged him persistently, but Derrick ignored it, convinced that he was just a nuisance. Finally, an elderly, weathered man named Alejandro chuckled and said, "This is embarrassing. Pedro is the donkey. Give him the carrots, and let's go."

Derrick's face flushed with embarrassment as he handed the carrots to the donkey, who eagerly munched on them. Lydia laughed softly beside him.

"Well, that's one way to make an impression," Derrick said, trying to laugh it off as they followed Alejandro out of the village.

The trek to Everest Base Camp was both grueling and breathtaking. The rugged beauty of the Himalayas surrounded them, with towering peaks and vast glaciers that seemed to stretch on forever. The thin air made every step a challenge, and by the time they reached their midway point, they were both exhausted.

As night fell, Derrick and Lydia settled into their tent, the cold seeping through their layers of clothing. They huddled together for warmth as their breath was visible in the frigid air.

"This reminds me of when Madeline was born," Lydia said softly, her voice carrying a hint of nostalgia.

Derrick smiled, the memory warming him more than the shared body heat. "You thought it was just heartburn," he recalled. "We were cuddled up on the couch watching TV, and then... your water broke."

Lydia laughed gently. "I still can't believe you delivered her yourself."

"You didn't give me much of a choice," Derrick replied with a chuckle. "I tried to get you to the car, but you just wouldn't hold her in anymore."

Lydia grinned playfully. "Yeah, that's how it went down. I recall it being a little different."

"I'm just glad your parents showed up when they did. I was hoping to be the one comforting you, but your mom was amazing. Your dad, on the other hand..." Derrick shivered, remembering the scene. "Who would have thought Mr. Big Bad Marine would be squeamish over a little blood and... other gooey stuff?" Derrick paused and then shuttered. "Why are they always so gooey?"

Lydia chuckled as she snuggled closer to him. "You being there was more comforting than you give yourself credit for. Madeline is lucky to have you as her dad."

They lay in silence for a while. The sound of the wind whipping around their tent was the only noise breaking the stillness. Despite the cold and the altitude, they felt a deep sense of peace. They had come a long way, not just on this journey, but in their lives together.

"Tomorrow's another long day," Lydia said, her voice growing drowsy. "Let's get some sleep."

Derrick nodded, holding her close. "Goodnight, Lydia. I love you."

"I love you too, Derrick."

...Derrick found himself walking through an empty, echoing warehouse. The cold steel door ahead of him creaked open, revealing a dark room where Lydia lay lifeless on the floor, surrounded by a dark, ominous circle. His heart pounded in his chest as he rushed to her side, cradling her in his arms, praying that it was all a nightmare.

But the sight of her pale face and the entrance wound in her forehead told him otherwise. As he wept, a hooded, faceless figure emerged from the mist, its breath foul and hot as it whispered, "Do not try to take what is mine." The figure reached out with a bony hand to claim Lydia, and no matter how hard Derrick tried to barter for her life, the figure simply said, "I will see you soon enough," before disappearing into the darkness with her...

Derrick woke with a start, his body tangled in the sleeping bag. His heart raced as he looked around, disoriented, until he saw Lydia sleeping peacefully beside him. Tears filled his eyes as the relief washed over him, and he silently thanked whatever force had allowed him to wake up from that nightmare.

The early morning sun began to rise over the jagged peaks of the Himalayas, casting long shadows across the Khumbu Glacier. Derrick and Lydia emerged from their tent, the cold, crisp air biting at their faces. They bundled up in their thick jackets, scarves, and hats, preparing for the final leg of their journey.

The camp was alive with activity, the sounds of climbers preparing for their ascents filling the air. The mingling scents of freshly brewed tea and the earthy aroma of the surrounding mountains added to the sensory tapestry.

Still shaken from his nightmare, Derrick felt Lydia's reassuring squeeze on his hand. "You ready?" she asked, her voice laced with excitement.

He took a deep breath and nodded. "Yeah, let's do this."

Alejandro met them at the camp's edge, his warm smile against the cold morning. Together, they set off on the trail and through the otherworldly landscape around them. The sky was a brilliant blue, the sun glinting off the snow, making everything sparkle like a scene from a dream.

They walked carefully, the crunch of their boots on the icy path the only sound as they took in the awe-inspiring views. To their left, the imposing face of Nuptse loomed, its sharp ridges cutting into the sky. To their right, the Khumbu Icefall lay like a frozen river, a treacherous path that many climbers would soon face.

"How are you holding up?" Derrick asked, squeezing Lydia's hand.

"It's incredible," Lydia replied, her eyes wide with wonder. "I never imagined it would be this beautiful."

Alejandro turned back to them with a smile on his weathered face. "We're almost there. Just a little further."

They continued, the path winding up and down, each step bringing them closer to their destination. Cresting a small rise, Derrick and Lydia finally saw it: Everest Base Camp. A cluster of brightly colored tents dotted the glacier, fluttering prayer flags adding splashes of color against the stark white landscape. The air was thin, but the exhilaration of reaching their goal gave them a second wind.

Alejandro led them to a large tent at the center of the camp. Inside, it was surprisingly warm, the smokiness of the yak butter tea and cooking rice welcoming them. Climbers and Sherpas chatted, exchanging stories and preparing for the days ahead.

"Wait here," Alejandro said, handing them a small thermos of hot tea before disappearing into the crowd.

Derrick and Lydia sat on a bench, warming their hands by a small heater and sipping the tea. Derrick felt a nudge on his back and turned to see Pedro nuzzling him. Lydia chuckled at the sight. "He likes you," she said, smiling.

Outside, the sounds of the camp continued—a mix of voices, the flapping of tent fabric in the breeze, and the distant rumble of ice shifting on the glacier. After a few minutes, Alejandro returned, a small, folded piece of paper in his hand.

He handed it to Derrick with a nod. "This is what you came for. I've arranged a lift to take you back down."

Derrick unfolded the paper, his heart racing. The note was written in neat, precise handwriting:

> *"Find the 'Cots of Blue.'*
> *The girls here are cold.*
> *Maybe they can't afford coats.*
> *See if Jackson, save two, will help*
> *Cinnamon.*
> *Declare the Black Lotus."*

Thanking Alejandro, they gave Pedro a pat and stepped back outside, the cold air hitting them once more. The view from the camp was breathtaking. To the north, the summit of Everest rose majestically, shrouded in wisps of cloud. The sheer scale of the mountain was humbling.

A distant whirring sound grew louder, and Derrick and Lydia looked up to see a helicopter approaching, its rotors chopping through the thin air. It touched down gently on a cleared patch of ice, and the pilot signaled for them to board.

"Ready to go back?" Derrick asked, helping Lydia with her pack.

"I'm ready to be warm," she replied, though she couldn't help but take one last look at the awe-inspiring surroundings.

Climbing into the helicopter, they secured their seatbelts and gave the pilot a thumbs-up. Derrick then waved goodbye to Alejandro and Pedro as the aircraft lifted off. They soared over the Khumbu Glacier with the vast expanse of the Himalayas stretching out in every direction. Lydia gasped at the breathtaking panorama of peaks and valleys. "We need to come back here again sometime," she remarked.

The ride back to the airport was smooth as the helicopter skimmed over ridges and through valleys. The roar of the rotors was loud in their ears, but Derrick and Lydia sat in silence, absorbing the incredible journey they had just experienced. The landscape below changed from snow and ice to rocky slopes and eventually to the greenery of lower altitudes.

As they approached the airport, Derrick glanced at Lydia. "Another clue down. We're getting closer."

Lydia smiled, her face flushed from the cold and excitement. "Let's just hope the next location is a little warmer."

The helicopter touched down gently, and they disembarked. Jet exhaust mixed with the fresh, cold mountain air as the sounds of the busy airport surrounded them.

After collecting their packs, they walked toward the terminal. The heated indoors made Lydia sigh in relief as they walked in.

Derrick found a seat and started studying the clue as Lydia grabbed them a couple of coffees. Since they had a few hours before the flight would depart, Derrick searched the internet for any location that sounded like "Cots of Blue."

Lydia returned and, handing him one of the cups, asked, "You figure anything out yet?"

Derrick looked at her dejectedly and replied, "I haven't figured out the entire clue, but I managed to determine where..."

Noticing his pause and the look on his face, Lydia realized she wasn't going to like it. "And...?" she asked, trying to pry the answer out of him.

"Kotzebue... Alaska."

Lydia sighed heavily. "Can you at least get a tent that has a hot tub this time?"

CHAPTER 11

Derrick slid the key into the door of their suite, and as it clicked open, Lydia's eyes widened in delight. She had insisted on this specific room when she saw it online, especially when she learned about the private hot tub on the balcony overlooking the Bering Sea. The thought of relaxing in warm water while gazing out at the vast, icy ocean had been too tempting to resist.

As Derrick set their bags down on the bed, Lydia couldn't wait any longer. She pushed past him and rushed to the large windows. With a swift motion, she threw open the blinds, revealing the breathtaking view beyond. The vast expanse of the Bering Sea stretched out before them, a wild, cold beauty that was both awe-inspiring and intimidating.

"Derrick! Look at this! It's just like Virginia Beach!" Lydia exclaimed, her voice filled with joy as she took in the scene.

Derrick smirked, unable to resist teasing her. "Yeah, except we're in Alaska, and the water is just above freezing. But sure, I can see the resemblance," he replied with a grin.

But Lydia wasn't deterred. She rushed back to the bed in search of her bathing suit, shedding her clothes as she went.

"Honey! At least shut the blinds first," Derrick called after her, laughing at her enthusiasm as he watched her disappear into the bathroom.

Later, Lydia lounged in the hot tub on the balcony, steam rising around her as she soaked in the warmth. The cold air outside only made the water feel more inviting. She sighed contentedly, letting the heat seep into her bones. Her phone sat on a ledge nearby with Derrick on speaker. Inside, Derrick sat on the bed, staring intently at the clue they were trying to solve.

"We know the town is Kotzebue, and I can see why anyone here would be cold," Derrick muttered to himself, frustration creeping into his voice. "But who are the 'girls,' and what on earth is the rest of this supposed to mean?"

Lydia, her mind wandering as she gazed out at the sea, offered a suggestion. "Doesn't everything stand for something else in these clues? Maybe 'girls' doesn't mean women."

Derrick continued to puzzle over the words, mumbling to himself. "Girls... coats... Jackson... Cinnamon..."

Lydia couldn't help but laugh at the last word. "Cinnamon... that almost sounds like a stripper's name!"

Suddenly, the pieces clicked into place for Derrick. His eyes widened as the realization hit him. "That's it! The 'girls' and 'coats' refer to strippers and...

well, you know. 'Jackson save two'... Jackson is on a twenty-dollar bill... 'save two'... eighteen dollars."

He quickly pulled out his phone and searched for strip clubs in Kotzebue. "Just as I thought, there's only one. We need to go there, find a stripper named Cinnamon, give her eighteen dollars, and do something involving declaring Black Lotus."

Lydia shot up from the hot tub, aghast. "Derrick Anderson! I was joking about that! I'm not going to let you go to a strip club alone and mess around!"

Derrick grinned playfully at her. "Then I guess you're coming with me."

***

The flight from Nome to Kotzebue was short, just fifty minutes, offering a fleeting glimpse of the rugged Alaskan landscape below. The strip club was only a few blocks from the terminal, but Derrick insisted on calling an Uber, citing the chilly weather that barely hovered above freezing.

When they pulled up in front of the club, the music's thumping bass leaked through the car doors. Derrick hesitated as they approached the entrance, feeling a surge of nerves. The bouncer, a burly figure with a scrutinizing gaze, looked them over.

"Two, please," Derrick requested, his voice betraying his unease.

Rolling her eyes, Lydia interjected with a grin, "Excuse him. He's a bit... new to all this."

The bouncer chuckled, his stern demeanor softening. "Ah, a rookie in the wild. Well, brace yourself, buddy. You're in for a shock. Go on in," he said with a nod of approval.

Inside, the smoky air was thick, tinged with the scent of cheap perfume, almost drowning out the pulsating bass and the kaleidoscope of flashing lights. Feeling entirely out of place, Derrick shuffled over to a table and sat with his back to the stage, trying desperately to blend into the dimly lit ambiance. But his attempt at inconspicuousness was short-lived. A scantily clad woman, wearing little more than the tag on her thong, sauntered over with a sultry smile.

"Hello, stud! You looking for a little fun tonight?" she purred, sliding onto his leg.

"Um... no. I'm just looking for Cinnamon. Is she around? I need to talk to her about... her taxes," Derrick stammered, feeling his cheeks flush with embarrassment.

The woman grinned mischievously. "How about a little Brown Sugar instead?" she offered, but Derrick cringed at the suggestion.

Lydia, trying to stifle her laughter, quickly intervened. "It's his birthday, and Cinnamon has a 'special gift' for him."

Brown Sugar rose from his lap with a smirk. "Oh, it's your birthday? Wait right here, then."

As she walked away, Derrick spun around to Lydia, who was now laughing uncontrollably. "Why did you tell her that?! That was so gross! I could practically feel her butt cheeks on my leg! Do you have a hand wipe?" Unfortunately for Derrick, there was no time for cleanup.

The announcement of a birthday celebration filled the air, and before Derrick could protest, two scantily clad dancers whisked him onto the stage. "Let's show him a good time, ladies!" Brown Sugar cheered.

Feeling like a deer caught in the headlights, Derrick pleaded, "No, I'm good. Please, I just want to talk to Cinnamon." But his plea fell on deaf ears as the dancers continued their provocative routine around him, singing a sultry rendition of "Happy Birthday."

Finally allowed to retreat to his seat, Derrick buried his head in his arms while Lydia erupted in laughter.

Just then, a striking redhead with piercing green eyes approached Derrick. "Nice moves, hot stuff. I heard you were looking for me. I'm Cinnamon."

"Of course you are," Derrick muttered wryly under his breath.

Feeling bad for embarrassing him, Lydia explained their purpose to Cinnamon. "Our friend, Tae, mentioned you might have some information for us. We're supposed to give you some money and…"

"Oh, the short, funny guy with the goofy grin?" Cinnamon interrupted with a chuckle. "I remember him, especially his soft hands." Derrick groaned as Cinnamon continued, "He did give me something, but here's the thing—we can't accept money unless we're dancing. It's kind of a law in this town. I'm on in a few minutes, though."

With a playful nudge, Cinnamon sat beside Derrick. "Why don't you just enjoy the show? Slip me the right amount of money and the code during it, and let Cinnamon take good care of you." She moved uncomfortably close, her ample bosom nearly brushing against his face.

Derrick squeezed his eyes shut tightly, thinking of the consequences. "Nope. Don't do it, Derrick. Lydia's watching. Choose life!"

The pulsating rhythm of the music filled the air as Cinnamon made her grand entrance from behind the curtain, clad in what seemed like less than nothing. Derrick buried his face in his hands and muttered, "I hate you, Tae."

Overhearing him, Lydia laughed. "You got this?"

Looking utterly flustered, Derrick replied, "I'm not even sure she has the clue. There's not enough fabric for it to be hidden anywhere!"

A few minutes into her routine, Cinnamon sauntered over in front of Derrick and started dancing for him. He awkwardly attempted to hand her the eighteen dollars, but she refused to take it.

Amused, Lydia said, "You're supposed to put it in her G-string."

Derrick winced as he carefully slipped the money under the scant fabric on Cinnamon's hip, trying to avoid any unwanted contact. When she asked for the code word, he leaned in and whispered, "Black Lotus?"

With a playful smile, Cinnamon reached down and revealed the top of a small piece of paper hidden in the front of her underwear, moving it within arm's reach for Derrick to take. "Ooooh! That is SO unsanitary!" he thought as he forced himself to reach out and grab it.

Lydia, who had been enjoying the night until now, warned, "Careful!"

Derrick's antics didn't escape the notice of a bouncer, who started making his way over to them. Sensing the impending trouble, Cinnamon quickly removed the clue and placed it in Derrick's hand. "Missed that class back at Langley, did ya?" Derrick looked at her very suspiciously before hiding the note under the table. "Langley?!?" he whispered under his breath. Before he had time to ponder it further, his body shuddered.

As Cinnamon danced back over to the pole on stage, Lydia noticed Derrick's face. "What's with the look?"

Grimacing, Derrick gagged. "Why is it so moist?!?" he asked, holding the clue up with two fingers. "Can we get out of here now?"

As they stood to leave, a couple of loud pops echoed from the entrance, and a thick fog began to fill the club. Catching a whiff of the smoke, Derrick recognized it as tear gas.

"It's Nightfall! How do they always know where we are? Quick, backstage!" Derrick exclaimed, grabbing Lydia's arm and pulling her along as they ran.

Derrick struggled to navigate through the darkness and the choking gas, the acrid smell stinging his eyes and throat. Dancers and patrons were scrambling for safety, adding to the chaos.

"Give me your bra," Derrick demanded between coughs, the tear gas taking its toll on him.

"Mine?! Use one of theirs! They certainly aren't," Lydia shot back, incredulous.

Derrick gave her a look of disgust. "Gross! Do you have any idea where those things have been?!"

Lydia retorted sarcastically, "I've got a pretty good idea."

"I can't use those. They're made of lace and barely exist. I need a cotton one," Derrick insisted.

Finally, Lydia resigned and slipped out the pink polka dot undergarment from beneath her shirt. "Here, but I don't think it's your size," she joked.

Derrick quickly opened his knife and sliced up the middle of the bra between the cups, cutting it in two.

Shocked, Lydia protested, "You know I needed that back, right?"

Derrick, focused on the situation, handed her one-half. "Put this over your nose and mouth," he instructed as he secured the other half to his own face.

"Did you seriously just tell me to shut up?!" Lydia exclaimed.

"JUST DO IT!" Derrick snapped as he continued scanning for an exit.

Spotting one through the haze, Derrick led Lydia outside, and they sprinted several blocks back to the airport.

As they neared the terminal, Derrick glanced over at Lydia and noticed something. "Um, honey… they're… um…"

Lydia quickly closed her jacket and exclaimed, "It's Alaska! What'd you think would happen? THEIR coat is still on your face!"

Remembering he still had the pink polka dot undergarment strapped on, Derrick was thankful they hadn't passed anyone on the dimly lit road. "Oh, here, give me the other part, and I'll tape it back together," he said as he removed his half from his face.

Lydia glared at him in disbelief. "You know, duct tape holds a lot, but..."

As they approached the terminal, they spotted a couple of Nightfall agents in tactical gear standing by the front doors.

"Well, that's a problem," Derrick said, thinking quickly.

Just then, he heard a ripping sound and turned to see Lydia holding the torn bra.

"Yep... so is that," she said dejectedly.

Seeing a nearby hangar, Derrick had an idea. Lydia noticed the look on his face and sighed, "Fine, just tell me what we're doing first, so I'm not in the dark."

After Derrick explained his plan, Lydia rolled her eyes and sighed again. "This is a horrible idea, but I guess it's karma for the strip club. Just don't get caught."

She opened the door to the Air Cargo lobby, making sure her coat was open. The teenage boys behind the counter noticed her predicament immediately, their attention fully captured. They fumbled over each other, trying to be the one to assist her.

Meanwhile, Derrick slipped into the hangar, ensuring it was unoccupied. He quietly made his way to a rack of overalls and hats on the wall. Grabbing two of each, he began to slip back out through the hangar door and disappear into the darkness.

He was almost home free, carefully sneaking alongside a Beechcraft undergoing maintenance. But as he passed the nose, his foot caught on something solid. Looking down in horror, he saw the jack handle jutting out from beneath the aircraft. Before he could react, he tripped, sending the handle skidding across the floor. The jack, which had been holding the tireless landing gear of the plane, toppled over. The gear crashed onto the ground with a resounding thud.

Derrick held his breath, hoping no one had heard. He started walking toward the doors, breathing a sigh of relief when no one came running. But then, he heard a creaking sound behind him. Derrick turned slowly, his face contorting in dismay as the landing gear collapsed, and the nose of the Beechcraft fell to the floor with a thunderous crash.

Knowing someone had to have heard that, Derrick bolted for the door. Just as he was about to escape, a massive figure emerged from the darkness—a large, burly mechanic wielding a wrench that looked more like a T-rex's thigh bone than a tool.

Derrick quickly scanned the area and saw the jack handle lying nearby. He stomped on the end, flipping it into the air and catching it mid-flip. "That was so cool! Did you see that?!" he exclaimed, turning to the mechanic… who looked anything but amused. "Oh… sorry about the plane," Derrick said apologetically. The mechanic growled and started advancing toward him.

Derrick lost his footing as he dodged the swinging wrench, the heavy tool whistling past his ear. As he hit the ground, the hand holding the jack handle slammed down—directly onto the mechanic's foot. It hit with such force that it penetrated through the boot and into the foot. The mechanic screamed in pain, dropping the wrench. This commotion alerted the two teenagers in the lobby, who came running.

As Derrick scrambled to his feet, he accidentally knocked over a rack of oil cans beside the door. The cans came crashing down, spilling their contents all over the floor. The teenagers, rushing in, slipped on the freshly spilled oil and fell, sliding under the crippled aircraft.

Derrick grabbed the clothes and ran for the hangar door, where Lydia watched the scene unfold. She was clearly struggling to find words but was at a loss.

"Don't ask. Just run!" Derrick exclaimed, tossing her a jumpsuit.

Derrick quickly zipped up his and adjusted the hat on his head. But when he turned around, he was surprised to see Lydia looking less like she was wearing a jumpsuit and more like she was swimming in a parachute.

"Uh… it'll be fine. We just need to get past those guards, then you can ditch it."

They tried to blend in with a group of passengers entering the Alaska Airlines terminal. Derrick was spouting off random aeronautical terms, trying to play the part of an airline mechanic. "I was having trouble with my altimeter, and it turns out my pitot tube was clogged. A couple of blasts of air cleared it out." The guards watched them as they entered the terminal, then relayed through their throat mics, "Elmo and Venus back at the airport."

After ditching his jumpsuit in the restroom, Derrick bought two return tickets to Nome and sat down next to Lydia at the gate.

"How do they always know where we are?!" he asked her, frustration evident in his voice.

The next morning, as the sun rose over their lodge in Nome, Derrick was still studying the clue. Lydia had just changed into her bathing suit and was heading for the hot tub. "Take your time, Honey. I like it here!" she called back to him.

After multiple Google searches and reading the clue aloud for the eighth time, Derrick was still stumped.

"Go to the land of the unforgiving,
where the fields no longer Bloom.
Seek your enemy where the monsters
loom."

He usually deciphered Tae's clues quickly, but this one made no sense. "Who is my enemy? And why is 'Bloom' capitalized?" he asked aloud to himself.

Hearing his dilemma, Lydia called out from the balcony. "Doesn't a capitalized word usually mean it's a proper noun? Like a person or a place?"

Derrick pondered her words for a few more minutes before dread washed over him like a bucket of ice water. "It's Bloomfield," he said with resignation.

Lydia sat up in the hot tub, despair written all over her face. "Oh, Derrick, tell me you're joking. Please don't make me go back there!"

CHAPTER 12

"...This is KIOW. Twenty-four hours ago, hundreds of people in southern Iowa were waking to a beautiful Sunday morning. Little did they know what lie in store. Mere hours after that serene sunrise, the sleepy little town of Bloomfield would be erased off the pages of time by the deadliest tornado in Iowa's history. In a matter of minutes, two hundred and thirty-five residents would lose their lives.

I'm standing outside of what used to be a church, where the parishioners huddled in the basement as the monster tornado roared overhead. Forty-nine of those... over three-quarters of the congregation... perished when they were torn from their place of safety and hurled into the raging torrent...."

***

Derrick's gaze shifted to the window, looking out at the barren landscape that had once been Lydia's hometown. The scar left by the tornado was still visible from the air, stretching endlessly across the horizon. Memories from that fateful afternoon flooded back, hitting him with the force of the storm itself.

Lydia stirred beside him as the plane's wheels touched down on the runway, her eyes blinking open with groggy confusion. "Are we in Bloomfield?" she asked, her voice thick with sleep.

"No, honey. They decided it was better to land in Ottumwa," Derrick replied, trying to keep his voice steady.

Overhearing their conversation, the co-pilot shot Derrick a puzzled look, clearly aware of the real reason they hadn't landed in Bloomfield. Derrick met his gaze and shook his head slightly, signaling the co-pilot to keep quiet. The co-pilot nodded in understanding and turned back to the controls, completing the shutdown procedures.

Lydia rubbed her eyes, still trying to shake off the remnants of sleep. "Why Ottumwa? I thought we were going straight to Bloomfield."

Derrick forced a smile. "Ottumwa has better facilities. We'll be there soon enough."

As they taxied to the terminal, Derrick stole a glance at Lydia, who was now fully awake and staring out the window. He could see the worry etched on her face and the apprehension in her eyes. He wished he could protect her from the pain that awaited them.

Once they disembarked, the small, quiet airport in Ottumwa felt like a stark contrast to the bustling terminals they were used to. It was almost too peaceful, as if the world hadn't noticed the tragedy that had unfolded nearby. Derrick signed the paperwork at the rental car desk, his thoughts drifting back to that terrible day, and they headed toward the car.

***

Derrick lay awake in bed, anxiously awaiting the 2 am update from the Storm Prediction Center. Despite the forecast downplaying the severity of the storms, he couldn't shake off his unease.

"Can you turn that off, please? It's too bright," Lydia grumbled from beside him, her voice laced with irritation.

"I can't. Something's not right," Derrick murmured, his mind flashing back to a similar feeling he had once felt on a muggy May morning in Oklahoma City.

"Okay, but there's nothing you can do about it right now. We have church in the morning, and you're going to wake Madeline."

Derrick reluctantly turned the brightness of his phone down and pulled the blanket over his head, the dim light barely illuminating the small space beneath.

"Seriously?!?" Lydia exclaimed, annoyed by his persistence.

"Give me just two minutes. I want to review the t-skew again," Derrick replied, his voice muffled by the blanket.

"I thought we agreed you wouldn't use that kind of language around me anymore. How many times have I told you? Bloomfield doesn't get tornadoes. The storms go around the county. It's been at least a hundred years since one came through town."

Oblivious to her frustration, Derrick simply muttered, "Huh?"

With a sigh of exasperation, Lydia rolled over and yanked the blankets from his side of the bed, trying to find some peace.

Downstairs, Derrick paced frantically, his phone clenched in his hand as he scrolled through weather updates. He had come down for breakfast, but he never made it to the kitchen. Instead, he found himself circling the living room, running into the couch twice as his mind raced. Sitting at the table, Jeb watched him with concern, noticing how a sense of urgency had replaced Derrick's usually calm demeanor.

"Son, you look more uptight than Jimmy at last year's county fair before he rode Tombstone. Rest his soul," Jeb remarked, trying to break the tension.

"I just need to check the low-level jet again. The dry line... with the station... triple point..." Derrick muttered, his words stumbling over each other as his thoughts raced ahead of him. He finally stopped pacing and exclaimed, "Where's the moisture at?!?"

Mary stepped out of the kitchen, wiping her hands on a dish towel as she approached. "Hun, what's going on?" she asked, her voice gentle but filled with concern.

Without looking up from his newspaper, Jeb answered, "Derrick done snapped."

At church, the Sunday service seemed to drag on forever for Derrick. Each minute ticked by painfully slow, and he shifted uncomfortably in the wooden pew, checking his watch every few minutes. Lydia noticed his restlessness and leaned over, whispering, "Would you cut it out?" Her eyes flickered with annoyance as she noticed the goosebumps on his arms.

"I... uh... It's here. I know it. I can feel it... I'm just going to check my phone. Two seconds is all I need..." Derrick whispered back, his voice laced with an edge of panic.

"You do, and you will be chasing it in a body cast," Lydia threatened, her eyes narrowing as she turned back to the preacher.

Just as Derrick reached for his phone, the calm of the morning service was shattered by the sudden blare of the Emergency Alert System alarm. The shrill sound echoed through the church, causing everyone to jump in their seats. Scrambling to cover the speaker, Derrick cursed himself for allowing his new weather app to override the silent feature on his phone.

Unable to turn the alert off quickly enough, he bolted to the back of the auditorium and out the front doors. His eyes locked onto the alert on his screen, and he froze as the words sank in.

A few moments later, Lydia burst through the doors, her face flushed with anger. "Seriously, Derrick?!?"

Before she could unleash her frustration, Derrick held up his phone to show her the alert. Her anger shifted to confusion as she read the message. "What does 'PARTICULARLY DANGEROUS SITUATION' mean?"

Without breaking his gaze from the horizon, Derrick replied in an uncharacteristically serious tone. "It means I was right."

"But the sky is so blue," Lydia remarked, her voice tinged with uncertainty.

Derrick didn't respond. His attention was fixed on the horizon, his heart pounding in his chest.

Feeling a surge of concern, Lydia placed her hand on his arm. "You're starting to scare me now. Service is almost over. Come back inside, and we can keep an eye on it during the potluck."

But Derrick couldn't shake the feeling of impending doom. His eyes scanned the sky, searching for any sign of the approaching storm.

After the service, everyone made their way down to the basement for the meal... everyone except Derrick. He dashed outside again to check the skies, his heart racing with anticipation.

Lydia hurried after him. Her voice filled with astonishment as she took in the scene. "Wow... it really clouded up in fifteen minutes, didn't it?"

Derrick remained silent with his eyes locked on the dark and ominous clouds that were now streaming overhead.

Lydia smacked his arm in frustration. "Derrick!"

Startled, he turned to her, his mind still on the storm. "What?!"

"Have you not heard a word I've said? It's time to eat. Come on."

"I'm not hungry," he replied dismissively, his eyes drifting back to the sky.

Lydia's patience was wearing thin. "Derrick Hezekiah Anderson! Get your butt downstairs and eat. If it's going to be as bad as you say, you'll need the energy!"

Reluctantly, Derrick followed her back inside, but his mind was still on the storm.

They were just about to fill their plates when Derrick's phone erupted with another alert, startling everyone nearby. Mortified by the disruption, Lydia scolded him to silence it, but Derrick didn't hear a word she said.

His heart pounded as his phone announced the alert. "THE NATIONAL WEATHER SERVICE IN DES MOINES HAS ISSUED A TORNADO WARNING FOR DAVIS COUNTY IN

*SOUTHEASTERN IOWA UNTIL 1:30 PM. AT 12:45 PM, A
TORNADO WAS CONFIRMED BY SPOTTERS TWO MILES EAST OF
COATSVILLE, MOVING NORTHEAST AT 15 MPH. TOWNS IN THE
PATH OF THIS STORM INCLUDE: RURAL DAVIS COUNT, WEST
GROVE, AND BLOOMFIELD. RESIDENTS..."*

Derrick sprinted up the basement stairs, taking three at a time. When he stepped outside, his worst fears were confirmed. The blue sky that had clouded up just fifteen minutes earlier was now the darkest black he had ever seen.

Lydia walked out the door just as the town sirens began to wail, the eerie sound sending a chill down her spine. She gasped as she saw the jet-black clouds rapidly spinning like a malevolent carousel in the sky.

"I know," Derrick replied, his voice filled with dread.

"Adam just made an announcement telling everyone to head home before the storm hits. Momma is cleaning up, and then we'll make for the house."

Derrick's eyes widened in alarm. "NO! They can't leave. This is the safest place right now. There's no way they could make it home in time."

Trusting Derrick's instincts, Lydia turned to stop those who were trying to leave when his phone went off again.

"Derrick... we know there's a tornado warning. Can you turn that thing off now?" Lydia pleaded, her nerves fraying.

"But they don't usually issue warnings twice...." His voice trailed off as he listened to the alert.

"THIS IS A TORNADO EMERGENCY FOR BLOOMFIELD. At 12:55 pm, a confirmed large and extremely dangerous tornado was five miles southeast of Bloomfield, moving northeast at 20 mph. This includes Bloomfield Regional Airport and Downtown Bloomfield..."

The color drained from Lydia's face as the words sank in. She grabbed Derrick's arm, her voice trembling. "What do we do?"

Derrick didn't hesitate. "We get everyone to the basement. Now."

They raced towards the stairs, their hearts pounding in fear. As they reached the entrance, they ran into Hailey, who was determined to leave.

"Get to the basement, now!" Derrick commanded, leaping down the stairs.

Hailey hesitated, her eyes wide with fear. "I think I'll be safer at home."

Lydia grabbed her arm, urging her to stay. "There's no time, Hailey! The tornado is already huge, and it's coming this way!"

Derrick jumped onto one of the tables and tried to convince everyone to stay and take cover.

"You don't have time to get home! You will be safer if you stay here!"

Torrents of rain started cascading down, mixing with small hail… and then growing larger.

Lydia flinched with each distant thud as the roof of the church building was being assaulted.

"Derrick, we got the damage waiver on the rental, right?" she asked, cringing at the sound of the hail.

"That's the least of our worries right now," he replied, ushering everyone away from the windows.

Adam approached, explaining that the door to the basement that led outside had a broken latch, and he didn't think it would hold against the storm. Examining it, Derrick assured him that he could fix it in time. Grabbing two metal folding chairs, he crisscrossed them through the handle on the door and wedged them against the wall.

The rain and hail suddenly subsided, and a few people started celebrating, thinking the storm had passed. But Derrick knew better. The room fell silent again as a low rumble began to shake the glasses by the sink. Derrick swallowed hard as the wall he was leaning against started vibrating.

"EVERYONE TO THE BATHROOMS! NOW!" he screamed, his voice cracking with urgency.

The rumbling grew into a deafening roar as the tornado approached. Though Derrick urged everyone to seek shelter, only a few heeded his warning. Placing

Lydia and Madeline in the corner between the toilet and wall, he wrapped his leg and arm around the toilet as an anchor and covered them both.

"This is going to get really bad in a few moments. Keep your heads down and hold on," Derrick instructed firmly.

Jeb, Mary, Adam, and a few others huddled in the stalls next to them while William and Caleb took shelter in the kitchen with their friends, hoping to catch a glimpse of the funnel for their YouTube channel.

The church building groaned under the assault of the wind. The windows shattered as debris tore through the siding.

"Hold on tight to my babies there, Derrick!" Jeb shouted as he anchored Mary to a neighboring toilet.

A rapid succession of gunshot-like cracks echoed through the building as the wood structure of the old church snapped, board by board, followed by a vacuum-like whoosh of the roof being lifted off.

The metal chairs Derrick had used to secure the door began to bend under the pressure. William, still filming, tapped Caleb on the shoulder and pointed toward the door. They both ran over, excited by the spectacle.

"We're going to go viral with this! Look at how much they are bending! You better be getting this!" William exclaimed.

A few seconds later, Caleb's face paled as he saw the door itself begin to bow outward. "Maybe we shouldn't be over here," he suggested just before they both dashed back for cover.

The immense winds outside finally overwhelmed the makeshift barricade, and the door blew off its hinges and was sucked into the vortex. Everything... and everyone in the basement fellowship hall was pulled into the gale-force winds. Derrick winced as he heard the door give way, followed by screams from outside the bathroom and then... silence.

Lydia breathed a sigh of relief as the roaring suddenly stopped. "It's over!" she exclaimed, her voice trembling.

Derrick paused a moment and gave a grim reply, "It's not over. EVERYONE HANG ON!"

The tornado had lifted momentarily, only to slam back down directly on top of the church building, obliterating the remaining walls. The flooring was now its target, as it was ripped away, plank by plank.

Derrick felt like a monstrous force had grabbed ahold of him, trying to pull him through the ceiling. Lydia struggled to breathe under Derrick's crushing grip he had on her and Madeline. She had never seen his face so red, veins bulging, as he fought to hold on.

A scream pierced the air from beside him. Derrick opened his eyes to see Ava huddled with her parents in the stall to his left. Her screams grew more *intense as her terrified face suddenly disappeared as she was pulled into the violent vortex above. Derrick looked back at Lydia and saw, for the first time, fear… true fear… in her eyes.*

The clock tower from the courthouse put up a valiant fight but finally yielded to the torrent and was ripped from its foundation. Cartwheeling across two now empty blocks, it landed in the parking lot, bricks crumbling into pieces, and rolled into the void that was the basement. A large metal beam from the clock's inner workings fell onto Derrick's back, relieving the upward suction but now trapping him in the tiny stall.

Lydia thought the roar would never end, but after several minutes, it finally did. The bathroom fell into an eerie silence.

Derrick slowly relaxed his vice-like grip on the toilet but refused to let go of Lydia and Madeline. "Are you two okay?" he asked, his voice shaky.

Lydia didn't respond. She just stared at Derrick, her lower lip quivering as Madeline screamed her head off.

Derrick leaned closer, his voice gentle but insistent. "Honey! Are… you… okay?"

Again, she remained silent, her eyes filled with shock.

Hearing movement nearby, Derrick shouted, "Is everyone okay?" Several people responded, confirming their safety, but he didn't hear anything from her parents.

"Jeb... you okay?"

"Yeah, we're here, son. We're okay. Are you guys trapped, too?"

Adam's voice echoed from a couple of stalls down, "I think Hailey's hurt!"

CHAPTER 13

The drive from Ottumwa to Bloomfield was heavy with silence. Lydia stared out the window, her thoughts swirling with memories of a past that felt like it had been torn away. Derrick focused on the road, his eyes flicking to her now and then, ready to offer comfort when she needed it. But for now, he let her sit with her thoughts.

As they drew closer to Bloomfield, the devastation grew more evident. Once full of life, the trees were stripped bare, their branches reaching out like skeletal fingers against the sky. Buildings had been reduced to rubble, and the landscape was scarred, a reminder of the tornado's unrelenting fury. Lydia searched the horizon for something familiar, but there was nothing.

"Where's Bo's Auto… the car wash… True Value?! There's nothing here! It doesn't even look like there used to be anything here," she said, her voice trembling with disbelief.

Derrick's heart ached as he watched her childhood memories vanish before her eyes, leaving behind only empty spaces where they used to be.

As they turned onto North Street, Lydia gasped again, her eyes wide with shock.

"Derrick! Downtown is gone! The courthouse, the movie theater, the farmer's market... everything is gone! It looks like one big parking lot! They haven't rebuilt yet?!"

Derrick slowed the car to a crawl, allowing her to take in the scene. The heart of Bloomfield, once vibrant and full of life, was now a vast, empty expanse. It looked like a place that had been forgotten, a stark reminder of what the tornado had taken.

"They've been slow to rebuild," Derrick said quietly. "Funding issues, arguments over what should be prioritized... it's been a mess."

Lydia's eyes roamed over the desolate landscape. "I can't believe it. It's like... it's like Bloomfield never existed."

They drove past the ruins of what used to be her favorite spots, the places where she had made countless memories. The devastation was overwhelming, and Lydia felt a mix of sorrow and anger bubbling up inside her.

"How could they let this happen?" she whispered. "How could they just... give up?"

Derrick parked the car near what used to be the town square. They sat in silence for a moment, the weight of the loss settling in around them.

"Do you want to take a walk?" he asked gently.

She nodded, and they stepped out of the car. The air was thick with an eerie silence, broken only by the crunch of gravel underfoot. They walked slowly, hand in hand, through the remnants of Lydia's past.

Approaching where the church building used to be, they ran into Adam, who was overseeing the designs for the new building. He greeted Lydia with the warmth of an old friend, but when his eyes fell on Derrick, his smile dimmed into a scowl.

"Well, hello, Lydia! I didn't expect to see you back here after your parents moved last year. How are you doing?" Adam said, his voice friendly, though his eyes tightened just a bit when he looked past Lydia at Derrick.

"We're in the area for a few days, and I just wanted to see where y'all are meeting now. I thought we'd come to services on Sunday before we headed out," Lydia replied, trying to maintain her composure.

Adam put his arm on her shoulder and said, "Let me show you what we're planning for the new building." Derrick hung back, feeling the sting of being unwelcome in a place that once felt like home.

After showing Lydia a few of the new designs, Adam finally turned to Derrick. "Lydia, while we'd love for you to join us on Sunday, I'm not sure it would be a good idea for Derrick to come. There are a lot of people here who… haven't gotten over the incident. I don't think it would… be a good idea if you catch my meaning."

Lydia stepped back, her face pale with disbelief. "Are you saying Derrick isn't welcome to come back to church here?!"

Adam waved his hands in a futile attempt to soften his words. "It's not that he's not welcome. I just don't think it's the best time right now. People are still trying to heal, and his presence might not be... beneficial."

Lydia felt like she had just been punched in the stomach. "Very well," she replied sadly. "Let everyone know I said hi," she said turning and walking back toward Derrick.

As they drove past the Bloomfield Airport, Lydia finally understood why they had landed in Ottumwa. "How does a tornado destroy an airport?" she asked in amazement, still trying to process the level of destruction.

They continued down Key Blvd to the site of the Evans' home, where Derrick felt a knot of apprehension tightening in his stomach. The memories of that day weighed heavily on his mind, and he stole a glance at Lydia, whose face was a mask of determined hope mixed with the dread of what they might find. Having been in Des Moines with Hailey, Lydia hadn't come back to town since that day and didn't know what awaited.

Turning into the long, gravel driveway, Lydia's composure shattered. Tears streamed down her cheeks as she took in the scene before her.

"Are you sure this is the right place?" she asked in shock, her voice trembling. "Where's the house? Where's my tree and swing? Where's... anything?"

Before them lay an empty field with a lone concrete stoop standing sentinel amidst the encroaching grass. Debris from the tornado still littered the pasture where she used to lie and gaze at the stars. The sight was both surreal and heartbreaking.

Lydia got out of the car and headed to the stairs. It was the first construction project her dad had let her help with.

...Ten-year-old Lydia sat on the porch, watching her dad mix the mound of wet, gray concrete. She loved watching him work on the house. He always explained things and made her feel like she was part of something important. But today was different. Her dad looked up from where he was kneeling, wiping his brow, and said, "Alright, kiddo. Today's the day. You're going to help me pour this stoop!"

Her heart raced with excitement. She was finally going to be able to help him with a project! She stepped off the porch and looked at the outline in the dirt where the old one had stood for decades.

Handing her a hammer and some nails, her dad explained the process. "I've already cut the wood. That saw is a bit dangerous. What I need you to do is create the form we'll use to pour the new stoop. You remember what the old one looked like, right?"

Lydia nodded eagerly.

"Good. Now, take the pieces of wood and make a mold that will shape the new one once the concrete is poured. Don't hammer anything in yet. I just want to see how your mind works."

Jeb watched as Lydia maneuvered the pieces into position, her young mind diligently working through the problem. He could almost see the gears turning as she calculated the best way to assemble the mold.

Finally, she stepped back, proud of her work. "Okay, I think I got it!"

Jeb smiled, his heart swelling with pride. "That's perfect! Now... you ready to nail it together?"

As they finished pouring the last batch of concrete, they both stepped back and admired their work.

"I love you, Daddy!" she said, hugging him. Jeb's rough exterior softened as he hugged her back. "Hey, let's put our handprints in the concrete so we can keep this moment," Jeb suggested.

Mary stepped out of the house just as they were planting their hands into the top step. "Oh, my! What a wonderful way to mark this!" she exclaimed, her eyes twinkling with pride.

Lydia ran her hand over the two sets of prints, now worn by time. She had grown so much since that day. Her hand was almost the size of her dad's now. A lump in Derrick's throat made it hard to swallow as he watched tears fall from her eyes. He felt helpless, wanting to comfort her, but she had asked to be left alone.

She began searching through the overgrown weeds around the empty slab for any remnants of the life she had once known there. As she moved a tuft of grass, she uncovered a round piece of plastic. Bending down, she flipped it over to reveal a scuffed-up eye from a stuffed animal. A blue eye... from a stuffed dolphin. Lydia clutched it to her chest and fell to her knees as her sobs echoed across the empty field.

Derrick approached her cautiously, not wanting to intrude on her moment of grief. Kneeling beside her, he placed a gentle hand on her shoulder. "Lydia," he whispered, his voice filled with sorrow. "I'm here."

She looked up at him, her eyes red and swollen. "It's from Madeline. I can't believe this is all that's left."

Derrick pulled her into his arms, holding her tightly as she wept. "I know it hurts," he murmured. "I wish I could make it better."

"How can one storm do all this? It killed so many... so many that were only feet from us. How did we live?!"

Derrick's chin began to quiver. "I don't know."

"What would we have done without you?"
Lydia's voice was soft yet filled with a depth of
gratitude.

"What are you talking about?! I didn't do
anything," Derrick replied, confused.

"Don't pretend like you didn't spend weeks
rescuing people from the rubble. I was worried sick
when I didn't hear from you. Then I turn on the TV, and
there you are, hanging out of a helicopter by a rope,
pulling people from the collapsed City Hall."

***

*...Derrick wiped the sweat from his brow as he
stood at the church entrance after loading Hailey into a
medivac helicopter heading for Des Moines. Lydia joined
her friend, providing support. He waved as they flew
away. The building was now cleared of the last
remaining survivors.*

*The eerie calm that followed the devastating
storm was shattered by the frantic calls for help from
City Hall. Being the city's designated storm shelter,
numerous people became trapped inside when it
collapsed.*

*Jumping onto the back of a fire truck responding
there, Derrick got his first glimpse of what was left of
the historic building. The formerly three-story structure
was now just a pile of unrecognizable rubble.*

*Incident command was across the street, where
Fire Chief Harris was directing operations. Above him,*

the rhythmic thump of helicopter blades cut through the air as a news crew captured the drama below.

Derrick had an idea. Running over to the chief, Derrick urged, "We need to get that helicopter down here, now!"

The chief's eyes widened in anger. "Who do you think you are giving orders? And it's far too dangerous to set that thing down here."

Derrick didn't back down. "You want to save those people? Just do it!"

Hearing the argument, Jeb happened to be nearby and walked over to the chief. "If he tells you to do something, you better do it. He's your best shot right now."

Reluctantly, Chief Harris radioed the helicopter pilot on the emergency frequency and asked them to land at the school for the rescue. Officer Johnson grabbed Derrick by the shoulder and said, "Come on! I'll give you a lift over there."

They arrived just as the helicopter was touching down, the car's strobes flashing in the whirlwind of dust that spread out from the landing zone. Grabbing the emergency traffic kit from the cruiser, Derrick made for the helicopter.

Rigging a harness out of the rope in the kit, Derrick secured it around his waist and then to the skid. Giving a thumbs up to the pilot, he held on as the helicopter lifted off the ground. Derrick felt his stomach drop as the ground fell away, and the destruction became fully visible.

As the helicopter pulled into a hover over the courthouse, Derrick sat on the skid, trying to build the courage to lower himself down. A gust of wind made it easier as he lost his grip and slid down the rope. Everyone on the ground cheered as he descended into the rubble. Good thing the blades were so loud, or they would have heard him screaming. He still hadn't kicked that fear of heights yet.

Once his feet finally reached the exposed top floor, Derrick quickly unclipped from the rope.

Working his way down the rubble-filled staircases, Derrick worried about how he would extract any of the injured.

A few hours passed when he reached the reinforced sheltered room in the basement. The door was cracked open but blocked further by debris. He was relieved to find everyone mostly uninjured.

After removing the rubble and opening the door, Derrick led the twenty-three survivors up the twisted escape path to the opening he came in. A helicopter from the Des Moines Fire Department, equipped with a rescue basket, was overhead now. They made quick work of recovering everyone and taking them to safety.

Night after night, Derrick manned one of the search and rescue helicopters, scanning the area with *thermal cameras. When a target was identified, the helicopter would come into a hover, and a team would rappel to check the signature. More often than not, they were deceased bodies. GPS trackers were left for later recovery, and they resumed their mission. A few survivors were found, but Derrick's team came up empty. He had been on many disaster scenes, but nothing compared to the devastation he observed throughout those days. After the third day, the rescue effort shifted to recovery, as the thermal cameras could no longer identify bodies.*

Derrick had been working nonstop, only catching a nap when his body finally shut down. He sat on the front steps of the destroyed church building, seeking a moment of refuge from the death and destruction around him. Still wearing his dress clothes from that day—now ripped and stained—he glanced down at the wet and dirty butterfly stuffed animal he was holding. It had belonged to Ava. Utterly exhausted, his mind was a lifetime away from that rubble when Adam sat down beside him.

"You okay?" Adam asked gently.

Staring off into the distance, Derrick handed the butterfly to him and numbly said, "We found her parents."

Taking it, Adam replied solemnly, "I know, I heard."

A few church members approached, and Adam embraced them tightly. Tears flowed as they thanked him for his tireless efforts. Derrick couldn't help but notice the glare he got as they walked by him without a word.

Feeling the tension, Adam placed his hand on Derrick's shoulder. "God will forgive. It's people that might take a little longer."

Exhaustion taking over, Derrick's eyes welled with tears.

Adam patted him on the shoulder and then walked away without another word...

***

Derrick's shoulders slumped under the weight of her words. The memory of those frantic days was still fresh in his mind, a blur of desperation and determination.

"Forty-nine people died because my door didn't hold," he said, his voice barely above a whisper.

Lydia turned towards him, her eyes wide with disbelief. "Derrick... the wall where the door was, isn't there anymore. I don't care if you welded that door shut; it wasn't going to hold. None of that was your fault. The ones that survived would have been on their way home when that monster hit, and the number dead would have been higher."

Derrick's mind replayed the events over and over. The door he had tried so hard to secure, the one he believed would keep everyone safe, had failed. The guilt gnawed at him relentlessly, a constant reminder of the lives lost.

"I should have done more," he said, his voice breaking. "I should have found a way to save them."

Lydia stepped closer, her hand resting gently on his arm. "You did everything you could, Derrick. You saved so many lives. You can't blame yourself for what the storm took. None of us could have predicted the destruction it would cause."

He looked at her, the pain and guilt reflected in his eyes. "I can't stop thinking about it, Lydia. Every time I close my eyes, I see their faces. I hear their screams. It's like I'm still there, trying to pull them out."

Lydia's heart ached for him. She knew the weight he carried was immense, but she also knew that he had to find a way to forgive himself. "Derrick, you're a hero. You put your life on the line to save others. That's something to be proud of, not something to regret."

He shook his head, the words not quite reaching the part of him that felt responsible. "I don't feel like a hero. I feel like a failure."

Lydia cupped his face in her hands, forcing him to look at her. "Listen to me, Derrick. You are not a failure. You are a brave, selfless man who did everything he could in an impossible situation. You saved lives. Don't let the ones you couldn't save overshadow that. You're human... let yourself be human."

Tears welled in his eyes as he listened to her words. Slowly, the wall of guilt began to crack, allowing a glimmer of hope to seep through. "If I don't know how to forgive myself, how can others?"

The clue replayed in his mind: "*Go to the land of the unforgiving, where the fields no longer Bloom. Seek your enemy where the monsters loom...*"

His mouth dropped open as something clicked this time.

"Hailey! That's the answer to the riddle."

Pulling into the driveway of Hailey's house, Lydia asked, "You ready for this?"

"No. You think she's forgiven me?"

"Derrick... of course she has..." Lydia said as her voice trailed off, uncertainty creeping in. "I hope..."

He took a deep breath and knocked on her door. The latch unlocked, and the door slowly opened. His eyes panned down to the woman in the wheelchair who answered the door.

"Morning, Hailey. How have you been?"

The door slammed shut in his face.

"I'm guessing the answer is no."

Derrick sat in the car while Lydia went in to talk with her friend.

"Hailey, you know he was right. You wouldn't have made it home," Lydia explained, placing her hand on Hailey's leg.

"It would have been nice if I could have made that decision for myself."

"You still had the choice. No one could have known how bad that storm was."

Turning her head, Hailey struggled to hold in her frustration. "You kept telling me how smart he was and knew everything about the weather. I believed he actually knew what he was talking about."

"Hailey... the winds were 311 mph. The second fastest ever recorded on earth. You're lucky to be alive."

"Why are you here? To rub it in that you made it out uninjured and that I'm paralyzed from the waist down?"

Lydia was taken aback. "Seriously? I sat in that hospital room with you for an entire month. I held your hand through every single one of those tests they put you through. We're best friends."

"Were... We WERE best friends."

Hailey's comment stung like a red-hot knife plunged into her chest. Lydia tried not to show how much it hurt and got down to business.

"Well then… the real reason we're here is that we are trying to find Tae. We think something has happened to him, and something we found said that he may have sent you a clue to his whereabouts."

"I did get a text from him a couple of weeks ago. It didn't make any sense at the time. I was going to delete it, but for some reason, I kept it." She pulled out her phone and searched through the text messages.

"Here it is:

> *'There's a light at the end of the world*
> *that will lee-you-in.*
> *Don't be a dingo and fall out the*
> *window.'"*

As she was leaving, Lydia tried to reassure Hailey that they had tried their best, but her anger still brewed strong, and she shut the door as Lydia was explaining.

Derrick could tell it didn't go well from her expression as she walked back to the car.

"I'm sorry, honey. I thought she'd be safe there," he said with remorse.

"I'm not sure it's you that she's angry at. Anyway, I have the clue. Can we get out of here now? This is definitely not home anymore."

***

Lydia stared out the window as they approached the city limit sign, the familiar landscape of her devastated hometown receding in the rearview mirror. The road ahead led back to Ottumwa, but the past lingered heavily, casting long shadows over their departure. Derrick slowed the car and turned into the cemetery, the gravestones stark against the summer sky. Lydia's face tightened with distress as she realized where they were.

"Honey, you don't have to get out. I just need to pay my respects to a few people," Derrick said softly.

Lydia nodded, but her eyes were filled with unspoken sorrow. Derrick parked near the tornado memorial and stepped out. The granite sculpture was simple yet solemn, engraved with the names of those lost in the tragedy. He traced the names with his fingers, each one a stab of pain.

"So many names," he whispered, his voice barely audible over the gentle rustling of leaves.

To his surprise, a voice answered him. "So many friends."

He turned to find Lydia standing beside him, her eyes red from holding back tears. She offered him a small, sad smile. "There's a few I need to as well..."

They walked together to the rows where the victims were laid to rest. The cemetery was quiet, save for the distant hum of a lawnmower. Derrick didn't know many of the names on the graves, but those he did recognize hurt more than he could bear. They moved down the row, one by one, saying their goodbyes.

"Olivia... Mia... Natalie... Zoey..." he murmured, each name a piece of his heartbreaking off. "Ava..." He paused at her grave, a marker without a body. They searched for weeks, but they never found her. At her funeral, Adam told a story about how she became a butterfly after being lifted into the monster tornado and flew away to Heaven. It was a comforting tale, but Derrick knew it wasn't true. The emptiness of her grave echoed the emptiness in his soul.

But it was the names of William and Caleb that struck him the hardest. Despite his urging, they had decided against taking cover with them. Their bodies were found over seven miles away in the town of Floris. Derrick knelt by their graves, the weight of their loss pressing down on him.

"What I wouldn't give right now to be annoyed with your stupid questions," he whispered as his voice broke.

Lydia knelt beside him, placing a hand on his shoulder. He shook his head, the guilt overwhelming. "I should have tried harder. I should have made them come with us."

Lydia's eyes were full of compassion as she looked at him. "You did everything you could. Sometimes... it's just not enough."

They sat silently for a long time, the memories of their friends and neighbors swirling around them like the wind that had once torn through their town. Finally, Derrick stood, pulling Lydia up with him. He placed a hand on the memorial, a silent promise to remember and never forget the lives that had touched his.

Sitting back down in the car, Derrick's gaze fixated on the ridge in the distance.

...*The sky turned gray, and rain started falling. Seeing a headstone standing off by itself, Derrick made his way to it. Weeds were growing up around it. Getting closer, he moved the leaves, and it read 'Anderson.' It had Lydia's and Madeline's names on it, and they had the same date of death. Something was odd, though. He looked closer at the dates. They were in the future... a month from now. Then, from behind him came a faint voice, as if from a ghost, saying, "We had a beautiful life together. How'd we end up here?"*

"Derrick! Are you okay?" Lydia yelled as she shook his arm, snapping him back to reality. "You were just staring off and not responding to me." Then she felt the goosebumps covering his body. "Was it another flashback?" she asked, her voice lowering in intensity.

"Kinda," Derrick replied shortly as he started the car.

The sun had just gone down as they made it back to the airport.

"What does that clue mean?" Lydia asked.

Derrick sighed. "Well, I only know of one place that would have 'dingoes.'" He pulled up the map and searched the coastline until he found the Cape Leeuwin Lighthouse... in Australia.

"Ah, man... we have to go back there?!"

CHAPTER 14

Lydia gazed out the car window, a wide grin spreading across her face as Derrick turned off the engine. The lighthouse was perched on a rocky cliff where the Indian and Southern Oceans met. At one hundred and twenty-eight feet, it had stood guard over the southwestern tip of Australia, silently protecting sailors for over a century.

As they stepped out of the car and approached the base of the lighthouse, its grandeur became even more apparent. Derrick paused to take a deep breath, letting the salty sea breeze fill his lungs. The wind brushed against his face, carrying with it the scent of the ocean. It had been a long time since he had felt such peace. No ringing phones, no blaring horns—just the distant crash of waves against the shore and the cries of seagulls overhead. Derrick glanced at Lydia, who smiled and took his hand. "You ready, Hun?" she asked.

Opening the large, white doors, they entered a small room filled with historical photographs and artifacts, with a spiral staircase winding up the brick walls.

A grizzled man met them with a warm smile. "The name's Mr. Morrison. Welcome to Cape Leeuwin Lighthouse! I'll be your guide today," he said, leading them to the staircase. "This lighthouse was built in

1895, and it's been guiding ships safely to shore ever since. It's the tallest lighthouse on mainland Australia, standing at 39 meters."

One hundred and seventy-six stairs later, Derrick found himself gasping for air as they reached the top of the staircase and stepped out onto the balcony. The panoramic view that greeted them took his breath away. The ocean stretched endlessly before them, and the massive rotating light above cast long shadows across the balcony. Lydia, captivated by the sight, turned to see Derrick lingering inside, his attention caught by the intricate workings of the light.

"Derrick!" she called. "Are you coming out here? The view is amazing!"

Derrick quickly shook his head. The thought of stepping out onto the high balcony made his heart race.

"There's a railing—you'll be fine. We need to find the clue," she coaxed.

But Derrick shook his head again, more firmly this time. "I'll check for it in here," he muttered.

Lydia rolled her eyes and grabbed his arm, gently pulling him toward the door. His resistance was profound, as he muttered, "No, no, no, no, no!" dragging his feet as she led him outside.

Looking into his eyes, Lydia spoke softly, "Derrick." Her voice was soothing and calmed the storm of fear inside him. "I'll be right here with you. Please, just come out and look at this."

With Lydia by his side, his fear began to ebb. Stepping onto the balcony, he was met with a breathtaking view of the merging oceans. The vast expanse of water, where the two seas met, astonished him.

"See? I told you it was great!" Lydia exclaimed. Her joy was contagious.

As Mr. Morrison headed back downstairs to greet another arriving tour, Derrick began searching the balcony, mumbling to himself, "The clue has to be around here somewhere."

Lydia watched him, amused, as he crawled around, searching every nook and cranny. Just then, Mr. Morrison returned, noticing Derrick's peculiar behavior. "What's that bloke doing?" he asked.

Lydia smiled and explained, "He's looking for our next clue and afraid of heights. We've been following a trail of them left behind by a friend."

Mr. Morrison chuckled. "Well, if it's a clue you're after, you might be interested in this." Reaching into his pocket, he pulled out a folded note and handed it to Lydia.

She unfolded it, her eyes widening in surprise. "This is exactly what we're looking for!"

Mr. Morrison nodded knowingly. "I figured as much. It was left here by someone who seemed to know you'd come looking."

Calling out to Derrick, Lydia waved the note in the air. Scrambling back to her, he asked eagerly, "Is that it?"

"Sure is," Lydia replied, handing him the note. Derrick unfolded it and read aloud:

> "In the city of wealth,
> where fortunes dance on green,
> Seek the palace of chance,
> where the stakes are keen.
> Upon the wheel of fate,
> a number bold and true,
> Place five hundred forty-one
> on double-zero,
> and the path will come to you."

"The city of wealth... that sounds like Las Vegas," Derrick pondered. "And the palace of chance—Caesar's Palace, I bet."

As they headed back down the spiral staircase, Mr. Morrison bid them farewell. "Wherever your adventure takes you, may you find what you're looking for. Safe travels," he said warmly.

After leaving the lighthouse, Derrick and Lydia strolled along the rugged coastline, the powerful waves crashing majestically against the rocky shore. Derrick reached down and took Lydia's hand, the warmth of her touch grounding him in a way that calmed his ever-present anxieties. They found a grassy knoll nearby and sat down, watching as the sun dipped below the horizon in a blaze of orange and pink, reflecting off the ocean's surface.

Lydia leaned into Derrick, resting her head on his shoulder. "It's so peaceful here," she whispered, her voice barely audible over the rhythmic sound of the waves.

Derrick nodded, but his mind was elsewhere. The beauty of the sunset felt like a stark contrast to the darkness that lingered inside him.

Lydia could sense that something was troubling him. She took his hand, gently rubbing her thumb over the scars that marked his skin. "Is it still bothering you?" she asked softly.

Derrick stared out at the ocean, a tear forming in his eye. They had promised each other never to keep secrets, and he had kept that vow in everything—except this.

Lydia felt his body tremble slightly, her concern growing. "It's not the crash, is it?" she asked, her voice filled with sympathy.

Tears began to stream down Derrick's face. "I didn't get these scars from the accident."

...It was the first anniversary of the crash that killed Emily, and it was a rainy night in Boston. Derrick sat in the bathtub with a bottle of Kentucky poison, which was now running through his veins, resting on the rim. A broken plastic handle from a razor lay on the sink nearby. Grasping for the bottle of whiskey, it slipped from his fingers and crashed to the floor. As he reached for it, the sight of his palm being covered in a red, viscous fluid caused him to stop. He pulled his arm closer to his face to examine it as blood continued to flow out from the open wounds on his lower extremity. Grabbing a towel, he applied pressure, only to find his other wrist matched the first in lacerations and hemorrhaging. The edges of the room around him started to close in with a gray fog until he could no longer hold his head up. The room went dark...

"I don't know how I got out of that," Derrick confessed, his voice heavy with emotion. "I remember waking up in the ICU, handcuffed to the bed. I screamed in anger through my breathing tube when I realized where I was."

He paused, the memories too painful to revisit easily. "I spent weeks in that hospital, then at a recovery center, trying to put the pieces of my life back together. I tell people I stopped flying because of the memories, but the truth is... the FAA pulled my wings. They said I wasn't 'fit for duty' anymore. I was punished for being human."

Derrick's voice wavered as he continued. "I returned to my apartment that day, but the locks had been changed. A month in the hospital with no contact, and they auctioned off everything I owned, including my mom's Bible."

He took a deep breath, trying to steady himself. "I needed money to get my car out of impound, so I sold my dad's watch. He'd saved for years to buy that Omega and was wearing it the night of the crash. Every time I saw the crack in the crystal, it reminded me of him and that night."

Derrick's tears flowed freely now. "I lost everything—my family, my job, my friends... my sanity.

But then the Agency called. They gave me a second chance. They saved me in just about every way possible." He turned to Lydia, his gaze filled with love and gratitude. "And they brought me the greatest help anyone could ever ask for."

Lydia's face crumpled with emotion, and she buried her head in his chest, sobbing. Derrick held her tightly, his own tears mingling with hers.

"The nightmares have returned," he admitted, his voice barely above a whisper. "But they're different now. They're not flashbacks... they're foreshadows. I lose you in every one of them."

He swallowed hard, the memories of his dreams making his throat tighten. "In one, you're captured. I hear you screaming, but I can't find you. Then the screams stop. In another, we're back home, and the house is on fire. I'm outside, watching it burn with you and Madeline inside... I wake up in a cold sweat, heart pounding, and I can't shake the fear that one day, it might come true."

Lydia cupped his face in her hands, pulling him close. "Derrick, I'm here. I'm safe. You always make sure of that. Nothing is going to happen, okay?"

"I know," Derrick whispered, his voice trembling. "But the fear is always there. Every time we go on a mission, every time we face danger... I can't help but think, what if this is the time I lose you? I can't go through that again."

CHAPTER 15

The lights of the Las Vegas Strip shimmered against the desert night sky as their plane touched down at McCarran International Airport. Derrick couldn't help but let his curiosity get the best of him. "Do you think the pilots would take us up to Area 51 when we're done?" he asked, half-serious.

Lydia shot him an unamused glance. "Derrick..."

"But it's just over that way," he persisted, but her glare was enough to stop him mid-sentence. "Well, it is. I just wanted to see the aliens."

As they stepped outside the airport and joined the line for a taxi, they were surprised to see that limousines were more common than regular cabs. Derrick caught Lydia's eye and raised an eyebrow. "You wanna?"

Before she could respond, Derrick flagged down a sleek, black Maybach limo. As they climbed into the luxurious backseat, Derrick sank into the plush leather, letting out a contented sigh. "I could get used to this," he remarked, stretching out.

Lydia, sprawled out on one of the side benches, nodded in agreement. "No kidding!"

As they pulled up to Caesar's Palace, it was as if they'd stepped into another world. The entrance, framed by Roman-inspired arches and adorned with elaborate decorations, was bustling with activity.

Multiple valets hurried over, tripping over each other to assist. Lydia stepped out onto the red carpet, squeezing Derrick's arm excitedly. "I've never felt more like a celebrity in my life!" she exclaimed, waving at the bystanders like they were someone important. The crowd waved back, pointing and whispering as if they should recognize her.

After checking in, their luggage was whisked away to their suite while Derrick and Lydia ventured onto the casino floor. Having never set foot in a casino before, Derrick wasn't sure where to start. "Everyone's using chips... where do we get those?" he asked Lydia, who shrugged, equally clueless. "I've never been to one either."

Getting directions from a helpful passerby, they found the cashier's cage and exchanged their money for chips. As they walked toward the roulette tables, Derrick realized the clue didn't specify which table to play at. "Um... any ideas?" he asked.

Lydia looked around, equally uncertain. "I guess we just pick one and hope for the best."

Derrick placed five hundred and forty-one dollars' worth of chips on the green space marked '00' at the first table they found. The dealer spun the wheel, and as it clicked around, Derrick held his breath. The ball landed on 23, and the dealer moved on as if they weren't even there.

Leaning closer to Lydia, Derrick whispered, "What now?"

She shrugged again. "I guess we move on to the next one?"

They repeated the process at several tables, but each time, they were met with the same disappointing outcome. Finally, stepping out into the lobby, Derrick was at a loss. "What do we do now? We followed the clue, right?"

Lydia scratched her head, just as puzzled. "I don't know. Maybe we got the wrong place? Is there another city known as the 'City of Wealth'?"

Exhausted from the long flight and their fruitless efforts, Derrick sighed. "Let's just head to the room, regroup, and try again tomorrow."

The next morning, the desert sun began to creep over the horizon, waking Derrick from his deep sleep. It had been a long time since he'd slept in such comfort—the king-sized bed was dressed in silky sheets and a plush comforter that made him reluctant to leave. He rolled over to face the other side, surprised to find Lydia still nestled beside him. She was usually up and about, with two cups of coffee already consumed by this hour. He watched her for a moment, still amazed that someone so beautiful had chosen to spend her life with him. With that thought, he drifted back to sleep.

Hours later, Lydia gently shook him awake. "Honey, it's past 11 am. Time to get up."

Derrick groggily rolled out of bed, muttering, "We need one of these beds at home," as he stumbled toward the bathroom.

After grabbing some much-needed coffee, they set out onto the Strip, searching for one of the many buffets they had seen the night before. "I can't decide if I want the all-you-can-eat steak or the all-you-can-eat crab legs," Derrick mused.

Lydia spotted a sign across the street and smiled. "How about... BOTH?"

Stepping out of the restaurant, Derrick looked disappointed. "It shouldn't say 'all-you-can-eat' if they're going to run out of food!"

Lydia laughed, taking his hand. "Let's go for a walk and check out some stores. If you're still hungry, we can find another place for dinner."

Wandering down the crowded street, Lydia pointed out a jewelry store across the way. But when she turned back to Derrick, he was gone.

Derrick had spotted a store advertising Agent Inept merchandise and darted inside. The place was a treasure trove of shirts, action figures, and memorabilia from his favorite show. By the time Lydia found him, his arms were overflowing with items.

"Oh, dear," she sighed, seeing the childlike excitement on Derrick's face. Resigning herself to the inevitable, she grabbed a basket.

"Look at this action figure! It almost looks like me!" Derrick exclaimed, dropping it into the basket before disappearing back among the racks.

An hour—and five hundred dollars worth of stuff later, Derrick was finally ready to check out. As he placed his items on the counter, a familiar voice behind him said, "Wow, looks like we've got a serious fan here!"

Derrick's body froze as he turned around to see Duke Jacoby, the star of Agent Inept, standing behind him. His knees nearly gave way as he tried to speak, unsure if the squeal he heard came from him or someone else in the store. Duke extended his hand with a smile. "Hi there! The name's Duke. What's yours?"

Derrick struggled to get his name out, his voice shaking with excitement. Lydia, seeing how starstruck he was, stepped in with a grin. "Mr. Jacoby, I think you've met your biggest fan. He's never missed an episode... not even a re-run."

Duke beamed. "My biggest fan! Well, we definitely need a picture together, then. It's not every day you meet someone so dedicated."

Lydia lined up the shot as Duke put his arm around Derrick, who looked like he was about to burst with joy. "I guess it's redundant to tell you to smile," she joked before snapping a few pictures.

"I'm glad you enjoy the show," Duke said. "We've got a new episode tonight, but I'm sure you already know that. How about I sign something for you before I head out?"

Derrick eagerly handed over the action figure box. As Duke signed it, he added, "Well, Derrick, stay awesome! Hope you enjoy the rest of your time in Vegas."

Later that night, after saving the world again with Duke, Derrick woke to the annoyance that it was a dream. Groaning, he reached out for Lydia, but his hand found only the sheets beside him. Confused and a little concerned, he checked the time—4 am—and noticed that Lydia's phone was also gone.

Following the location of her phone, Derrick headed downstairs to the casino. The bright lights and constant noise were jarring at this hour. "Don't you people ever sleep?" he muttered as he scanned the floor for Lydia.

Finally, he spotted her at a coin pusher machine, completely engrossed as she watched the coins teeter on the edge. She even blew on the glass, trying to coax the coins to fall. "Come on! Fall already! Momma needs some new shoes!"

"What are you doing?" Derrick asked, trying to suppress a laugh.

Lydia jumped, turning to him with a sheepish grin. "Oh... uh... I couldn't sleep," she said, clearly unconvincing.

Derrick raised an eyebrow, amused.

Turning back to the machine, Lydia kept working on the stack of coins. "I figured you'd be fine all snuggled up with your new stuffed sleeping buddy."

Derrick rolled his eyes. "You leave Dominic out of this!" His protest was cut short by the sound of coins tumbling over the edge.

"YES!" Lydia cheered, turning toward Derrick as the machine's bells rang. "I just won $100!"

Derrick's eyes widened as he noticed the shirt she was wearing. "And you're a thief! That's my 'Ineptitude at its Finest' shirt!"

Lydia held out the shirt, giving Derrick a better view. "You mean this old thing? It matched my skort," she teased with a grin.

Derrick was still aghast. "I haven't even had a chance to wear that one yet!"

Feigning innocence, Lydia offered, "Oh, I'm sorry. Would you like me to take it off?" She slowly lifted the hem past her belly button, a mischievous glint in her eye.

Derrick's eyes bulged as he tried to stop her. "Lydia!"

"So... no?" she asked with a giggle.

Later that day, Derrick stood by the pool, deep in thought, trying to piece together the clue. "City of Wealth," he muttered before diving into the cool water. Each stroke helped clear his mind of the clutter from the past few weeks.

Lydia watched him through her oversized sunglasses as she reclined on a plush lounge chair, soaking in the sun. Her red and white polka dot bikini accentuated her relaxed demeanor.

As Derrick swam, his thoughts churned. "City of Wealth. Where else could that be? It has to be somewhere wealthy, with casinos." He pushed himself harder, trying to swim through his own frustration.

After finishing his laps, Derrick climbed out of the pool, water dripping from his body. He walked over to Lydia, who was still lounging in the sun. Despite his efforts to focus, his breath still hitched every time he saw the scar on her shoulder from Baghdad. She no longer tried to hide it, but it was a constant reminder to him of how close he came to losing her.

Plopping beside her, he let out a deep sigh as he toweled off.

"Any ideas?" she asked, noticing his mind still working.

"Not yet," he admitted. "It's like my brain's in a fog. There's so much running through it, I can't think straight."

She squeezed his hand, offering a reassuring smile. "You'll figure it out. You always do. Just relax. Maybe catch a few more rays, and it'll come to you."

Derrick smiled at her and then leaned back on the lounger, staring up at the clear sky. As he closed his eyes and let the warmth of the sun melt away his worries... if just for a moment.

Hours later, Lydia gently nudged him awake. "Honey, it's almost time for Agent Inept. Do you want to go wash up first?"

Sitting up with a groan, Derrick felt a familiar sting on his skin.

Lydia gasped when she saw the redness. "How many times have I told you to use sunscreen?!"

"I did!" Derrick protested, reaching into her bag to pull out the tube he had used. His face fell when he realized it wasn't sunscreen at all—it was moisturizing lotion.

Lydia raised an eyebrow, fighting back a smile. "The aloe is back in the room waiting for you."

Later, Derrick sat on the edge of the bed, eagerly waiting for the new episode of Agent Inept. He had changed into one of the shirts he'd bought the day before. This one had the show's tagline across the front: "Accidentally Awesome: Agent Inept."

The episode began with Dominic Storm uncovering a money-laundering scheme at the Monte Carlo Casino in Monaco. As the scene unfolded, Derrick sat up straighter. When the host welcomed Dominic to the casino, he said, "Welcome to the City of Wealth, Mr. Storm!"

Derrick's eyes widened. "Did you hear that?" he asked Lydia, grabbing his phone. A quick search confirmed that Monaco was indeed nicknamed the "City of Wealth."

"It's Monaco, not Vegas!" Derrick exclaimed.

That night, Derrick couldn't sleep. His mind raced with anticipation for their next move. But first, they needed to buy some new clothes suitable for the upscale Monte Carlo Casino. His usual shirt and tie wouldn't cut it there.

Thankfully, there was an upscale mall right next to Caesar's Palace.

The next morning, as they entered the mall, Derrick was struck by the gleaming marble floors and the high-end boutiques lining the corridors. He led Lydia to a tailor shop known for its bespoke suits.

Inside, a well-dressed man greeted them warmly. "Welcome! How can I assist you today?"

Derrick smiled. "I need a tuxedo. Something classic, with a modern touch—like James Bond would wear."

The tailor nodded, understanding precisely what Derrick meant. He began showing him various fabrics and styles, and after some deliberation, Derrick chose a sleek black tuxedo with subtle satin lapels. The tailor took his measurements with meticulous care, promising a perfect fit.

Meanwhile, Lydia wandered into a boutique specializing in evening gowns. The saleswoman greeted her with a knowing smile and immediately began pulling out dresses that matched Lydia's height and figure. After trying on several, Lydia found the perfect one. "Derrick is going to lose his mind when he sees this!" she thought with a grin.

She headed back to the tux shop just as Derrick was finishing up. "Perfect timing!" she exclaimed.

He turned to see her carrying a garment bag over her shoulder. "What did you get?" he asked excitedly.

"You'll just have to wait and see," she replied with a mischievous glint in her eye.

CHAPTER 16

The Gulfstream touched down smoothly on the runway in Nice, France as the Mediterranean coastline glistened under the afternoon sun. Monaco, being a tiny yet glamorous country, didn't have its own airport, but the short distance from Nice made the journey seamless.

Derrick wrestled with his tuxedo, fumbling with the unfamiliar fabric and intricate folds. He was never one for formal wear, and the task was proving more challenging than he anticipated. "How do people make this look so easy?" he muttered, struggling to adjust his bowtie, which felt more like a noose than a fashion accessory.

In the adjacent lavatory, Lydia was putting the final touches on her makeup. Her reflection in the mirror showed a woman of poise and elegance, but the slight tremor in her hands revealed the nerves beneath the surface. She took a deep breath, steadying herself before replying to Derrick, who had just called out to see if she needed any help.

"No, I'm good. I want to surprise you," she said, her voice carrying a hint of mischief. "Wait for me at the car when you get back."

Derrick finally managed to wrangle his tuxedo into submission and headed out to pick up their rental.

Thirty minutes later, the roar of a powerful engine announced his return. A dark gray Lamborghini Aventador, sleek and polished to a mirror-like finish, slid to a stop at the base of the plane's stairs. Derrick stepped out, a grin spreading across his face as he admired the car's aggressive lines and the way the sunlight danced on its surface.

"Such a beautiful car," he whispered to himself, running a hand along the fender. Leaning casually against the passenger side, he crossed his arms and adopted a confident smirk, waiting for Lydia.

When she appeared at the top of the stairs, Derrick's breath caught in his throat. Lydia moved with the grace of a starlet from a bygone era, her burgundy sequin dress catching the fading light, turning her into a vision of fiery embers against the dusk. Derrick's attempt at maintaining his cool demeanor faltered as his face betrayed his admiration.

"Madam," he greeted with a playful tone, holding the car door open for her. Lydia chuckled softly, her eyes sparkling as she slid onto the leather seat.

The drive to the casino was an exhilarating experience, with the Aventador's engine purring beneath them, the tires gripping the winding roads with precision. When they arrived at the casino's grand entrance, Derrick pulled up to the valet with a sense of flair, the engine's growl drawing the attention of passersby. He stepped out, adjusting his bowtie and sunglasses, feeling every bit the suave super-spy he had always dreamed of being.

As he tossed the keys to the valet, Derrick made his way to Lydia's side. He opened the door, watching as she emerged with an effortless elegance, her black silk-covered legs catching the last rays of the sun. For a moment, Derrick was lost in the sight of her, the mission forgotten.

Lydia, noticing his distraction, gently linked her arm with his and whispered, "Later," as her voice brought him back to the task at hand.

They walked into the casino, and the opulence of the place hit them immediately. Crystal chandeliers hung from the ceiling, casting a glow over the marble floors and rich velvet drapes. The air was thick with the clinking of glasses, the rustle of expensive clothing, and the soft murmur of gamblers focused on their games.

Derrick felt a surge of nerves as they approached the roulette table. The instructions from the clue were clear: *Put $541 on '00'.*"

With Lydia by his side, he counted out the chips and placed them on the green space marked '00.' The dealer's eyes flicked to Derrick, his curiosity mingling with professionalism as he spun the wheel.

Lydia leaned in close, her voice barely above a whisper. "This had better work."

As the wheel spun, Derrick's heart pounded in his chest, its sound almost drowning out the clatter of the ball as it bounced along the numbers. Just as the tension reached its peak, the dealer casually slid a small envelope across the table toward Derrick. Picking it up, he quickly glanced at the contents: a new clue, written in elegant script.

Before he could pocket the clue, the ball dropped into the slot marked '00.' Gasps rippled through the crowd as the dealer announced the win. Derrick's stack of chips multiplied in an instant, drawing the attention of everyone nearby.

Lydia's eyes darted around, noticing several men in dark suits moving toward them. "This isn't good," she muttered.

Derrick recognized them immediately. "Nightfall," he whispered. "We need to move. Now!"

In a calculated move, Derrick threw the winnings into the air, the chips scattering like confetti. The resulting chaos among the casino patrons gave them the precious seconds they needed. Grabbing Lydia's hand, Derrick led the way as they sprinted toward the exit.

Outside, Lydia grabbed the keys from the valet, and they ran for the car. Derrick gasped as she slid across the hood and jumped into the driver's seat.

"Careful! You're going to scratch it!" Derrick protested, but his words were lost in the roar of the V12 engine as Lydia started the sports car. Derrick barely managed to shut the door before they peeled out from under the porte-cochère, the tires screeching against the pavement.

The streets of Monaco blurred past as Lydia navigated the narrow, winding roads with the precision of a professional driver. Derrick's eyes flicked to the rearview mirror, trying to catch sight of their pursuers. "Are they following us?" he asked, his voice tense.

His question was answered by a bullet shattering the back window. "Yep," Lydia replied, her tone calm as she downshifted and maneuvered the car more aggressively.

Derrick glanced at the broken glass, wincing. "There goes my deposit."

Hitting a stretch of four-lane road, Lydia pushed the car to its limits, the car weaving through the thinning traffic. Derrick clutched the seat, his knuckles white as he prayed they wouldn't collide with anything. Looking out the passenger side mirror, Lydia saw one of the Range Rovers pulling up alongside them.

"Did you use your real name or an alias when you rented this?" she asked, her voice steady despite the situation.

"An alias, why?" Derrick replied, puzzled.

"Just curious," Lydia said, her eyes narrowing as she swerved to the right, sideswiping the Range Rover and sending it careening off the road.

"LYDIA! This is an Aventador!" Derrick exclaimed, his voice marked with horror.

"And it still is… mostly," she shot back, her focus unyielding as she steered them back on course.

Derrick scanned the car's interior, looking for anything that could help them out of this mess.

"What I wouldn't give for a gun right now," he muttered.

"Upper right thigh," Lydia replied, her tone casual.

"What? Where?"

Lydia nudged her leg closer to him. "My upper right thigh. There's a holster."

Derrick blinked in disbelief. "How in the world are you hiding ANYTHING under that dress?"

"Derrick, just grab it!"

Reaching over, Derrick found a tiny .380 pistol strapped to the inside of her thigh. "This thing is embarrassing!" he exclaimed, holding up the small weapon.

"Got a better idea?" Lydia quipped.

"Maybe…" Derrick unbuckled his seatbelt and turned to remove the headrest from his seat. Sitting back down, he looked at the finely stitched Italian leather, feeling a pang of regret for what he was about to do. "Well, I guess if I'm not getting my deposit back anyway..." he muttered, pulling out his knife and cutting a slit in the bottom of the headrest, fluffing the foam inside.

Distracted by his actions, Lydia nearly missed a traffic light that had turned red. She slammed on the brakes at the last second, sending Derrick flying forward into the dashboard.

From his new position on the floor, Derrick spat out the headrest and glared up at Lydia.

"That's why you're supposed to wear your seatbelt," Lydia remarked, her tone dripping with sarcasm.

Grumbling, Derrick climbed back into his seat and rummaged through the emergency roadside kit. Finding a road flare, he turned to Lydia. "Where are they?"

"Two cars back," she replied, her eyes never leaving the road.

"Get ready to go when the light turns green," Derrick instructed, rolling down his window.

Lydia's lips curled into a grin as she anxiously revved the engine.

Derrick lit the flare and shoved it into the headrest. He then fired three shots into the grill of the car behind them. Steam erupted from the engine as oil began pooling under the car. Derrick tossed the flaming headrest onto the oil slick, igniting a fiery explosion that sent the occupants scrambling for safety.

"Bullseye!" Derrick shouted as the light turned green, and Lydia launched the vehicle through the intersection.

Just when Derrick thought they were in the clear, the remaining Nightfall vehicles swerved over the median and resumed the chase.

"Your friends are back," Lydia noted, her voice calm as they approached the on-ramp to the A8.

One of the SUVs clipped the rear of the car, but Lydia quickly recovered and opened up the behemoth engine. It thundered down the on-ramp, reaching over 100 mph in seconds, leaving the SUVs far behind.

The open highway was where the Aventador truly came alive, the engine's roar echoing through the tunnels as they sped toward Nice. Derrick's stomach lurched every time he glanced at the speedometer, watching the needle climb past 240 km/h. The tunnels, in particular, amplified the car's ferocious growl with each downshift sending a shiver up Derrick's spine.

As they neared one of the last tunnels, Derrick noticed the tachometer redlining at 8,600 rpm. His eyes widened in panic. "SHIFT! SHIFT! You've got to shift, or you're gonna blow the engine!" he shouted.

Lydia smacked him on the leg. "I've got this! Stop side-seat driving!"

The lights of Nice Côte d'Azur Airport loomed in the distance as they raced through the final stretch. Lydia quickly dialed their pilot's number and, as if discussing dinner plans, calmly asked, "Hey, Cap, would you be a dear and start the plane for us? We'll be there in about three minutes, and we need to leave in a hurry."

Derrick's heart leaped into his throat as Lydia skidded through yet another intersection.

"Curb... um... CURB... LYDIA, CURB!!!" he yelled in horror as the car launched over the curb and into oncoming traffic.

Without missing a beat, Lydia added, "Make that about two and a half. Thanks, dear!"

The sports car skidded to a stop at the bottom of the plane's stairs, and smoke billowed from the engine. Derrick opened his door, only to have it fall off its hinges and clatter to the ground. Stumbling out, he surveyed the wrecked supercar with dismay. "How are we going to explain this to the rental place?!"

Lydia didn't slow down, grabbing Derrick's arm as she bolted for the plane. "Let THEM explain it!" she shouted, pointing to the convoy of SUVs crashing through the gate.

Derrick barely had time to secure the plane's door before yelling, "GO, GO, GO!"

The aircraft rumbled down the runway just as Obadiah and his team pulled out onto the tarmac. He slammed his rifle to the ground in frustration as the plane lifted off.

Behind them, the Aventador exploded into a fiery inferno, knocking Obadiah's men to the ground. Derrick winced, watching the car he had so briefly enjoyed melt into a heap of metal. "I guess we won't be coming back to France anytime soon."

As the plane leveled out, Derrick sat down and undid his bowtie, his mind replaying the events that had just unfolded. He pulled out the new clue and read it aloud:

> "In the land where cherry blossoms bloom,
> And cities buzz with lights in gloom,
> The capital's heart, you must go,
> For a journey fast, with secrets to know.
> At 8:04, catch the express,
> To the City of Water
> You'll find the next quest.
> Seek a man whose name is Yoshi.
> He holds the key to this grand odyssey.
> Then to the castle, strong and grand,
> Where ancient tales of honor stand,
> Look into the barrel deep,
> For inside the cannon is what you seek."

The familiar chime of a Facetime call interrupted his thoughts. Lydia's mother's face appeared on the screen, her smile brightening when she saw them.

"Wow, you two look snazzy! Been somewhere fancy?" Mary asked.

Lydia, looking a bit sheepish, replied, "Kinda…"

Madeline's excited face appeared next, tugging at the phone. "Maddie has something she wants to tell you," Mary said, turning the phone toward her granddaughter.

"I went poopie in the potty!" Madeline announced proudly. Lydia cheered, her eyes welling up with tears of both pride and regret. "You're such a big girl now! I'm so proud of you!"

Derrick saw the pain in Lydia's eyes that she tried so hard to conceal. He excused himself and walked to the front of the plane, giving her some privacy.

After the call ended, Lydia broke down, her emotions finally spilling over. Derrick returned, sitting beside her and pulling her close. "I'm sorry, Honey. I know how much you want to be there."

"I don't think I can do this anymore," Lydia sobbed. "Madeline needs her momma."

Derrick held her tightly, his voice gentle but firm. "I know. That's why I've told the pilots to change course. We're not going to Japan. We're going home."

Lydia looked up at him, her eyes searching his face. "You're giving up on Tae?"

"No, not exactly," Derrick replied. "I'm taking you back so you can be with Maddie. This life... it's not fair to you. I'll go to Japan alone."

Her voice trembled as she asked, "How long are you going to keep doing this?"

Derrick sighed, the weight of the question pressing down on him. "I don't know. I keep telling myself it's just one more place... one more clue... but I don't know when it'll end."

CHAPTER 17

After weeks of traveling the world, Derrick couldn't help but smile as the wheels of the plane touched down on the familiar runway. Shining from inside the hangar, he saw the hood of his Mustang.

As soon as the plane rolled to a stop, Lydia hugged him tightly, her voice filled with excitement as she exclaimed, "We're home!"

When they finally pulled up to their house, Lydia was out of the car before Derrick even had a chance to put it in park. She paused on the porch, her breath catching as the front door swung open. Madeline squealed with joy and toddled toward her, arms outstretched. Lydia scooped her up, spinning her around before hugging her close. Tears streamed down her face as she whispered, "I missed you so much, sweetheart."

Inside, the smell of home-cooked food filled the air. Mary was bustling in the kitchen, adding the final touches to dinner. She greeted them with warm hugs and a welcoming smile. "Welcome home, you two. Dinner's almost ready!"

Later that evening, after a satisfying meal, Derrick stood quietly in the doorway of Madeline's room. He watched as Lydia sat on the bed, reading Madeline her favorite bedtime story. Her voice was soft and soothing, and it wasn't long before both mother and daughter's eyes grew heavy, and they drifted off to sleep together.

Derrick slipped out of the room and into their bedroom, where he began packing for his next trip. As he folded the last of his clothes into the suitcase, Jeb appeared in the doorway, leaning against the frame.

"Heading off again so soon?" Jeb asked, his voice filled with concern.

Derrick could see the worry in Jeb's eyes, and he sighed, leaning back against the desk. "We're close... I hope."

Jeb paused, choosing his words carefully. "We all love Tae. Funniest guy I've ever met. But how do you know he's still one of the good guys? I've seen many good men change over the years."

Derrick ran his fingers through his hair, the question weighing heavily on him. "I don't know for sure. That's why I have to find him. If he's still good, he needs help. If he's not... he needs justice."

Jeb nodded slowly, understanding the gravity of Derrick's mission. "Fair enough. But remember, son, that little girl in there needs her daddy more than this world needs justice. Make sure you come home."

***

The next morning, after saying goodbye to Madeline, Derrick hugged Lydia. "I wish you didn't have to go," she said, her voice tinged with sadness.

Derrick held her close, wishing he could stay. "I know," he replied, "but I promise, I'll be back soon."

At the airport, Derrick checked in for his flight to Tokyo. With Lydia staying behind, it made more sense to fly commercially this time. It was less conspicuous and easier to explain to customs.

Derrick's thoughts drifted back to Jeb's words as he settled into his business class seat. This mission wasn't about the thrill or the danger—it was personal. Tae was his best friend, and Derrick couldn't shake the gnawing fear that something had gone terribly wrong. The idea that Tae could have turned ate away at him, leaving a heavy weight in his gut.

Derrick gazed out the window as the plane lifted off, and the familiar landscape of home disappeared again beneath the clouds. The excitement he once felt at the start of this journey was now replaced by a sense of longing and dread. This time, leaving everything he loved behind felt like a burden he wasn't sure he could bear.

Even with his seat laid out flat, Derrick struggled to sleep. His mind kept drifting back to happy times with Lydia and Madeline.

...It was 3 am when Derrick felt something moving beside him. He opened his eyes and saw Madeline crawling over onto his stomach. She made it up to his face, grinned, and then stuck her finger into his ear. Derrick's reaction made her giggle. She then laid her head down on his chest and went to sleep...

"How could anyone be angry about getting woken up like that?" he asked himself.

His thoughts then wandered to when he and Madeline had replaced the dishwasher.

...Being something he had never really done before, Derrick found out his kryptonite... plumbing! Days before, he received a surprise one morning when he walked into the kitchen to brew the coffee. Stepping into a cold puddle of water on the floor, he knew what his next project was going to be. While he was sure he could fix the old plumbing of the dishwasher, Lydia was insistent they just get a new one. Since Derrick knew her vote counted twice, he cleaned up the water, and they headed off to the hardware store.

Lydia hated going with him there because it was always like he had ADHD at a squirrel convention. After twenty minutes of grabbing things they "needed," Lydia finally got him to the appliance section.

Finding the cheapest washer on display, Derrick grabbed the ticket and said, "$349, not bad. Looks like we're done here!"

"That one doesn't match any of the other appliances!" she explained.

"So?" When he saw Lydia put her hands on her hips, he knew it was going to be a long day.

Derrick managed to sneak away to the toilets so he could at least have somewhere to sit while she inspected each and every one with a fine-tooth comb.

After twenty minutes, he heard his name called over the intercom. "If there is a Derrick Anderson in the store, can you please return to Appliances?" At that moment, he seriously considered making a run for the car.

"Where have you been?!?" she scolded as he returned with his tail between his legs.

"I was checking out the toilets. I figured we might need a new one, too... since we're here. I found one that will talk to you while you do your business."

Looking at him confused, she asked, "Derrick...why would we need that?"

Derrick just shrugged.

"Anyway..." she said with a tint of ire in her voice, "I found the perfect one for us!"

Derrick's eyes widened when he saw the price tag. "1,299?!?"

Grabbing his arm and pulling him closer, she explained, "Stay with me here! This washer has a third rack! It will also sanitize Maddie's bottles. It even has a window on the front so you can watch it working!"

"Why would you want to..." Derrick stopped mid-sentence when he saw Lydia's glare. "Sure... sure. Makes sense. So, when can they install it?"

A sheepish grin appeared on Lydia's face. "Well... they can't get someone out there for a week, so I told them my big, strong, smart husband would do it for me."

"He sounds amazing... you'll have to introduce him to me sometime," Derrick halfheartedly joked. "Honey, I've never installed a dishwasher before. What makes you think I can? I hear they are rather difficult."

Lydia's lip pouted. "Are you saying you can't? I was under the impression there wasn't anything you couldn't do."

That afternoon, Derrick unloaded the dishwasher from Jeb's truck. After watching a few YouTube videos, he got down onto the floor and began removing the old unit. Crawling into the kitchen, Madeline sat down to watch.

"Hi, Sweetie! You wanna see Daddy at work?" She clapped her hands excitedly.

After thirty minutes, and multiple cuts, Derrick finally had the water and electrical lines removed. The *old washer pulled out rather easily compared to what he had done so far. As he prepped the new one, he realized it was a little taller than the last. "That's okay," he said. "Nothing a little proper application of force can't fix."*

Derrick shoved and wiggled the new unit until it was thoroughly wedged into the opening. "Well, crap!" he exclaimed. To his surprise, Madeline repeated him. "Whel cwap!"

"Uh, that could be a problem," he thought, looking at her.

A few more hours passed, and Derrick tried just about everything to get the washer into the hole. Finally, he called for Lydia to come help. "I need you to push while I lift the counter," he explained. "One... two... three!" Derrick lifted as hard as he could while Lydia pushed. The washer finally popped free and slid into place... smashing Derrick's fingers between the counter and the washer. Derrick screamed in agony and exclaimed, "Hezekiah on a horse!"

Lydia rushed to his aid, trying to help however she could. From behind her, she heard a small voice call out, "Whel cwap!" The color left Derrick's face as Lydia's sympathetic look turned to a suspicious glare...

Derrick smiled at the memory. He then laughed, remembering the first time Maddie yelled that out in church after the preacher dropped his Bible. Lydia glared at him so hard that day. He was already in trouble, but if the laughter he was holding got out, she might have killed him right there in front of everyone.

"We sure have had some good times," he thought, drifting off to sleep.

CHAPTER 18

Derrick stepped out of the Metro at Shinagawa Station, the cool evening air brushing against his face as he made his way through the bustling crowds. The station was alive with the hum of commuters and the occasional announcements echoing through the corridors. He approached the ticket office and secured seat 46D on the 8:04 pm express to Osaka, just as the clue had instructed.

As the sleek, silver bullet train cut through the dark Japanese countryside at nearly 200 mph, Derrick sat by the window, watching the world outside blur into streaks of light. The street lights were a fleeting flash of light, and the traditional houses seemed to flicker past like ghosts of a simpler time. The rhythmic hum of the train's engines provided a steady, almost hypnotic backdrop.

Beside him, a young Japanese man sat quietly, absorbed in a novel, only occasionally glancing up to exchange a friendly nod. Confused, Derrick finally introduced himself. He was greeted with a slight nod of acknowledgment. The man then introduced himself as Yoshi.

Leaning in, Derrick whispered cautiously, "Did Tae give you something for me?" Yoshi glanced his way, a slight smile playing on his lips. He nodded almost imperceptibly before returning to his book, leaving Derrick more confused than before.

As Derrick's phone buzzed with a message, he glanced down to see a text from Lydia: "Stay safe. I love you." A small smile tugged at the corners of his mouth as he quickly typed a response and tucked the phone back into his pocket.

When he looked up again, he noticed Yoshi's hand subtly covering a small, white piece of paper on the seat between them. As Derrick reached for it, Yoshi whispered, "Hide it. There are many eyes here."

The train continued its smooth journey toward Osaka, the gentle rocking and muted noises of passengers around them creating a false sense of calm. Derrick's thoughts were interrupted when a sudden, deafening explosion ripped through the tranquility. The carriage lurched violently, the screech of twisting metal filling the air as the train careened off the tracks.

Derrick's world spun out of control as he was slammed against the window. Pain shot through his side, and his breath was knocked out of him. The lights flickered once, twice, and then went out, plunging everything into darkness.

When Derrick regained consciousness the air around him was thick with heat and the smell of smoke. Groaning, he tried to push himself up, only to realize he was pinned under a mangled seat. Every movement sent sharp stabs of pain through his body, but with a grunt of effort, he finally managed to free himself.

Using the faint light from his phone, Derrick scanned his surroundings. The train was a twisted wreck, and the once-quiet carriage was now filled with the muffled cries of injured passengers. He felt a deep gash on his arm and winced as he realized how bad it was.

"Yoshi?" Derrick called out, his voice hoarse.

"Here," came a strained reply. Derrick crawled over the debris, finding him trapped but seemingly unharmed. He quickly helped free him, and the two men exchanged a grim look, knowing they had to get away.

"We need to find a way out," Derrick said, his mind racing. Spotting an emergency medical kit, he had an idea. "Stay with me, Yoshi. We're getting out of here."

Rummaging through the scattered bags, Derrick found hydrogen peroxide, a highlighter, and a bar of soap. Working quickly, he created a makeshift chemical light, casting a dim, eerie greenish glow over the wreckage. It revealed the full extent of the devastation, and Derrick felt a knot tighten in his stomach as he saw the fear on the faces of those around them.

"We need to open those," Derrick pointed to the now upward-facing doors. Yoshi nodded, and they rallied a few able-bodied passengers to help. With a concerted effort, they pried the doors open, letting in the cool night air and a much-needed breath of relief.

As they helped the passengers out of the wreckage, Derrick caught a familiar, acrid scent. His nose crinkled as he recognized the smell of C4. His pulse quickened. "This wasn't an accident," he muttered just before the first bullets pinged off the metal.

"Get down!" Derrick shouted, yanking Yoshi off the car and leading him toward the sparse cover provided by the underbrush. Panic erupted among the survivors as Derrick spotted the telltale glow of the Nightfall operatives' goggles closing in on them.

"We have to move," Yoshi said urgently, hastily wrapping a makeshift bandage around Derrick's injured arm. "You can't stay here."

Before Derrick could respond, Yoshi's head snapped back, a bullet tearing through his skull. The shock of it froze Derrick in place as Yoshi's lifeless body slumped to the ground. Anguish and fury churned inside Derrick, but he knew he had to get out of there.

With no time to mourn, Derrick spotted a narrow gap in the wreckage. He slipped through it, crouching low as he made his way toward the faint lights of a nearby town.

Derrick stumbled into the outskirts of the town, his breath ragged and his vision swimming from the blood loss and exhaustion. An elderly couple stood outside their small, traditional home, their eyes widening as they took in his disheveled appearance.

"Please," Derrick rasped, barely able to speak. "I need help."

The couple didn't hesitate. They quickly ushered him inside, where they tended to his wounds with the quiet efficiency of those who had seen hardship before. In broken Japanese, Derrick explained that he was being hunted. The couple nodded solemnly, understanding the danger he was in.

As the night deepened, the couple led Derrick to an old, beat-up truck hidden behind their house. The old man handed Derrick a worn hat and a jacket. "Keep your head down," he said in heavily accented English. "We'll get you to safety."

The truck rumbled to life, the engine coughing as it pulled away from the small town. Derrick glanced back at the lights fading into the distance, his mind heavy with thoughts of Yoshi and the other passengers left behind.

The elderly couple dropped Derrick off at a nearby bus station. After purchasing a ticket for him, they wished him safe travels and sent him on his way.

Derrick stared out the window as the sun began to rise, casting a warm glow over the landscape. The charter bus had just crossed into Osaka's city limits, and Derrick felt a small sense of relief. Despite the comfortable seats and air conditioning, the long journey had taken its toll. The woman sitting next to him kept glancing at his bandaged arm, her expression a mix of curiosity and concern. Derrick knew he looked like a mess—bloodstained and exhausted—but he was too tired to care.

He found a Courtyard hotel just down the street from Osaka Castle and booked a room under an alias, desperate for a shower and some rest.

Once inside his room, Derrick collapsed onto the bed, pulling out the clue Yoshi had given him. He studied it in the dim light.

Whisper through the hidden lines
Go to the number of Venice
Dial the code and you find
Nightfall's path through shadows wide.

Derrick groaned at the cryptic nature of the message. "Maybe the dream fairies will tell me what it means," he muttered to himself as exhaustion pulled him into a deep sleep.

***

The next morning, Derrick struggled to get out of bed. His arm throbbed with pain, and he suspected it was on the verge of infection. He groggily logged onto the castle's website and booked the earliest ticket he could get. "It's a beautiful country, but I'd much rather be back home," he thought, the longing for Lydia and Madeline gnawing at him.

Derrick stood before the imposing Osaka Castle, its ancient walls standing as a testament to centuries of history. The clue from Tae, "Inside the cannon is what you seek," echoed in his mind as he eyed the massive cannon displayed in front of the castle. The sun gleamed off its dark metal, making it stand out against the backdrop of the bustling castle grounds.

As he approached, the two guards stationed nearby watched him with suspicion. "Sir, please step away from the cannon," one of them said sternly.

Derrick quickly surveyed the area, searching for a way to distract the guards. His gaze fell on a small shrine nestled within the castle grounds. He hesitated, knowing that what he was considering could cause significant damage. But with no other option presenting itself, he approached the shrine, heart heavy with guilt.

After ensuring no one was watching, Derrick lit a small piece of paper and placed it inside the shrine. The flames quickly caught, sending plumes of smoke curling into the air. Derrick's stomach churned with regret as he watched the fire spread, but he had no time to dwell on it.

The rising smoke and the panicked crowd drew the guards away from their posts. Seizing the opportunity, Derrick sprinted to the cannon, hoisting himself up onto the barrel. His hands were shaking as he peered into the darkness within. There, hidden in the shadows, was a small, weathered scroll.

Derrick snatched the scroll and quickly unrolled it, revealing yet another clue. Before he could fully comprehend it, the guards returned, spotting him on the cannon. "Halt! What are you doing?" one of them barked, reaching for his radio.

Thinking fast, Derrick put on his worst British accent. "Oh, I'm terribly sorry, sirs. I was just trying to avoid the fire and the stampeding crowd. Didn't want to get trampled, you see."

The guards were not amused. They demanded he come down, intending to detain him. Derrick complied, but as soon as his feet hit the ground, he bolted into the crowd of tourists fleeing the shrine.

Weaving through the crowd, Derrick made his way to the line of buses shuttling visitors back to the city. Spotting an unattended bag, he quickly snatched a baseball cap and sunglasses, slipping them on before boarding one of the buses.

Once they were on the move, Derrick pulled out the scroll and read the new clue:

> By the Dome of Great renown,
> Seek the tunnels underground.
> In the depths where shadows loom,
> Discover the clue within the tomb.

Later, Derrick approached the ticket counter at the airport, trying to appear casual as he requested a ticket to Boston. The clerk behind the desk smiled politely, her fingers dancing across the keyboard as she searched for flights.

As she worked, she attempted to make small talk. "Did you hear some tourists set fire to the castle today?"

Derrick swallowed hard, trying to keep his expression neutral. "Who would do such a thing?" he asked, feigning shock.

The clerk shook her head, printing out his ticket. "I don't know. People have no respect for history these days."

***

Meanwhile, back home, Lydia was scrolling through the news on her phone when a headline from Japan caught her eye.

"Historic Osaka Castle Set Ablaze by Tourist."

She groaned, reading the article that described an unidentified tourist—who matched Derrick's description—setting a fire at one of the castle's shrines.

Derrick was almost asleep at the gate when his phone rang. "Hey, honey," he answered, trying to sound more alert than he felt.

There was a pause before Lydia's voice came through, a mix of amusement and exasperation. "Why did you set the castle on fire? I saw it on the news. What did the Japanese ever do to you?"

Derrick sighed, rubbing his tired eyes. "Why do you always assume it's me when you read something bad in the news?"

"Well, was it?"

"Of course it was! But why do you always assume it's me?!"

Lydia's laughter echoed through the phone. "Because it usually is!" she teased.

Derrick couldn't help but smile despite his exhaustion. "I needed a distraction, and it was the only thing I could think of. I didn't mean for that much to burn."

Hearing the weariness in his voice, Lydia's tone softened. "Honey, do you think it's time to give this up? How much longer can you keep doing this?"

Derrick sighed deeply, the weight of her words pressing down on him. "I don't know. I really don't. This next clue points to Boston. MIT, specifically. I thought about hitting one more spot since it's in the U.S. Maybe I could visit my alma mater and catch up with some old friends. But... if I give up now, Tae's on his own."

Lydia hesitated before offering a suggestion. "My dad offered to meet up with you and help out. I think he's tired of being stuck at home and wants to get out for a bit. Maybe he could meet you in Boston so you don't have to be alone. You know, have some guy time. What do you think?"

Derrick considered the idea. It could be a bit awkward having Jeb tag along, especially with the kind of trouble he tended to get into. But the thought of not being alone for a while was appealing. "Okay, honey. That sounds like a good idea."

He could hear the relief and excitement in Lydia's voice. "Oh, thank you, sweetie! Text me your flight info, and I'll make sure he meets you at the airport."

As Derrick ended the call, he felt a sense of calm settle over him. Having Jeb with him might just be what he needed to get through this next part of the journey.

CHAPTER 19

Derrick jolted awake as the plane touched down with a solid thud on the runway. His mind was still foggy from the long flight as he gathered his things and made his way through the bustling terminal. The fluorescent lights overhead buzzed softly as he took the escalator down to the baggage claim. The sight of Jeb waiting there, with his broad shoulders and easy smile, brought Derrick a surprising wave of relief.

As Derrick approached, he extended a hand for a handshake, but Jeb had other plans. With a grin, Jeb pulled Derrick into one of his signature bear hugs, nearly lifting him off the ground.

"How was your flight, son? Set any lavatories on fire?" Jeb teased, his voice warm and familiar.

Still feeling the weight of jet lag, Derrick managed a chuckle as he grabbed his bag from the conveyor belt. "Not this time, thankfully."

The line at the rental car desk seemed to stretch on forever. The air felt thick and stifling, and by the time Derrick finally reached the counter, he was sweating through his shirt. He handed his reservation to the clerk, who began typing away on her computer. A frown creased her brow.

"I'm sorry, sir, but it appears we've sold out of the vehicle type you reserved," she said, her voice apologetic.

Derrick felt a flash of irritation. How do you sell out of something that's been reserved? He bit his tongue, holding back his frustration.

The clerk continued typing before looking up with a bit of relief. "We do have a Camaro available if that works for you—no extra cost."

Derrick's scowl quickly faded, replaced by a smile. "That'll work just fine."

Jeb spotted the bright yellow Camaro as they walked out to the lot and gave Derrick a sidelong glance. "Uh, how am I supposed to fit in that?" he asked, eyeing the car's low roof and snug interior.

Derrick hadn't considered Jeb's larger build. After some creative seat adjustments and a few good-natured grumbles, Jeb finally squeezed into the passenger seat. Derrick slid into the driver's side, glanced over at his father-in-law, who looked like a jumbo sardine packed in a tin can, and shrugged. "They were out of the normal cars," he said with a smirk.

Boston's rush hour traffic was as unforgiving as ever. As sleek and fast as it was, the Camaro wasn't much help in the gridlock. Derrick's fingers itched to open up the engine and fly down the highway, but instead, he found himself inching along, tapping the steering wheel in frustration.

Finally, after what felt like an eternity, they pulled into the Boston Marriott Cambridge parking lot. The hotel towered above them, a sleek, modern structure that dominated the skyline. After checking in, Derrick and Jeb made their way to their room, eager to relax after the long day.

Derrick remembered the countless meals he had enjoyed around Boston during his time at MIT, but his favorite was always Santarpio's, a small, family-owned pizza place. Knowing Jeb's appreciation for good pizza, Derrick decided it would be the perfect introduction to Boston's culinary scene.

However, he preferred to avoid Boston's traffic, especially with the new episode of *Agent Inept* airing soon. So, Derrick called in their order for delivery instead.

When the pizza arrived, Jeb had just taken a big bite when the familiar theme song of *Agent Inept* started playing. Derrick, clearly excited, began bobbing his head and singing along—terribly out of tune.

> *"Agent Inept's a master of mayhem,*
> *He gets the job done again and again.*
> *Genius in chaos, he reigns supreme,*
> *Dominic Storm lives the secret dream..."*

Jeb, halfway through his slice, stared at Derrick in mock horror. "Son... that almost scared me. Never do that again," he teased, shaking his head.

As the episode unfolded, Dominic Storm found himself setting fire to a Russian embassy in a daring escape. Jeb couldn't help but notice how deeply engrossed Derrick was in the show, sauce still smeared on his face.

During a commercial break, Derrick asked Jeb what he thought of the show. Jeb nodded thoughtfully. "It's pretty funny. I can see why you like it." He paused, then grinned, "Were you a consultant on it? This guy seems an awful lot like you."

Derrick looked confused. "But I've never even been to Russia."

Jeb chuckled. "You know, Mary used to know a guy named Dominic Storm. She might have had a little thing for him, but she'll never admit it."

Later that night, as Derrick was getting ready for bed, Jeb walked over and placed a hand on his shoulder. "Son... we need to talk."

Derrick froze, a knot of anxiety forming in his stomach. These kinds of talks usually didn't end well. He sat down on a nearby chair, and Jeb pulled up another one, sitting across from him.

"There's something you need to know about me... about what I used to do for a living," Jeb began, his tone serious.

Derrick watched him closely, intrigued but unsure where this conversation was going.

"Before I retired and settled down, I was in the Marines," Jeb continued. "Served for a good number of years."

Derrick nodded, his interest piqued.

"After I left the Marines, I was recruited to continue working with radios... for the CIA."

Derrick's jaw dropped. "You were in the CIA?! Why haven't you ever mentioned it?"

Jeb chuckled. "It's not exactly something you bring up in casual conversation."

Derrick sat there, absorbing this new information. "So, you were commo? Just like me and Lydia?"

"Exactly," Jeb replied. "Did a lot of the same things you two do. Covert operations, setting up secure communications, you name it. That's why Lydia joined. She wanted to follow in her Daddy's footsteps."

Derrick grew solemn. "Why did you leave?"

Jeb sighed, the weight of his words heavy. "For the same reason you did. It took a toll on our family. The long weeks away with no contact, the close calls where I almost didn't come back... it was too much."

After turning out the light, Derrick lay in bed, staring at the ceiling. The quiet hum of the hotel room's air conditioning did little to drown out his thoughts. Since getting married, there had been very few nights he'd slept without Lydia by his side. Now, with her so far away, the emptiness felt even more pronounced.

Jeb, also struggling to fall asleep, broke the silence. "This reminds me of that night when Hurricane Luna made landfall."

A smile tugged at Derrick's lips as he remembered. "I remember. We all slept in the living room. It was so hot after the power went out."

"Who knew you snored so loud?" Jeb joked. "That was a long night, but do you remember the day before? That ranks up there for me!"

...Lydia, Mary, and Madeline had just left to grab supplies before Hurricane Luna hit. The storm had shifted suddenly, and now it was only hours away. After securing his own home, Jeb came over to help Derrick batten down. They stood on the pier, looking at Derrick's fishing boat bobbing in the water.

"What are we going to do with that?" Jeb asked, nodding toward the boat.

Derrick's mind was clearly working on a solution, and Jeb knew that look all too well. "I've got an idea!" he said, grinning.

Derrick had a trailer for the boat, but with a Mustang and a Beetle in the driveway, they didn't have anything to tow it with. Jeb sighed, already anticipating what was coming next. "What tools do you need?"

After a quick trip to the junkyard, Derrick began working on his solution. He attached an extra set of wheels to the front of the trailer and rigged a makeshift transmission and a drivetrain that would allow him to steer using the boat's wheel.

"You think this will work?" Jeb asked as he tightened the last few bolts.

Derrick stepped back, tilting his head as he eyed the contraption. "Maybe."

"Good enough for me!" Jeb replied, clapping his hands. "How are we going to get this to the ramp?"

"Remember how Fred from church towed it down for us when we bought it? He volunteered to take the trailer back down there for us," Derrick said with a smile.

Jeb looked puzzled. "Why didn't Fred just tow the boat back to the house for us too?"

Derrick paused, thinking it over. "Uh…"

Jeb laughed. "Don't hurt yourself. I'll grab the boat and meet you down there."

Fred backed the trailer into the water, and Jeb maneuvered the boat onto it. After securing it, Fred *pulled the boat and trailer up to the parking lot and disconnected. "You sure you've got it from here?" the old man asked, eyeing Derrick's creation skeptically.*

Derrick nodded confidently. "Yep!"

Fred shook his head but offered a word of caution. "Well, let me know if you need help. I'll be back in a couple of hours after moving Helen's trailer to higher ground."

As Fred drove off, Derrick and Jeb went to work. Derrick connected the rudder controls to the front wheels while Jeb finalized the drivetrain and brakes. Once everything was in place, Derrick fired up the engine and shifted into drive. To his delight, the trailer moved forward smoothly.

Jeb watched as Derrick clapped and jumped in excitement. "I've never seen a happier kid... I mean... man... before," he thought, grinning.

Climbing aboard, Jeb worked his way to the front of the boat, and Derrick "Took her to ground," playing on the phrase.

Meanwhile, Lydia and Mary were stopped at a red light on their way to yet another empty store. Lydia was scrolling through local news boards, trying to find stores that were still open, when Mary suddenly gasped. "Honey... don't look up."

Lydia glanced over at her mom, confused, but before she could ask why, she saw it. A boat was driving through the intersection, with her dad sitting on the deck, casually reading a newspaper. Lydia let out a long sigh. "Uh... what... how... ugh."

Derrick was almost home, just a few more miles, and everything would have gone off without a hitch. But then, they passed Officer Reed, who was parked outside the donut shop. Reed spit his coffee out on his patrol car's dash, wondering if he was hallucinating. He flipped on his lights and pulled Derrick over into a bank parking lot.

"Derrick Blackbeard Anderson," Officer Reed began, exasperated. "I don't even know which license to ask for. What are you doing?!"

Rappelling down from the boat, Derrick walked up to him with a sheepish grin. "Hey, Nathan! I was just trying to get the boat to safety. Didn't have a way to pull the trailer, so I made a way."

Nathan shook his head in disbelief. "You can't do this. It's illegal!"

Derrick chuckled. "How? It's got a license plate, headlights, and brake lights."

Nathan scrunched his nose and tilted his head. "What headlights?!?"

Derrick pointed to Jeb sitting up on the bow. He was waving two flashlights at them, laughing.

Nathan scratched his head, bewildered. "You got me. I'm not even going to write a report on this. The *boys back at the station would laugh me out of it. Let me at least give you an escort home."*

As Mary and Lydia pulled up to the house, they saw the patrol car leaving. Mary walked up to Jeb and smacked him on the arm. "What is wrong with you?!"

"Why am I in trouble? It was his idea!" Jeb protested, pointing at Derrick.

Lydia walked by with Madeline in one arm and a few bags of supplies in the other. "Because we expect it from him," she said, barely holding back a laugh.

Mary wasn't satisfied. "And why were you on the front reading a newspaper?!"

"I was controlling the headlights," Jeb replied, sheepish. "Oh, and IGA has a good deal on steaks next week."

Back in the hotel room, Jeb chuckled at the memory. "I like your new garage design far better."

Derrick sat up, flipping on the light beside his bed, laughing. "That was a great time... and one of the funniest."

Jeb grinned. "Wasn't as funny as the pier."

Derrick's laughter deepened as he remembered that story...

...Lydia stood at the end of her pier, watching the waves grow more turbulent as the storm approached. Her heart ached, knowing the hurricane would likely wash away her favorite spot in the world.

Jeb and Derrick were securing the last of the loose items when Jeb noticed Lydia standing alone. "It's a shame we can't pick up her pier and move it inside too," Jeb mused.

A lightbulb went off in Derrick's head. "Thanks for reminding me! You're going to love this!" he said, excitement bubbling in his voice. He led Jeb inside and pointed to a button on the wall by the back door. "Watch this!"

Derrick pressed the button, and the pier began to shift and separate into eight sections. Each section lifted, moved back, and stacked neatly on top of the one behind it. Once all the sections were stacked, they rotated and expanded out to create a protective wall around the sea-facing side of the house.

Jeb's eyes widened in amazement. "Not bad!" he said, genuinely impressed. But then, a thought occurred to him, and his expression turned to concern. "Wait... where's Lydia?"

Derrick laughed hard, his sides aching from the memory. "Oh yeah. I forgot about that! She was SO wet... and MAD!"

***

The next morning, Derrick led Jeb on a leisurely walk along the Charles River, heading toward Building 10. "That's the Great Dome," Derrick said, gesturing to the iconic library. "And over there is where we used to grab coffee between classes."

Jeb looked around, taking it all in. "This place is huge. How'd you ever find your way around?"

"Lots of trial and error," Derrick replied with a chuckle.

As they approached the library's entrance, they ran into a couple of Derrick's old instructors. Professor Lewis and Dr. Carter were deep in conversation when they spotted Derrick.

"Derrick Anderson!" Professor Lewis exclaimed. "It's been years! Who's this with you?"

"This is Jeb, my father-in-law," Derrick introduced. "Jeb, these are two of the best instructors I had here."

Jeb shook their hands, smiling warmly. "Nice to meet both of you."

Dr. Carter laughed. "Derrick was quite an inquisitive fellow when he went here. Did he tell you about the time his experiment almost burned down the lab?"

Jeb raised an eyebrow, turning to Derrick. "No, he hasn't."

Derrick rubbed the back of his neck, embarrassed. "Yeah, I had a few... incidents."

"Incidents?!" Professor Lewis echoed. "More like frequent visits from the fire department! They were talking about renaming the fire station after him!"

"I remember the one," Dr. Carter chimed in. "Derrick was synthesizing some new compound... what was it called?"

Blushing, Derrick muttered, "Phosphamite."

Jeb's mouth dropped open, recognizing the name.

"Phosphamite! That's it!" Dr. Carter continued. "He was heating it on a burner, but the fire wasn't hot enough for his liking. The mixture started boiling, and then—BOOM—a beam of white light shot straight up! We all stood there, amazed... for about two seconds until the beaker exploded, sending that stuff everywhere! That was the first and only time I've ever seen the sprinkler system go off in that lab."

Derrick turned bright red as Jeb nodded knowingly. "You know, none of that surprises me. What does surprise me is that you actually graduated."

Dr. Carter laughed. "He was one of my brightest students. He aced that project—got an 'A' and a few hours of community service, if I remember right."

The clock tower bell rang, and Professor Lewis checked his watch. "Oops! I'm late again. Good to see you, Derrick. Stop by anytime you get the chance. Maybe I'll let you teach a class... on lab safety."

Derrick snickered as the two professors walked away, still chuckling.

Continuing their tour, Derrick and Jeb finally reached the entrance to the underground tunnels, known to students as "the tombs."

"Here we are," Derrick said, his voice echoing slightly in the narrow passageway. He pulled a key from his pocket and inserted it into the door, unlocking it with a click.

"Do they know you still have that?" Jeb asked, curious.

"Of course. All graduates get to keep their keys. It's MIT's version of a challenge coin."

They slipped inside, the air cooler and tinged with the scent of machinery humming softly in the background.

"These tunnels have been here for decades," Derrick explained. "Students sneak down here to work on projects away from prying eyes."

They descended a narrow staircase, the light growing dimmer with each step. At the bottom, a long, winding tunnel stretched out before them, lined with old pipes and cables. Derrick handed Jeb a flashlight. "Stay close. It's easy to get lost down here."

Navigating the tunnels by memory, Derrick searched for the clue. "There's one spot where students like to do experiments. I bet that's where Tae left the it." He noticed the silence behind him and turned around, realizing Jeb wasn't following.

"Jeb!" Derrick called but got no reply. Turning back, he retraced his steps to an intersection. As he rounded the corner, he nearly ran into Jeb, who was hiding in the shadows, shining his flashlight up at his face. Derrick's scream echoed through the halls, followed by Jeb's laughter.

"Why?!" Derrick asked, exasperated.

Jeb shrugged. "Because I could."

They continued down a narrow section of the tunnel until they reached a large room filled with makeshift desks. Derrick pointed to a burn mark on the wall. "That's where I built my lab one summer. I conducted all sorts of experiments. Mostly harmless... although there was that one time I set off the fire alarms with some homemade rocket fuel."

Jeb shook his head, laughing. "You haven't changed a bit, have you?"

Derrick scanned the walls for the clue while Jeb paced back and forth, looking uneasy.

"You okay, Jeb?" Derrick asked, noticing his discomfort.

"Are you sure this place isn't haunted? There are some strange noises down here," Jeb replied, his voice low.

Derrick chuckled. "Ghosts aren't real, you know that." He continued searching until his flashlight passed over a brick that looked different from the others. Grasping it, Derrick slid the brick out of the wall. Behind it was a small note.

"I think this is it!" Derrick exclaimed, pulling out the note and reading it aloud:

> *"Oogie Boogie Daga Doo,*
> *Get yourself to Ouagadougou.*
> *Meet Amina at Chitir Chicken.*
> *Convince her to give you her hat."*

Derrick shook his head, smiling. "At least this one was easy to figure out."

***

Back at the hotel, Derrick packed his bags, getting ready for his next journey. Jeb emerged from the bathroom, wearing his new MIT t-shirt. "Looks pretty good if I do say so myself," he said, admiring the shirt in the mirror. "So, where are we going next?"

Derrick looked surprised. "We? I figured you were heading back home."

Jeb closed his suitcase and gave Derrick a determined look. "Why, this trip was fun. I thought about tagging along to the next one if that's okay with you."

Derrick was caught off guard by Jeb's sudden enthusiasm. "Well, the next spot is Ouagadougou.

We're supposed to find some hat. But there's somewhere I need to go on the way."

Derrick turned left off Commonwealth Avenue and entered the Evergreen Cemetery. Jeb was slightly confused as they slowly drove through the gravestones toward the south side of the cemetery. Derrick's face grew solemn as he put the car into park. "There's one more person I need to see before we leave."

After climbing out of the car, Jeb followed Derrick to a small, simple tombstone. The name "Hayes" was etched into the stone. Jeb placed a hand on Derrick's shoulder. "Emily, right?"

...*Derrick saw a gap between the glass and window frame. Unfortunately, it was too small for his fingers to fit in. Opening the large blade of his knife, he inserted it into the gap and twisted, trying to gain those precious few millimeters. Just as his fingers were about to slip into the opening, the blade tip snapped, causing the window to reseal into the frame.*

Emily saw the devastation on his face. In a final, desperate act, Derrick opened the reamer punch, placed the knife in his palm, and wrapped his fingers around the open blade. With the sharp punch now sticking out between his index and middle fingers, Derrick punched the window repeatedly as hard as he could. With each hit, he could feel the bones cracking and tendons

*tearing. Fire was starting to surround him, blurring his
vision from the heat... but the blood-smeared window
refused to relent.*

*The fire finally reached Emily's seat. Derrick
screamed in anguish and watched in helpless horror as
the fire began to consume her. The edges of her flight
suit caught first and then spread rapidly, engulfing her
in an orange and red inferno...*

A tear slid down Derrick's face as the memory
played out in his mind. "She was one of the good ones,"
he said softly. "Even with all the years she had as a flight
nurse, she never turned jaded. She truly cared about
people. If I could've just gotten that window open..."

Jeb swatted Derrick on the arm, breaking his
train of thought. "Don't do that! I never met her, but
from what you've told me, I know she wouldn't want
you living like this. She'd probably smack you harder
than I did."

As they stood in silence, Derrick heard the
sound of gravel crunching underfoot. He turned to see a
man with two children approaching—a teenage boy and
a younger girl. The man's eyes lit up when he saw him.
"Derrick? Derrick Anderson, is that you?"

Derrick's heart swelled as soon as he heard his
name. The girl came running, arms outstretched. "Uncle
Derrick!" she shouted. He knelt down to catch her in a
tight hug. The boy followed, a bit more reserved but
clearly happy to see him. Derrick pulled him as well.

"Amy! Terrance! It's been so long! I've missed you both!" Derrick said, his voice thick with emotion.

Amy pulled back, excited. "Daddy got us a puppy! Terrance named him Derrick, after you! He said it reminded him of you because he was always destroying everything."

Jeb chuckled. "Well, Derrick does look like a mutt," he thought to himself.

"What are you doing back up here in Boston?" Jim asked. "We heard you got some big government job and moved to D.C. You still a G-man?"

Derrick cringed at the term but nodded. "Kind of. I'm actually here on business and wanted to stop by since I was in town."

"I know it was hard for you when you left," Jim said, his tone softening. "But as you can see, things have changed. The kids found some pictures of you and Emily. I've been sharing stories with them about our time together."

Tears welled up in Derrick's eyes. "There's not a day that goes by I don't think about you guys. I just didn't want to cause any more pain. We have a flight in a bit, but I'll have to bring my wife and daughter back up to meet y'all."

After reminiscing for a bit, Derrick knew it was time to go. They said their goodbyes and Derrick and Jeb headed to the airport.

At the ticket counter, the clerk behind the desk greeted Derrick with a polite smile. "Good afternoon, sir. How can I assist you today?"

"I need two tickets to Ouagadougou," Derrick said, trying to sound casual.

The clerk's smile faltered as confusion crossed her face. "I'm sorry. Where did you say you're going?"

"Ouagadougou," Derrick repeated. "It's in Burkina Faso." He realized that might have made things worse as the clerk blinked at him.

"Would it help if I spelled it?" Derrick offered.

CHAPTER 20

Derrick settled into his economy seat, knowing the twenty-hour flight from Boston to Ouagadougou was going to be long and exhausting. The weeks of travel were starting to take their toll on his body. "What a time to decide to fly commercial," he thought, already missing the comfort of the private jet.

He adjusted the small pillow behind his neck and took a moment to glance around the cabin. It was a full flight. To his right, an elderly Japanese woman was quietly knitting, the soft clicking of her needles providing a rhythmic background noise. On his left, Jeb occupied the aisle seat, his long legs stretched out slightly, ready for his frequent trips to the restroom. Across the aisle, a young man in a business suit had already dozed off, his head bobbing gently with the plane's movements. The hum of the engines provided a steady, almost soothing backdrop that Derrick tried to focus on as he settled in for the long haul.

As the plane took off, Derrick gazed out the window, watching the lights of Boston slowly fade beneath the clouds. His thoughts drifted back to Yoshi, the unlikely friend he'd made and lost in such a short time. Yoshi's smile haunted him, a constant reminder of another life cut short. Up until now, Nightfall had only chased him, assumingly trying to find out where Tae was. But now, someone had died, and Derrick couldn't shake the feeling that the bullet was meant for him.

The hours passed in a blur of in-flight movies, sporadic naps, and brief conversations with the woman next to him, who turned out to be a retired schoolteacher visiting family in Africa. She shared stories of her travels, and Derrick found himself listening more than talking, grateful for the distraction.

Jeb, on the other hand, seemed to handle the flight with ease. A former Marine, he could sleep anywhere, in any position. He was out for most of the flight, even using Derrick's shoulder as a pillow for part of it. Derrick snapped a selfie with Jeb's head resting on him, thinking Lydia would get a kick out of it.

But for Derrick, the trip was far from comfortable. From the moment they took off, a kid seated behind him started kicking his chair incessantly. Derrick tried to ignore it at first, thinking it would stop after a while, but the kicking persisted, making it impossible for him to relax. He glanced back a few times, hoping to catch the eye of the child's parents, but they seemed blissfully unaware of the disturbance.

To make matters worse, the cabin was unusually warm. Derrick loosened his collar and fanned himself with the in-flight magazine, but the stuffy air made it hard to concentrate or rest. He tried reclining his seat and closing his eyes, but sleep eluded him. Every time he started to drift off, a sharp kick to the back of his chair jolted him awake, adding to his frustration.

The flight attendants made their rounds, serving meals and drinks. Derrick accepted a tray of food, unenthusiastically poking at the contents. Airline food was never his favorite, but he ate enough to stave off hunger, knowing that was all he was going to get for hours.

When the plane finally touched down, Derrick gathered his belongings and prepared to disembark. The air was warm and dry as he stepped out of the plane and onto the tarmac. It was a stark contrast to the climate he had left behind in Boston.

Jeb, ever the seasoned traveler, navigated the airport with ease. Derrick followed closely, grateful to have him there. He was exhausted, both physically and mentally, and hadn't had a good night's sleep in over a week.

Jeb hailed a cab and directed the driver to the restaurant where they were supposed to meet their contact. Derrick hated taxis... especially in foreign countries. He couldn't let his guard down, always wondering who the driver might really be working for.

***

Stepping out of the cab, they entered into the dimly lit interior of Chitir Chicken Burkina, a popular eatery in the heart of Ouagadougou. The cool air was a welcome reprieve from the blistering heat outside. The restaurant was bustling with locals and a few adventurous tourists, all drawn by the promise of mouthwatering fried chicken and the unique charm of the place. Derrick's eyes scanned the room, taking in the cheerful decor adorned with colorful murals of chickens and rustic wooden tables.

They made their way to an empty table near the back, trying to blend in. The restaurant's lively atmosphere buzzed around them, but Derrick's mind was focused on his mission. He needed to find a specific waitress, and to his surprise, the waitress who approached them was wearing a name tag that read "Amina."

As she approached with a bright smile, Derrick noticed the whimsical cloth chicken hat she was wearing—exactly the hat he was looking for. The hat had long ear flaps, and when she pulled on them, it made a clucking sound that blended with the lively atmosphere of the restaurant.

"Bonjour, monsieurs! Welcome to Chitir Chicken Burkina. What can I get for you today?" she asked, her eyes sparkling with warmth.

"Hello, Amina," Derrick replied, matching her smile. "We'll start with a couple plates of your famous fried chicken and some cold drinks. But I also have a bit of an unusual request."

Amina raised an eyebrow, intrigued. "Oh? And what might that be?"

Derrick leaned in slightly, lowering his voice. "I need your hat. It's very important. Could you give it to me?"

Amina laughed, her voice light and melodic, blending with the soft flapping of her hat's ear flaps as she absentmindedly tugged on them. "My hat? Why in the world would you want this ridiculous thing?"

"It's not silly to me," Derrick said earnestly. "It's a long story, but let's just say it's vital for something I'm working on."

Amina's expression shifted from amusement to suspicion. "Is this some kind of joke?"

"No joke, I promise," Derrick assured her. "I'll even buy you a new one, any hat you want. Please, Amina, it's very important."

She looked at him for a long moment, trying to gauge his sincerity. "I don't know. This hat is special to me. It's part of my uniform, and besides, it's fun for the customers."

Derrick sighed, realizing this wasn't going to be as easy as he had hoped. "What if I made it worth your while? I could offer you a generous tip in exchange."

Amina shook her head firmly. "It's not about money. This hat is part of who I am here. It brings joy to people."

Derrick admired her dedication but knew he couldn't leave without the hat. He needed a different approach. "Amina, I respect that you cherish the hat.

But there's more at stake here than just a fun accessory. I can't explain all the details, but I need your help. Please."

Her eyes softened slightly at his earnest plea. "You're really serious about this, aren't you?"

"I am," Derrick nodded. "More than you can imagine."

Amina sighed, clearly torn. "Alright, how about this? I'll give you the hat, but only if you can make everyone in this restaurant smile and laugh as much as this hat does. Think you can do that?"

Derrick grinned, accepting the challenge. "Deal."

He stood up quickly, knocking over his chair and catching the eyes of the patrons around him. He started by telling a few jokes, but with no one cracking a smile, he realized he needed to step up his game. Spotting a guitar in the corner, Derrick rolled his eyes, muttering under his breath, "I hate you, Tae," before asking if he could borrow it. The musician, seeing the earnest look in Derrick's eyes, handed it over with a smile.

Derrick strummed a few chords and began to sing a lighthearted, improvised song about the joys of Chitir Chicken Burkina. The crowd responded with laughter and applause; the atmosphere growing even more vibrant and lively. Amina watched with her arms crossed, but a smile tugged at her lips.

After a few more songs and some playful banter with the diners, Derrick felt he had fulfilled his part of the bargain. He handed the guitar back and returned to Amina, who was now smiling widely.

"Alright, you've convinced me," she said, removing the hat and handing it to him. "But you'd better take good care of it."

"I will," Derrick promised, taking the hat with a grateful nod. "Thank you, Amina."

As he placed the hat on his head, he felt something hard tucked inside the lining. Reaching in, he pulled out a small, folded piece of paper. It was the clue he had been searching for.

> *"Find me where it all began with Lydia.*
> *I'll be saving our seat."*

"Merci, Amina," Derrick said, tipping the hat to her. "You've been a great help."

She gave him a curious look but didn't press further. "Take care, monsieur, and tell Tae, '*Hello*' for me."

Derrick returned to the table, where Jeb was struggling to keep a straight face. "What's so funny?" Derrick asked, puzzled by his expression.

"That was horrible!" Jeb exclaimed. "I see now why Lydia says living with you is never boring!"

After their meal, they left the restaurant and took another taxi back to the airport. As they stepped into the terminal, Derrick walked up to the ticket counter.

"Good evening, sir! Where are we headed to?" the agent asked.

Sighing, Derrick said, "Home."

CHAPTER 21

Derrick stepped out of the Richmond airport and immediately felt the sticky Virginia summer air wrap around him like a blanket. He'd almost forgotten just how humid it could be here. Eighteen hours of flying and multiple connections later, he was finally back in the U.S. The heat, combined with the exhaustion of his journey, caused his limbs to feel heavy as he made his way alone to the rental car counter.

During their layover in New York, Derrick had convinced Jeb to head home. "We've finally found Tae… and if we didn't, I'm not chasing him anymore. This is the last place I'm going. You might as well go back. Mary and Lydia need you," Derrick had said, his tone more serious than usual. Jeb, who had enjoyed the time spent with Derrick but was clearly worn out from the relentless traveling, agreed.

Watching his luggage while he went to the restroom, Derrick changed the background on Jeb's phone to the selfie he had taken of them on the plane with Jeb asleep.

"That will teach him to use Lydia's birthday as the pin," Derrick laughed.

After returning, they'd shared a quick, firm hug before parting ways, with Jeb telling Derrick to stay safe.

Now, behind the wheel of a rental car, Derrick was on what he desperately hoped was the final leg of this crazy, globe-trotting mission. The roads leading into Lynchburg were familiar, and as he passed the city limit sign, a wave of doubt washed over him. "Buddy, you better be here because this is my last stop. I'm not going anywhere else but home," Derrick muttered to himself, almost as if Tae could hear him.

The city had changed little since the last time Derrick was here. Memories came flooding back as he drove through the streets. He found himself lost in thought as he parked outside the restaurant. This was where he'd first laid eyes on Lydia, where their relationship had slowly blossomed over weekly meals with friends. It was also the same place where they would sit with Tae before he was sent to Botswana. Derrick's heart ached as he stared at the familiar building, realizing how much had changed since those early days.

Taking a deep breath to steady himself, Derrick pushed open the door and stepped inside. "I'm with a party that's already here," he told the hostess, his voice calm despite the nervous energy thrumming through him. As he made his way to their usual table, his heart sank— the table was empty. A pang of loneliness hit him hard, and for a brief moment, he considered just turning around and leaving.

But then, out of the corner of his eye, Derrick noticed a familiar figure sitting in the booth where he'd first seen Lydia. Tae, with his usual goofy grin, was there, waving him over. Derrick's emotions were a tangle of relief and anger as he walked toward his friend. Part of him was happy to see Tae alive and well, but another part of him wanted to punch him in the face for putting them through all this.

"Hey, ya! Long time, no see! You look kinda rough. Got my hat?" Tae greeted him with his trademark nonchalance, his grin widening.

Without a word, Derrick pulled the chicken hat from his pocket and tossed it to Tae. "Souvenir from Ouagadougou," he said dryly.

Tae laughed as he put the hat on, pulling the ear flaps to make the chicken cluck. "I've wanted one ever since I saw it there!" he exclaimed, clearly delighted.

Derrick sat down, leaning in closer to Tae. "Alright... what's going on?" he asked, his voice low and serious.

For the next hour and a half, Tae laid it all out. He explained how he'd stumbled upon some suspicious activity in the network and started tracing it back to its source. The deeper he dug, the more dangerous it became. Eventually, it got the attention of some higher-ups, culminating in a physical attack from his own chief one night. "I knew it was something big, but I put myself out there too much," Tae admitted, his voice tinged with regret. "The night the tac team surrounded my house, I thought it was the end. I managed to escape out a window, but after that, I knew I couldn't keep going."

Tae looked down, guilt and worry etched into his face. "I'm sorry, Derrick. I needed someone I could trust, and there's no one else I could turn to."

Derrick shook his head, dismissing Tae's apology. "Don't worry about it, man. I would have been offended if you didn't think of me. If something's dirty in Langley, we need to figure out what it is and stop it... But what exactly are we looking for?"

Tae pulled out a small, worn notebook filled with his findings. His handwriting was as bad as ever, but Derrick could make out the details. "Did you notice there were two clues at some of the places you went? Those are the places I tracked this mole to. I found a weird alias: 'Sunaj.' That's what they go by. Does that mean anything to you?"

Derrick's brow furrowed as he thought it over. "The first thing I noticed is that it's 'Janus' backward."

"Janus..." Tae repeated. "Isn't that the name of the two-faced Roman god?"

"Exactly," Derrick confirmed. "Whoever this is, they're not even trying to hide their intentions. That makes this whole thing even scarier. Wait... the places with two clues were where you tracked them?" Derrick started flipping through his own notes, and his eyes widened when he realized those were the same sites where Nightfall had shown up.

"What's that face for? You figured something out, didn't you?" Tae asked, watching Derrick's reaction closely.

"What did the tac team look like that came to your house? Was Obadiah with them?" Derrick's voice was tense, his mind racing.

Tae frowned, trying to recall the details. "They looked like your typical clandestine tac team. Black, head to toe. Body armor and lots of guns. But now that you mention it... there was a voice I heard that seemed familiar..."

Derrick's stomach dropped as everything started to fall into place. "Nightfall. They were at those places we went to. Lydia and I couldn't figure out how they knew where we were going..." He paused, a cold realization hitting him like a freight train.

Seeing the terror on Derrick's face, Tae's eyes widened in alarm. "Dude, what?!? Is the Grim Reaper behind me... or worse... a SPIDER?"

Derrick paused for a moment, connecting the remaining dots in his head. "The chief," he said in disbelief. "It can't be, can it? He was the only one that knew where we were going. It was he who sent me on this quest to find you. He also wanted to make sure it was kept super-secret. It all fits." Derrick sat numb as his mind raced through the last couple of weeks.

"Did you tell him you were coming here?" Tae asked with fear in his voice.

Derrick shook his head slowly. "No. I haven't talked to him since Japan. I meant to give him an update, but I never got around to it."

Tae let out a sigh of relief. "Then he shouldn't know you're here... that is, if you're still in."

Derrick's heart ached at the thought of betrayal from someone he had trusted. The chief had been like a brother to him during his time with the Agency. The sting of betrayal was one thing, but the thought of him betraying his country was almost too much to bear. "Of course, I'm still in. I need to know for sure, and if he's a traitor, we have to stop him."

***

Later that evening, Derrick slipped into the hotel room Tae was staying in. He thought it best not to get his own room to avoid drawing any unwanted attention. With the school being in the same town, there could be informants anywhere.

As Derrick brushed his teeth, Tae was busy fluffing the eight pillows on his bed just the way he liked them. "You're weird, you know that?" Derrick mumbled through a mouthful of toothpaste.

Tae laughed, reminding Derrick that he should be grateful for the double room. "Otherwise, you'd have to respect the pillow fort."

Derrick chuckled as he pulled back the sheets on his bed, ready to collapse. But just as he was about to climb in, he paused, a thought crossing his mind. "There were only five locations that had two clues. Why did you send me to all those other places?"

Tae grinned, clearly enjoying the moment. "I used them as a distraction. It would've been too obvious if you only showed up at the places we knew they were targeting. Plus, it gave you and Lydia a chance to see the world. I was really hoping she'd go with you. You'll have to tell me all about your adventures."

Derrick jumped out of bed, flicking the lights back on and blinding Tae, who had already assumed his sleeping position. "Wait, you sent me to a strip club... FOR FUN?!?"

Tae burst into uncontrollable laughter. "I wish I'd been there to see that! Did you have any... trouble... getting the clue from Cinnamon?"

Derrick's glare only made Tae laugh harder. "Well, did you?"

"It was awful! The place reeked. Some 'lady' sat on my leg... without pants on! Then, to top it off, Lydia told them it was my birthday, and I got dragged onto the stage while they 'sang' Happy Birthday to me."

Tae was practically wheezing from laughter. "I wasn't expecting Lydia to get in on the action too! Man, I wish someone had recorded that. We'd make a fortune online!"

After they both calmed down, Tae was about to turn off the lights again when another question popped into his mind. "So... did Lydia like Antarctica and the penguins?"

Derrick shot him another glare.

"Seriously! What happened this time?" Tae asked, more curious than ever.

Derrick sighed, rolling over in bed. "I got attacked by one... out of the blue... for NO reason."

Tae stared at him, waiting for more. "And...?"

With a dismissive wave, Derrick muttered, "I choked it out. Good night."

***

Meanwhile, back at home, Lydia was winding down for the night, brushing her teeth when her phone buzzed. It was Izzy.

"Hey, girl! What's up?" Izzy's voice was bright and cheery, almost too much for this early hour in her time zone.

Lydia spit out her toothpaste and wiped her mouth before answering. "Not much, just getting ready for bed."

"Yeah, I figured as much. I was watching the news and saw something about a tourist setting that castle on fire in Japan. The first thing that came to mind was Derrick."

Lydia couldn't help but laugh. "How'd you guess?"

There was a brief pause, and when Izzy spoke again, she sounded genuinely surprised. "Wait, seriously? It was him? Can't you control that boy?"

"Are you kidding? I can't even control him when I'm with him," Lydia replied, chuckling.

Izzy laughed too, but there was a slight shift in her tone. "Wait... so you went back home? Finally got tired of him, huh?"

Lydia's laugh softened. "Not even close. Madeline needed me. Daddy's been watching him. He'll keep him in line... I hope."

There was another pause, and then Izzy's voice came back, more serious. "Jeb's with him?"

Lydia frowned, sensing the change in Izzy's tone. "Yeah... why?"

"Oh, nothing really," Izzy replied, trying to sound casual. "Just curious. Want them to stay safe, you know? But hey, I'll let you get some rest. Talk to you soon!"

As Lydia hung up, she stared at her phone, her frown deepening. "That was weird," she muttered, a nagging sense of unease creeping into her thoughts.

CHAPTER 22

Derrick had driven from Lynchburg to McLean many times before, but this time was different—this time, he was planning to break into CIA Headquarters. Even with the fake badge and logins Tae had made, he knew he was walking a razor's edge. The thought of getting caught loomed large in his mind, but there was no turning back now.

Finally arriving at the complex, Derrick found himself sitting in the left turn lane listening to the signal light clicking. The familiarity of the situation struck him, and he tried to lighten the mood by joking to himself, "Why does this seem so familiar?" But the humor fell flat as nerves crept up on him. If this plan was going to work, he had to convince everyone that he belonged there.

The line of cars inched forward, bringing him closer to the guarded gate. Derrick mentally prepared himself, repeating over and over, "You're grumpy and annoyed to be here. Traffic was horrible. Work is worse. You're just here for the paycheck."

When the car in front of him was waved through, Derrick's turn arrived. He noticed the cameras scanning every inch of his vehicle, feeling their scrutiny. "I don't remember there being so many of those," he thought, hoping the rental car he'd secured under an alias wouldn't raise any red flags.

The officer at the gate greeted him politely as he scanned Derrick's badge. This was the moment everything hinged on—would the badge work? If it didn't, he could be looking at a lot more time here than planned. The badge reader beeped, and a green light flashed. "Thank you, sir. Have a good day," the officer said, waving him through.

Derrick finally exhaled, realizing he'd been holding his breath. "That was awful," he thought, trying to calm the adrenaline surging through him. But as soon as he cleared the perimeter trees, he saw the parking lot and groaned inwardly. "Oh, crap. I forgot about this nightmare."

An hour later, after navigating the labyrinthine parking lot, Derrick finally reached the building. Walking through the doors, a wave of nostalgia hit him hard. The familiar seal and the Memorial Wall greeted him, and he felt a pang of sadness as he looked at the stars.

Standing in front of the memorial, Derrick's eyes scanned the names, and his heart sank when he saw how many new stars had been added since his last visit. He found Richie's, now a faded gray. They were designed to fade over time, a symbolic reminder of the passage of years and the shifting world. "Has it really been that long?" he whispered, his fingers brushing over the star.

...The night was quiet and on the cool side. Derrick rechecked Richie's tourniquet, making sure the bleeding was still under control. Richie seemed lost in thought, his gaze distant.

"You okay, man?" Derrick asked quietly.

Richie sighed. "Yeah, just... thinking.

Derrick nodded and waited. He knew Richie well enough to know when he was ready to talk, he would.

After a long silence, Richie finally spoke up. "You ever wonder why I left the Navy?"

Derrick was caught off guard by the sudden question. Richie rarely talked about his past. "Yeah, I did. But I figured if you wanted to tell me, you would."

Richie took a deep breath, his voice tinged with old pain. "There was this night in Hawaii, back when I was stationed there. I'd had a rough week and went out with some buddies. Got way too drunk. The town didn't have taxis or Uber, so I decided to sleep it off in my truck. The next morning, I woke up with the worst hangover. The buzz was gone, and I thought I could make it back to base. But as soon as I turned the car on, some cop lit me up and busted me for DUI... and that wasn't even the worst part. The Navy doesn't mess around with DUIs. The XO called me in and gave me a choice: either get demoted a rank and pay step or resign."

Derrick listened, shocked by the story. "Seventeen years of service meant nothing to them?"

Richie's voice trembled slightly as he continued. "I felt so betrayed… By my own people. I took the less disgraceful way out and resigned. I didn't want anything more to do with the Navy. It was the most ashamed I've ever felt in my life."

Derrick struggled to wrap his head around the injustice. "I'm surprised you came here, then. If it was me, I don't think I could've worked for the same type of people again."

Richie chuckled, but it was tinged with bitterness. "It was hard, but what other jobs were out there for people like me? All I know is commo and deployments. It's not like Microsoft was calling me back."

Looking down at his now missing arm, he sighed deeply. "And what now? OMS will never let me deploy again with my arm."

Derrick saw the despair creeping into his friend's eyes. He grabbed Richie's head and pulled him close, forcing him to focus. "Richie! Listen to me. We'll get through this. When you get home, we'll get you a new bionic arm. What comes after that, I don't know. But I can guarantee you one thing—the ladies go crazy for guys with war wounds. You're gonna need that mechanical arm to fight them off."

Richie smiled, laughing a little…

"Pull yourself together, Derrick," he muttered, clearing his throat and blinking away the memories.

"You've got a job to do, and every second here makes it more dangerous."

He swiped his badge and passed through the turnstiles in the lobby, heading up the short marble staircase. Turning right, he walked down the hallway toward the library. The familiar scent of the building hit him—a mix of sterile office air and something he could only describe as "the smell of history." His mind wandered to the days he'd spent walking these halls hand-in-hand with Lydia, her strawberry perfume lingering in the air.

"Come on, Derrick. Tighten it up. Wait... am I talking to myself?" He noticed two women giving him odd looks as they passed by. "Shut up, Derrick. People are gonna think you're crazy... maybe I am... wonder if they still have that pizza in the cafeteria. SNAP OUT OF IT, DERRICK!"

Entering the library, he went to a workstation in the back corner. Pulling out the slip of paper Tae had given him, he typed the login information into the computer. The screen flashed, and the main menu appeared. Opening the Intranet, Derrick typed in the phrase "Sunaj" and hit enter. Thousands of results scrolled past the screen, but none of them were exact matches—they were all autocorrected or irrelevant hits.

Frustrated, Derrick leaned back in his chair, thinking. He tried the search again, this time filtering for exact results. To his surprise, a few matches appeared. They were flagged with high-level classification banners, most marked SCI—above Top Secret. "I sure hope Tae added those clearances, or this isn't going to work," he muttered, hovering over the first link. He clicked on it, and a cold chill ran down his spine. It was a termination order issued by Sunaj, assigned to Nightfall—the target was Tae.

Derrick's heart pounded. "The chief said he was trying to bring Tae in for questioning... why is there an order to kill him from an Agency computer?" His mind raced, trying to make sense of it all.

It was becoming clear that "Sunaj" was an alias someone was using... but who? Beside the name on the termination order was a phone number with an area code Derrick recognized as being an encrypted line. "No point trying to call without the key," he thought, typing the number into the search bar. '0 results found'. He scratched his head, trying to think of his next move. "The phone system... what was its name? I remember it's on a separate network... but what was it called?"

He racked his brain, thinking of anything that might trigger the memory. "It was some stupid Roman or Greek god. I think it began with an H." Names started flashing through his mind. "Hercules, Hekate... Herpes... definitely not Herpes... but no one would probably guess that." His mind raced, trying to pull the right name from the recesses of his memory. Suddenly, it hit him. "HERMES!" he exclaimed out loud, drawing annoyed glances from the people around him. Derrick's face turned red as he mumbled an apology.

Launching the Hermes system, Derrick entered the login information again. To his relief, it worked. Quickly, he searched for the number and found a series of recent calls. Cross-referencing the numbers, he saw multiple calls to Obadiah's phone and several other landlines he didn't recognize. But then, one number caught his breath—it was Izzy's number. After doing some quick calculations, he realized the call had been made just minutes after he and Lydia had left her to catch their flight. As Derrick processed this, his heart started to race. Then he saw it—a string of numbers that looked painfully familiar. They were his.

"It can't be... I mean, I suspected, but I didn't really believe it," he whispered, trying to make sense of what he was seeing.

Movement at the front of the library caught his attention. Three federal officers had entered and were talking to the librarian. Derrick's heart pounded as he saw her point in his direction. He quickly logged out, gathering his things as calmly as possible while slipping out the back door.

Blending into the crowd in the hallway, Derrick tried to act natural, but his pulse was racing. He had almost reached the lobby when he noticed another group of officers scanning the crowd. Panicking, Derrick turned to start a conversation with a random passerby, but his abruptness startled the man, who let out a loud yelp. The officers' heads snapped in Derrick's direction.

Derrick bolted for the lobby, leaping over the turnstiles as alarms blared and the building went into lockdown. He burst through the front doors, his eyes locking onto a side entrance reserved for deliveries. The gates were beginning to close. Pushing himself to the limit, Derrick sprinted toward the narrowing gap. Just as the gates were about to seal shut, he dove through, hitting the ground hard and rolling to a stop on the other side. The officers frantically entered codes to open the gate, but the lockdown denied them access. Seeing them draw their sidearms, Derrick scrambled to his feet and disappeared into the woods.

Hopping onto a random series of buses and metro trains, Derrick tried to cover his tracks before finally pulling out a burner phone to call Tae. "Hey, it's me. I found something. I'm on my way back. We need to lie low for a bit. Meet me at the Lynchburg Airport in about two hours."

Grabbing an Uber, Derrick headed to the Manassas airport, where he chartered a small plane. As they taxied to the runway, he kept a watchful eye on the surrounding area. It wasn't until the plane lifted off the ground that he allowed himself to relax.

***

Obadiah strode into an office, his demeanor tense. "You called for me?"

A dark figure stood by the window, staring out at the officers resetting the gates. "He was here.

Somehow, he got inside and logged into a computer. He searched for 'Sunaj.' He even accessed Hermes. I don't have to tell you how dangerous this is."

"Where is he now?" Obadiah growled, his eyes narrowing.

"He boarded a plane in Manassas. We're tracking it as we speak."

A predatory smile spread across Obadiah's face. "Just give me the word."

The figure turned from the window, his glare piercing. "Whatever it takes."

Obadiah's grin widened. "It will be done, sir. You won't have to worry about Elmo or his little friend any longer."

CHAPTER 23

The steady hum of the plane's engines filled the cabin, a low rumble that mirrored the turmoil churning inside Derrick's mind. He glanced across the aisle at Tae, who was staring out the window, lost in his thoughts. It was hard to believe how much their lives had changed in the last few weeks.

Leaning back in his seat, Derrick ran his hands through his hair, trying to process everything that had happened. "I still can't believe it," he said, breaking the heavy silence between them. "The chief? Of all people... how did we not see this coming?"

Still gazing out at the endless sky, Tae replied with a hint of anger in his voice. "We trusted him. He was our mentor... our guide. To think he's been behind all this... makes everything we knew feel like a lie."

Derrick nodded, the weight of the betrayal pressing down on him. "We need to figure out our next steps. If he's really the one pulling the strings, we're facing a level of deception and danger we've never encountered before."

Tae sighed, rubbing his temples as if trying to massage away the headache of it all. "First, we need to understand why. Why would he turn against his own country? What's his endgame?"

"Power? Money? Maybe he was compromised," Derrick suggested, though each possibility made his stomach churn. "Whatever his reasons, he's put countless lives at risk. We can't let him get away with this." The thought of Richie's death sent a shiver down his spine. "Do you think... do you think he had anything to do with Richie?"

The plane hit a pocket of turbulence, jolting them slightly. Derrick took a deep breath, trying to steady his nerves. "We'll need to go underground for a while, keep a low profile until we can gather more intel. We can't trust anyone, not even our own people."

Tae nodded slowly. "Agreed. We'll need to reach out to our most trusted contacts, people we know are loyal. But we have to be careful. He'll come after us hard if he suspects we're onto him."

Derrick clenched his fists, the frustration and fear bubbling up inside him. "We'll find a way to expose him. We owe it to everyone he's betrayed and suffered because of him."

Tae reached out his arm for a fist bump. "Dang, straight!"

As they began their descent toward Williston Airport, Derrick turned to Tae. "When we land, let's head to my place. We can regroup there and start planning our next move."

Tae nodded, managing a small smile despite the gravity of their situation. "But who can we trust? We'll need someone with enough clout to get us back into Langley."

A half-grin crept onto Derrick's face. "I know a guy..."

***

Derrick pulled into the driveway, and the porch light flicked on just as he put the car in park. Lydia stepped out onto the porch, holding Madeline in her arms. The little girl's face lit up when she saw Derrick. Lydia set Madeline down, and they watched as she shuffled unsteadily toward him.

"Da Da!" Madeline exclaimed, her little arms reaching out eagerly.

Derrick dropped his bag and crouched down, ready to scoop her up. But just as she was about to reach him, Madeline spotted Tae stepping out from around the car. Her eyes widened with delight, and she suddenly changed direction, her tiny legs carrying her as fast as they could toward him.

"TA TA!!!" she shouted with glee.

Tae froze, clearly startled, as Madeline barreled into his legs, arms outstretched. He hesitated for a moment, then awkwardly bent down to pick her up. She wrapped her arms around his neck and hugged him tightly.

Derrick couldn't help but laugh at the bewildered look on Tae's face. "Not a fan of kids, huh?" he asked, giving Tae a playful pat on the back.

Tae looked down at Madeline, gazing up at him with wide, curious eyes. "Ta Ta?" she asked as if to confirm he was real.

"Yeah, it's still me," he replied, his voice tinged with nervousness. Madeline giggled and snuggled closer, her tiny arms gripping him tightly.

Derrick chuckled. "Looks like you're a natural."

Lydia, smiling at the scene, ushered them inside. "Dinner's almost ready," she announced, leading them into the warmth of the house.

Once inside, Tae carefully handed Madeline back to Lydia and looked around, still trying to shake the feeling of being out of place.

Derrick patted him on the shoulder. "Make yourself at home, man. You're family here. Let me show you to your room," he said, guiding Tae upstairs.

Later, Derrick sank into the couch with a sigh, feeling relief wash over him. Madeline toddled over and climbed into his lap, snuggling close.

Sitting in a nearby recliner, Tae watched with a mix of envy and something deeper—perhaps a longing he hadn't acknowledged before. "I'm sorry for dragging you away from all this," Tae said, his voice soft. "Seeing you with your family is like watching one of those cheesy Christmas movies. Tae paused as he lowered his head. "I just didn't know who else to turn to."

"Dude, don't apologize," Derrick replied, shaking his head. "I'm honored you trusted me. We'll get this sorted out."

Lydia emerged from the kitchen with two steaming bowls of chicken and dumplings, setting them on the table. "I figured you guys would be hungry after your trip."

Tae's stomach growled loudly in response, and he laughed, a genuine smile breaking through the tension. "I'm famished!"

For now, Derrick pushed aside the worries of what lay ahead, letting himself enjoy the comfort of home and the company of his friend.

***

The following morning, the air was cool and salty, with a gentle breeze rolling in from the water. Derrick was securing the last of the fishing gear while Tae checked the tackle boxes, making sure everything was ready.

Grinning, Derrick asked, "Ready to catch some big ones today, buddy?"

"You know it!" Tae replied, giving Derrick a playful shove. "But I'm not doing all the work this time. You're reeling in your own fish today!"

As they finished up, Lydia and Madeline approached on the dock. "Ta Ta!" Maddie exclaimed, stretching her arms out toward Tae.

Still slightly uncomfortable, Tae responded, "Uh... hi again."

"Ta Ta!" Madeline repeated, more insistent this time.

"Okay, okay," Tae relented, lifting her up and swinging her over the boat's rail. Madeline squealed with delight as she landed safely in the boat.

"WEEEEEEEE!" she shouted, waving her arms excitedly.

Lydia smiled, watching them interact. "She really loves having you here," she said, stepping onto the boat herself. With her wide-brimmed hat, oversized sunglasses, and a book in hand, her plans for the day were clear. "If you two need me," she added, pointing to the front of the boat where she planned to relax.

Once everyone was settled, Derrick eased the boat from the dock and headed out onto the open water. Throttling the engines, he glanced at Madeline, whose face lit up with joy. Tae held her securely as the boat picked up speed, the wind whipping around them and the spray of water adding to the excitement. Madeline's voice cut through the noise, "Fasta, Da Da! Fasta!"

They cruised for about half an hour before Derrick slowed the boat and dropped anchor at one of his favorite spots. The water was a deep blue, with gentle waves lapping against the hull. Still soaking up the sun, Lydia peeked over her sunglasses and smiled at the peaceful scene.

Derrick and Tae readied their fishing rods while Madeline watched with wide-eyed curiosity. "You want to try too, Maddie?" Derrick asked. She clapped her hands excitedly in response.

Derrick handed Madeline a small fishing rod and helped her cast the line out into the water. Madeline giggled as the lure splashed into the waves, her eyes sparkling with excitement.

Derrick was distracted, watching another boat in the distance, when he suddenly heard a commotion behind him. He turned to see Tae already behind Madeline, helping her with her fishing rod, which was bent sharply under the weight of something big. "Fish on!" Tae called out, grinning as they both struggled to reel in the catch.

Lydia sat up, pushing her sunglasses onto her head for a better view. "You can do it, Maddie!" she cheered.

After a few tense minutes, a large red snapper broke the water's surface. "Oh, wow!" Tae exclaimed. "Maddie's first fish is huge!"

With Tae's help, they pulled the fish aboard, and Madeline beamed with pride as she watched it flop around on the deck.

Ruffling her hair, Tae knelt beside her. "Not bad, kid… not bad."

Tae sat in the second captain's chair, Madeline fast asleep in his arms. "That fish really wore her out," he said, gently stroking her hair.

Derrick smiled, watching his usually tough friend handle the little girl with such care. "You're going to make a great dad someday."

Tae shook his head. "Nah, I can't see myself settling down. I'll just borrow your kids whenever I get the urge."

Gazing out at the endless ocean, Tae sighed deeply. "Thanks, Derrick. I really needed this. The last few weeks have been so intense, I almost forgot there were places like this."

As the boat rocked gently on the water, Tae's eyes caught the glint of a Glock on Derrick's hip, triggering memories of their training days.

"That was some class, wasn't it?" Tae mused. "I still can't believe that was the first time you ever picked up a gun."

...Derrick and Lydia sat down next to Tae in the cold classroom. "You'd think they could at least afford to heat this place," Derrick told Tae, shivering.

"Here, let me help," Lydia said, leaning over and giving him a long kiss.

Shying his gaze away, Tae smirked. "I bet you aren't cold now."

The morning dragged on with endless safety videos, and by the time they finally hit the range after lunch, Derrick was more than ready to shoot something. Grasping the pistol, he tried to get comfortable holding it, adjusting his grip repeatedly.

Down the firing line, a voice called out, "Dear God, they gave Elmo a weapon!" Derrick rolled his eyes, recognizing Obadiah's annoying voice.

"Everyone needs to stay focused while on the line," the range master reminded them, counting down to the fire order. The line erupted in loud cracks as gunpowder ignited.

Derrick concentrated on his target and squeezed the trigger. The sound was expected, but the recoil wasn't. His grip slipped, and his thumb accidentally hit the magazine release, sending it clattering to the ground. A wave of laughter spread down the line, causing Derrick's face to flush red with embarrassment.

"Cold range!" the range master called as he approached Derrick. "First time shooting?" he asked

with a sympathetic smile. Derrick nodded, feeling even more self-conscious. "Don't worry about it. Most people haven't fired a gun when they get here. You'll get the hang of it."

Obadiah leaned over to Richie and snickered, "I'm not sure I have enough life insurance to be shooting with that idiot."

"Need we start this again, sir?" Richie barked, his glare silencing Obadiah.

The class final was a simulated escape from an enemy facility, using paintball guns instead of live ammunition. Derrick, Lydia, and Tae were on the escape team, while Obadiah and Richie were hunters.

Obadiah had set a trap near the end of the course. Just as they were about to reach safety, he sprang out and opened fire. Lydia, leading the group, didn't see him in time, but Derrick did. Without thinking, he threw himself in front of the paintballs, taking the hits meant for her. As Derrick crumpled to the ground, Lydia got a clear shot and nailed Obadiah between the eyes.

"That red mark stayed on his face for a week!" Tae laughed.

"Served him right," Derrick replied, wincing at the memory. "I couldn't shower for days. My whole torso was one big bruise."

Tae grinned mischievously. "But you didn't complain much when Lydia 'nursed' you back to health, did you?"

***

As they headed back toward the dock, Derrick noticed a boat pacing about a hundred yards on their right. He handed Tae a pair of binoculars. "Check out that boat. It's been following us."

Tae raised the binoculars, focusing on the vessel. "Those are Nikon Action EXs," he groaned. "Nightfall."

"Yeah. I recognized one of them, too," Derrick confirmed, keeping his voice low. "We need to stay sharp."

CHAPTER 24

The morning sun was beginning to rise, casting a warm glow over the sleepy neighborhood. Derrick and Tae were on a quick trip to the local grocery store to pick up some milk for breakfast. The streets were still mostly empty, with just a few early risers out and about. As they approached the store, Derrick's phone buzzed in his pocket. He pulled it out and glanced at the screen. His heart skipped a beat as he saw the alert from his home security system: *"Perimeter Breach Detected."*

Derrick cursed under his breath, quickly unlocking his phone to access the live feed from the security cameras. Tae, noticing the sudden tension in Derrick's posture, leaned over to see what was wrong.

"What's up?" Tae asked, his voice edged with concern.

Derrick's eyes widened as he saw a group of operatives in tactical gear moving towards the house. "It's Nightfall. They're about to breach the front door," he said, his voice tight with urgency. Without wasting a second, he dialed Lydia's number, praying she would answer quickly.

The phone rang, each ring feeling like an eternity. Finally, Lydia picked up. "Oh, Derrick! I'm glad you called. Madeline is in the mood for some…"

Derrick cut her off, his voice trembling as he fought to stay calm. "Lydia, listen to me carefully. There are operatives about to breach the front door. Get Madeline and find somewhere to hide. Now!"

He heard a crash through the phone, followed by shouting and the unmistakable sounds of a struggle. "Lydia! Lydia!" Derrick yelled, panic clawing at his chest. The line went silent for a moment, and then a familiar, menacing voice came on.

"I warned you, Elmo," Obadiah sneered. "Now, give us the traitor, or I'll kill both of them." There was another loud crash, and the call abruptly ended.

Derrick's knuckles turned white as he gripped the phone, breaking its case. "We need to get back... now!"

They raced back to the house, Derrick driving like a man possessed, pushing the car to its limits on the winding roads. Every second felt like an eternity, the distance between them and the house stretching impossibly far.

The front door was ajar when they arrived, hanging crookedly from its hinges. Derrick's stomach churned as he approached the house.

Inside, the living room was a wreck. Furniture was overturned, and Lydia's phone lay shattered on the floor, its screen flickering weakly. As Derrick scanned the room, his eyes landed on Madeline's stuffed turtle, lying abandoned on the floor. The sight of it sent a jolt of fear and fury through him.

Tae, who had cleared the rest of the house, returned to the living room to find Derrick kneeling on the ground, clutching Madeline's turtle. The usually composed and focused Derrick was now a man on the edge.

"I'll just turn myself in," Tae said quietly, breaking the silence. "This has gone too far."

Derrick's jaw clenched so hard that his teeth ground against each other, the sound audible in the tense room. "No. We're getting them back," he replied, his voice simmering with rage.

Tae, taken aback by this fierce determination, hesitated. "But where do we even begin to look?"

Derrick pulled out his phone and opened an app labeled "BLUE-ICE." A map on the screen showed a blinking red dot moving down a nearby highway. Lydia's blue diamond earrings weren't just an expensive birthday gift—they had tracking devices embedded in them for emergencies like this. He never thought he'd actually have to use them.

"Let's go," Derrick said, his voice cold and resolute. The fire in his eyes made Tae's heart race, but he followed without question.

The roar of the Mustang's V8 engine filled the car as Derrick floored it down US-98, the speedometer needle hovering dangerously past the limit. Tae gripped the door handle, his knuckles turning white as they sped past the blurred landscape.

"Derrick, slow down! This isn't the track back at school!" Tae shouted, his voice barely audible over the roaring engine.

But Derrick's eyes were locked on the GPS tracker, the beacon pulsing steadily on the screen. His face was a mask of intense focus and barely contained fury, a side of him Tae had never seen before.

"She's moving, Tae. I can't slow down," Derrick growled, his focus unwavering. "If we lose her, we might never get another chance."

Tae swallowed hard, memories of their training at the driving track flashing through his mind. He had seen Derrick push the limits before, but this was different. This wasn't a controlled environment; this was real, and everyone's lives were at stake.

"They're airborne," Derrick muttered as the dot suddenly sped northward. He veered off the highway toward Ocala International Airport, tires screeching as he came to a halt by the General Aviation hangars.

Barely waiting for the car to stop fully, Derrick jumped out and started scanning the area for a plane they could "tactically acquire."

Still reeling from the breakneck drive, Tae caught up with Derrick, slightly dizzy. "Wouldn't it be easier… and safer… to just hire someone to fly us?"

Derrick spotted a pilot doing a pre-flight check on his plane. He approached him with determined urgency. "We need to charter your plane immediately," Derrick said, pulling out a wad of cash.

The pilot, a grizzled man in his fifties, raised an eyebrow but nodded, pocketing the money. "Where to?"

"Follow this," Derrick said, showing him the GPS with the pulsing beacon.

Within minutes, they were airborne, the small plane climbing quickly into the sky. Tae sat beside Derrick, who stared out the window with an intensity that hadn't faded.

"Derrick," Tae began cautiously, "we'll get them back. I've never seen you so... consumed. But we need to stay sharp."

Derrick took a deep breath, forcing himself to stay focused. "I know, Tae. I just can't lose them. Not like this."

CHAPTER 25

The sleek, black sedan sped through the small town of Wilson, North Carolina, with the tracker beeping steadily from the dashboard. Derrick's jaw tightened as they neared a warehouse on the outskirts of town. "This is it," he said, glancing at Tae.

The warehouse loomed ahead, an imposing structure surrounded by a tall chain-link fence. The tracker's signal pointed straight to it—Lydia and, hopefully, Madeline were inside.

Tae parked the car a safe distance away. He turned to Derrick with a serious look. "I'll check the perimeter. Wait here, and don't do anything stupid," he ordered, sternly.

Already on edge, Derrick racked the slide on his Glock, the cold metal a reminder of what was at stake. Tae repeated himself, more firmly this time, "Derrick... Don't... do... anything... stupid. Okay?"

Without responding, Derrick watched as Tae slipped out of the car and disappeared into the shadows. As soon as he was out of sight, Derrick made his move toward the main entrance. The fear gnawing at him made it impossible just to sit and wait. His heart pounded in his chest as he approached the door, his footsteps eerily quiet.

He entered a small reception area where a woman sat behind the desk, her eyes widening slightly as she noticed him.

"Can I help you?" she asked, her voice steady, but her eyes had an underlying tension.

Derrick moved closer to the desk, his gaze icy and unyielding. "Where's my family?"

The receptionist blinked, feigning confusion. "I don't know what you're talking about. This is a shipping company."

Derrick's patience snapped. He drew his gun and aimed it directly at her, his expression darkening. "I'm not here to play games. Tell me where they are."

Her face turned pale, and she stammered, "I—I don't know anything about that—"

Derrick leaned in closer, the barrel of the gun now inches from her face. "Last chance," he growled.

Her eyes darted nervously toward a door behind her. "They're in the back. Please, don't hurt me."

Derrick didn't waver. He grabbed the desk phone, ripped the wires from the wall, and slammed it against the side of her head, knocking her out cold. Tossing it aside, his mind raced. The door she had indicated was too obvious, too easy. It had to be a trap. He needed another way in.

Derrick looked at the door she pointed to and then went down the hallway to the left. "That was a setup if I've ever seen one."

Moving cautiously, Derrick slipped down a side hallway, scanning every corner and every shadow for signs of movement. The air was thick with tension and every creak amplified his heightened senses. Finding another door, this one less conspicuous, he pushed it open quietly.

Inside the warehouse, he spotted Obadiah seated casually in a chair, a rifle resting across his lap. The sight of him sent a surge of rage through Derrick. Using the shadows for cover, Derrick crept closer, his gun trained on Obadiah's head.

"Drop your weapon," Derrick commanded, his voice cold and steady.

Obadiah didn't flinch. "Elmo. Knew you'd show up," he said calmly, as if they were meeting under normal circumstances. He slowly lowered his rifle to the ground.

"Where are they?" Derrick's voice was a low growl, his patience hanging by a thread.

Obadiah smirked, raising his hands in mock surrender as he turned to face Derrick. "I'll take you to them. But first, you're going to want to hear my proposal."

"No," Derrick snapped, his gun steady. "You're taking me to them now, or your head will disappear."

Obadiah's smirk didn't fade. "Come on, Elmo. You really think we didn't plan for this?"

From the darkness behind him, Derrick heard the unmistakable sound of a rifle being cocked. He was outnumbered, but his focus remained on Obadiah.

"Like I said, I just want to talk. Then you're free to go." Obadiah said, lowering his hands as his grin widened.

Derrick crouched down, placed his gun on the ground, and kicked it toward Obadiah. The move surprised him, but before he could react, Derrick spun around, sweeping the legs out from under the operative who had crept up behind him. The agent dropped his rifle and fell to his knees, Derrick looming over him. In one swift motion, Derrick grabbed the man's head and twisted until he felt the sickening snap of his neck breaking. The body crumpled to the floor, leaving Derrick holding the rifle.

Obadiah slowly approached, clapping sarcastically. "Wow! You've learned a few things since school. Totally unnecessary, but impressive."

Derrick's laser-like gaze now matched the barrel of the rifle. Both were directed at Obadiah's head. "Take me to my family."

Obadiah's tone turned more insistent as he began to explain. "Elmo, you think you know the truth, but you've been blinded. This whole operation, everything you think you're fighting for… it's all a farce.

Your friend Tae? He's not the savior he claims to be. He's the reason Nightfall exists."

Derrick's glare didn't waver, but doubt flickered in his mind. Obadiah continued, his voice smooth and persuasive. "We're the ones cleaning up the messes left behind by so-called heroes like Tae. We are the true protectors of this country, the ones who get our hands dirty so that others can sleep soundly at night."

Obadiah began to close the distance between them, his voice taking on a more conspiratorial tone. "You had to know something was off about Tae. Join us, Derrick. Unlimited resources, cutting-edge technology... you could do so much more with us. All you have to do is say yes."

Derrick's mind flashed back to the countless times Tae had risked his life for him and their shared loyalty. "I recall a pitch like this before... where did I read that... Oh yeah... Genesis. That was basically the same speech the serpent told Eve. Didn't work out too good for her, as I remember."

Obadiah took another step closer, his eyes gleaming with anticipation. "Tell me where Tae is, Derrick. Help us take him down, and you'll see that we're not the villains here. We're the ones keeping this country safe."

Derrick raised the rifle to his eye as he made his decision. "Why don't you take me to my family instead?"

Obadiah's expression darkened. "Now, Elmo, we both know what would happen if I did that."

Derrick didn't see the metal bar Obadiah had hidden behind his back until it was too late. He swung it hard, striking the rifle out of Derrick's hands. The metal clanged against the concrete floor, and he swung again, aiming for Derrick's head. Derrick ducked, rolling away and sweeping Obadiah's legs from under him. As Obadiah fell to one knee, Derrick delivered a powerful roundhouse kick to the side of his face, following up with several quick punches.

Obadiah managed to block one of the blows, countering with a jab to Derrick's side that left him gasping for air. Desperate, Derrick spotted his Glock lying on the ground a few feet away. He lunged for it, grabbing the weapon as Obadiah stumbled toward a nearby rifle.

With a final burst of energy, Derrick slammed into the back of Obadiah's knees, tearing the ligaments and sending him crashing to the ground. Derrick didn't let up, grabbing Obadiah's head and repeatedly slamming it into his knee. Obadiah's face was a bloody mess, but he still managed to grin through the pain.

Breathing hard, Derrick pressed the Glock against Obadiah's forehead. "My family. NOW!"

Obadiah, his voice weak but filled with malice, spat out a mouthful of blood and reached for his throat mic. "Execute."

Derrick barely registered the words before he heard two gunshots echo from the far side of the warehouse. The sound sent a jolt of horror through him, but Obadiah's sadistic grin only widened.

He felt his finger retract against the trigger and a loud gunshot resonated. Obadiah's eyes dimmed and then fixed as he slumped over onto the floor, the smile still etched on his face.